CAMORRA

CAMORRA

ORIGINAL NOVEL BY
ANTONIO FRANCESCA

Camorra
Copyright © 2020 by Antonio Francesca. All rights reserved.

No part of this publication may be reproduced, stored in a retrieval system or transmitted in any way by any means, electronic, mechanical, photocopy, recording or otherwise without the prior permission of the author except as provided by USA copyright law.

This novel is a work of fiction. Names, descriptions, entities, and incidents included in the story are products of the author's imagination. Any resemblance to actual persons, events, and entities is entirely coincidental.

The opinions expressed by the author are not necessarily those of URLink Print and Media.

1603 Capitol Ave., Suite 310 Cheyenne, Wyoming USA 82001
1-888-980-6523 | admin@urlinkpublishing.com

URLink Print and Media is committed to excellence in the publishing industry.

Book design copyright © 2020 by URLink Print and Media. All rights reserved.

Published in the United States of America
ISBN 978-1-64753-281-9 (Paperback)
ISBN 978-1-64753-287-1 (Hardback)
ISBN 978-1-64753-282-6 (Digital)

10.03.20

The word "Camorra" means gang, a word used for the Neapolitan Mafia (based In Naples) It appeared in the mid-1800s in Naples Italy, as a prison gang. Once released members formed clans in the cities and continued to grow in power.

Dedications

To my late uncle Antonio, the inspiration

To my late wife Abbey who encouraged me to write this book

To Clorinda and Emilio, my late parents, who were my guiding lights

To my partner Diane, who never lost faith

It is written that throughout history certain men of power within the Italian Government would, masquerading as good and decent leaders, go to diabolical lengths in order to defeat those who were thought to be enemies of the men in power. Many times as a result of those endeavors those unfortunate men who were thought to be part of the political opposition were wrongly accused and many were imprisoned.

It was also noted that some of the unlucky few who were imprisoned would garner strength in the hope that their government might see the error perpetrated on them and as such might set them free. As time passed many of those imprisoned, seeing that the system leaned favorably to the very culprits who caused their imprisonment, ultimately resigned themselves that their fate was sealed.

The accused, ultimately resigned to political retribution and imprisonment, now faced the fact that freedom might be impossible. These men facing the improbable odds of release aligned themselves with other imprisoned politically labeled brethren. As time passed and feeling that all hope was gone many of the newer more vocal and violent inmates joined older inmates, who were once politically powerful leaders when they were on the outside, to form a combined outpouring of hatred for their oppressors. In the end this group of politically discontented inmates both young and old prayed that somehow someway, if given the opportunity, they would gain revenge against those who were responsible.

PROLOGUE

1920

The Italian Government issued a decree that itinerant farmers who worked for large estates situated south of Rome, submit to a Government intervention. This massive effort launched by the authorities was an attempt to weed out and target dissidents as well as outside agitators and troublemakers who, for over a year, demonstrated and demanded that farmers receive a larger proportionate share of crops they picked in the region.

The Government labeled radicals demanded that they, the workers who did 100% of the work, be compensated with a bigger percentage of what they sowed compared with the current system whereby the overseer, or Gabelotto as they were called, decided how the crops were to be distributed. Traditionally the Gabellotto, employed by the wealthiest landowners, had to keep the peace on the property as well as making sure that the men who worked directly under him scrutinize the percentage of fruits and vegetables picked always favoring his employer.

Many dissidents were young people who felt that their future was tied to a system that enslaved its workers under an unfair government and that protesting the process was the only answer.

The idea of proportionate sharing was not a new idea it had its roots in medieval times when lords, Serfs and vassals all worked under a similar system. The land owner was the last word then came the Vassals who administered the everyday duties needed to keep the process going and lastly the serfs who tilled the soil and the byproducts grown were proportionately shared by all.

The Italian government's take on this was that the people of southern Italy were ignorant of how important a role that government needed to play in this story. A farmers struggle to eke out a living and stay alive was of the up most importance to him yet in the end the Government propaganda machine consistently put out the idea that they were not only for equality within the farmer's existence but that they were behind the farmer wanting only the best for them.

This propaganda might have been seen as plausible amongst the elderly and frail of the region simply because at their advanced age all that was left was survival but their young and impatient offspring did not share those views and they were willing to demonstrate against the Government to prove their point. The truth of the situation was that the farmers of the region had seen for many years the failed attempt by Government in trying to regulate this delicate balance between the needs of the farmers versus the demands of the wealthy land owners.

In the end the farmers believed that ultimately all disputes would and should be settled in a court of law. That would have made sense except that prior to any court mandated decree the will of the wealthy landowners in conjunction with corrupt officials of the Government saw to it that all cases died long before any argument was ever heard.

For the few farmers brave enough to fight the system there was prison, some were actually killed. Wealthy landowners acting through their own Gabelottos terrorized everyone until calm came to the region, of course the farmers who made up the dissident voices always held hope that there would eventually be freedom and rewards for their struggle.

Within the realm of what was Government propaganda and what was real emerged another group of young yet secretive Neapolitans who also vehemently objected to the way the Government and the wealthy landowners conspired to rob and cheat the farmers.

This new group of young men called themselves "Camorra" which when translated meant "Racket". The phrase was used as a reminder that to them the Government's handling of anything related to workers versus land owners was basically labeled a Racket.

In an attempt to explain how the Camorra became a part of Neapolitan life in the early to late twenties is like trying to put together a crossword puzzle in the dark. Rumor had it that Camorra had it origin from inside the prison walls of Castel DeMare evolving over the years into a movement. As each peasant farmer working the lands from sun up to sundown experienced transgression from the wealthy land owners Camorra, in turn, gained popularity and strength much as old English folk tales talked of Robin Hood, Camorra became the Robin Hood of the Neapolitans.

The outward motto of the Camorra was a free and unified Italy. But deep rooted in its very fiber was the taking, by any means, the power over everything that mattered in Italy. This thirst for power recognition and revenge was aimed at the wealthiest land owners.

The story continues.

Camorra had its beginning in prison. The old Roman prison called "Castel De Mare" Castle by the Ocean. The movement was started by men, from the farming community, who were incarcerated after being charged with crimes against Government.

The prison rules were fierce and even the smallest infraction would be met with severe treatment. Once the political label was placed to any inmate his fate was sealed. Basically the unofficial word for political prisoners was imprisonment as long as the government saw fit and moreover the only chance for the prisoner to return to his family was if he had learned the errors of his choices and publicly repent what he had done, other than that his stay would be indefinite.

BOOK ONE

CHAPTER 1

It was the 1920s and the Italian Government had stepped up its campaign against a radical element comprised of farmers and their sympathizers in their relentless pursuit of justice for all the itinerate workers in the region. Many of these men were eventually incarcerated and specifically labeled political agitators. The Government made sure that these individuals were to be kept in confinement indefinitely.

One such prisoner was Benito Crespi, named by the Italian government as the arch enemy of the state and the leading political activist in Southern Italy, had been incarcerated for over nine years. The government's contention was that he and his cohorts were the cause of strife and disobedient behavior throughout the entire Benevento valley. In reality the true cause of his being jailed had to do with him infuriating the most powerful land owner in the region, Don Francisco Jannace. Jannace was not only the largest land owner but also the most powerful man in the region. Jannace and a few of his powerful land owner friends controlled not only the ebb and Flo of life in Southern Italy but in so many ways they broke as many laws as the culprits they were supposed to be against. In essence they were the Government.

This small yet powerful group had total control over taxation, water rights, land deeds rights and voting not to mention the personal rights of each and every laborer in their charge who found, on a day to day basis, to suddenly be at the beck and call of those same land owners. They were law makers and lawbreakers by simply dictating to all that as long as they were the power nothing else mattered.

Any law enacted by the central government in Rome concerning the goings on in the Benevento Valley had to have this small yet powerful group of land owners in Benevento to sanction it. Every word of any document concerning Southern Italy initiated by that same Government in Rome had to have the go ahead by those same land owners. This small and powerful group of land barons ruled fiercely and Don Jannace was the face of this group.

To the downtrodden farmers of the region Don Francisco Jannace was looked upon as a tyrant. The Don always wanted respectability from the nobility caring less about how he was perceived by the work force. Everyone that worked within the boundaries of his estate as well as those who personally tended to his everyday needs also despised him. From the common laborer who tilled his estate to the government bureaucrats who needed his OK to function the end result was always the same, to a man he was feared.

Crespi, although an itinerant farmer, had always been looked upon as a formidable force to reckon, personality and fear with the all-powerful Jannace. Crespi, by his sheer force of power and personality, united most of the farmers of the valley in the belief that that their sweat and sacrifice was worth a little more than just be patronized by the Jannace clan.

In time Jannace realized that Crespi was more than a match for him. Crespi feared no man especially the shorter and ill-mannered land baron. Crespi actually held Jannace in such contempt that on numerous occasions, where demonstrations actually stopped fruit and vegetable picking, Crispi vocally denounced Jannace as a traitor to the Italian people. Crespi was the male Joan of Arc for everyone in the Benevento Valley.

The masses believed in him and this above all else petrified Jannace knowing full well that this small band of malcontents could in effect stop the progress that Jannace had so masterfully engineered since he officially took over as the last word in the region.

Crespi's message was simple. He believed that all hard working people in the valley needed fairness and their voice needed to be heard. Crespi and his loyalists became that voice.

Eventually Jannace had him imprisoned. Crespi's legions were many but after the arrest of their leader they went underground. Slowly his legend grew and eventually a name came out of the unrest solidifying all who believed in his message.

The name that all of Crespi's followers identified with was, "Camorra. Camorra to everyone involved signified hope, the translation said it meant "Racket". In reality Camorra unified everyone in mind and spirit.

The people of Benevento never mentioned the word Camorra in public. It was a society created by Crespi solely for identification from one member to another. Camorra was different than the Sicilian Mafia in that the Mafia's war against humanity took in all victims. The Mafia, even in its infancy, needed to create havoc in order for all of its goals to be met. The goals changed as the society grew and its original intent got lost and what was left was power and greed. The Camorra's only goal was to "Unionize" its people so that a fair proportion of goods and services were evenly distributed. To men like Don Francisco these demands were tantamount to tyranny and only imprisonment would suffice for anyone carrying the Camorra label

This secret society identified itself simply by its trademark, a tattooed cross between the thumb and index finger of the right hand. The stars above the cross marked time spent as a member. Each star stood for five years.

Benito Crespi at five feet eleven inches and weighing two hundred pounds was as formidable a foe to anyone who even remotely opposed his point of view. His height and general size made him a feared individual in and out of jail. His gruff demeanor and cold hard stare moved even the strongest. His thick black hair with small streaks of gray and piercing brown eyes together with his movie star looks and deep resonating voice made most women look at him with awe and most men look at him with fear.

Benito was not a talkative man and his powerful physique and general cold look could tell anyone interested that he was not to be trifled with. Based on his ferocious nature and strong personality he was allowed some isolated privileges in prison. The main interaction he was allowed, with a select few inmates and guards, took place during two periods during each day. That interaction was supervised and minimal amount of talking was allowed.

Over the years Crespi had befriended a few guards but even they were leery about his actions and motives especially after they had become friendly with him. If it became known about any friendship between Crespi and any of the men commissioned to guard him there would be consequences for all concerned. The utter finality of Crespi's future was the inevitable fact that he would never get out of prison. That fact alone made his everyday life caustic for him and his captors.

"He is one tough customer" One particular Guard was heard saying. Echoing what everyone connected with the Castel De Mare already knew.

In his mid-fifties Crespi had built a following that carried through to Castel De Mare. There the prison officials were instructed by the land barons to isolate him at every occasion but even in that restricted confinement he was still given leeway to do almost anything within the prison walls. Benito still managed to get his message out to the freedom fighters back in Benevento. The message was always the same; Never give in always remember worker equality comes before anything. As far as Benito's stature within the Camorra was untouchable, he was their leader to the death.

The soft positioning of the guards towards Crespi had to do with one fact, they knew that at days end they still had to go home to their families and the long arm of Camorra could reach anyone. In prison Crespi's legend got countrywide attention. His reputation reached far and wide as a man of respect.

Crespi's family, in Benevento, consisted of a wife Amalia and two daughters Anna and Vicenzina. His family were never political but because of who he was the Gabelotto was careful in all of his dealings with the family. After Benito's arrest his wife pleaded for help from the Gabelotto being that one of her two daughters, Vincenzia, had an eye ailment from birth that made her vision a problem. It is also noted that the rare beauty in the family, Anna, had not missed the eye of the Gabelotto boss Philip Testa.

Vincenzia was not able to work like the other girls of her age and so the burden fell upon Anna and Amalia to do the yeoman's work and create an environment to survive.

Amalia, three years younger than Benito, still had the charm and great smile that first won Benito's heart some 20 years prior. Vincenzia, with her long black hair braided and almost touching her backside, was short stout and big boned. Amalia still possessed that plain olive skinned beauty that became an Italian trademark amongst actress's years later best individualized by the likes of Anna Magnani and Silvana Mangano. These great Italian movie stars made 1950s America stand up and notice what the Italian Cinema called Cinema Verita. (True cinema)

Anna, at 19, was looked upon by all the young people of the village, as one of the most beautiful young women in the province. Like her mother and sister Anna was of the same height but that was where the comparisons ended. Anna was slim with an alluring figure that screamed maturity and surely not going unnoticed by every eligible male in the village. Anna possessed a lightness in her every move. In simpler terms her attitude could best be described as carefree and even. Her beauty and sweetness were at odds mixed with the agrarian culture that surrounded her and that alone made her stick out even more. Many young women who worked the land for more than a few years aged quickly and horribly. Attitude not to mention fatigue and bad skin were just for openers. People, especially women are supposed to age like fine wine. In this instance the working women within the Benevento farm workforce looked more like vinegar than wine. That was not the case with Anna, defying logic she acted as if her plight was not as drastic and hurtful as the other women portrayed it. In many ways Anna made it appear to anyone observing that she enjoyed and accepted her role and outwardly acted happy about it.

Anna was athletic in her gait and attitude. Unlike her mother and sister Anna was constantly cheerful. Working, talking or interacting with everyone in the village.

Anna, with anyone who came in contact with her, acted as if life was beautiful and tomorrow promised even more.

Anna, when doing chores, was constantly singing or humming the vast Neapolitan song book that every child of Italian decent knew by heart. Music and food were the two main ingredients in every Italian's life. With Benito's incarceration the future simply rested on Amalia. Amalia made sure to always speak of her husband with great pride and constantly talked about him to her children and how they should never forget what sacrifices he made for his family and countrymen.

CHAPTER 2

The Jannace estate, centered around a sprawling seventeen hundred acres, boasted vineyards that yielded some of the finest wine in southern Italy. The food stuffs produced ranged from Olive oil to dried figs from lemons to lettuce and from tomatoes to sweet potatoes. Viewing the enormous panorama of land and both natural and manmade lakes where the fish begged to be pulled out and eaten one might think that a family so lucky to have all of this might give thanks to the heavens for having such great fortune, sadly that was not the case.

It was said that back in the early seventeen hundred the Jannace ancestors carved out the land and made it their own. It wasn't lost on all of the people in the region that Jannace and his ancestors, because of the vast lands they either took or stole, became so politically connected that even the Vatican asked for their council on occasion. Jannace became the most powerful man in the entire southern region in Italy. His power and domain stretched farther than his estate. His queries were heard as far north as Switzerland and as far west as Spain and east to Greece, yet Don Jannace, out of choice, decided to stay close to his main source of power, which was his vast land holdings.

The Jannace estate had the Crespi family, as well as hundreds of other families, share cropping their land.

The Jannace clan consisted of the patriarch Don Francisco Jannace. Don Francisco was raised in the lap of luxury. Educated in Rome his aristocratic family had always driven the concept that they, the Jannace's, were from royal blood and as such deserved the best that life had to offer. Sadly, it often resulted at the expense of others. And the royal blood they consistently alluded became nothing more than wishful thinking eventually becoming a reality to family, friends and underlings.

The Don had two children a girl named Valentina and a son named Rodolfo. Each one of the children were named after historical figures in Italian Literature and art. The Don had married a woman who like himself came from aristocracy. But that did not stop him from being a selfish and self-centered man who was only interested in himself. The Don's appetite for women before, during and after his wife died was aggressive to say the least.

He poached on every available woman in the village. All women, from highbrow society types to farm girls, the Don was never satiated sexually. Few in the village who knew the Don and his family well surmised that his sexual appetite with many other women might have been the catalyst that eventually buried his poor wife.

The many single women who bed him down all had the same hopes in mind. The majority always held out hope that the Don might favor them and their families thereby making their life noble and worthwhile. The Don felt it was his birthright to do whatever he pleased no matter who was hurt by it. The end result for all the women whether pregnant or not was always the same. No one except his direct descendants could ever hope to become a Jannace.

Don Francisco, with his full head of salt and pepper hair and only standing five foot seven, acting a brute as if he were six feet seven and one hundred and sixty pounds instead of the over 200lbs of body weight he actually carried. The Don, clad with his custom made clothing, did in fact carry himself well within that 200 plus body. Totally confident in his manner and direction he stood hard and robust unlike many of the wealthy land owners who, through the years, allowed themselves to get fat and lazy. Early on everyone in the region began to see that Don Francisco would was a force to be reckoned with. Although he was raised desiring nothing and having everything and anything done for him he never allowed himself to fall into what he described as the rich man's quicksand. From the outset of his being referred to as the lord of his domain he never allowed the Gabelotto's, who managed his estate, to ever have the upper hand or make decisions without his final approval.

The Don represented a new force in the Jannace lineage. For the first time in the history of The Jannace clan The Don, whose outward appearance fashioned as an aristocrat, actually was ruthless and hands on fierce with retribution to anyone who opposed his will.

In many ways compared to the many wealthy land barons the Don's actions were in complete defiance of how an aristocrat was supposed to conduct business. The rest of the wealthy conducted themselves like the tail wagging the dog. And in no manner was this evident than the Don's relationship with the head Gabelotto on his estate, Philip Testa.

Traditionally the Gabelotto on most estates took care of the everyday duties that the head of the household felt was beneath him. And as a direct result of that action the Gabelotto, in time, would eventually have his way with the employer of record. Whether through fear or intimidation the Gabelotto became the force behind most owners. Their experience as law enforcement officers in the Italian Army gave them more respect than they deserved. The land owners desired peace and to enjoy their prosperity and so because of this as years passed and the reins of the family's went from one generation to another the power slowly shifted from land baron to Gabelotto.

As the 1920's were fast approaching the scene on largest estates allowed the Gabelotto to run roughshod over their property. Soon what was left was that the Gabelotto became the last word on the estate. Many land owners, seeing the errors of their ways, tried to reverse the reign of power and bring it back to its rightful owner but too many years had passed and for many it was too late. As the years passed many owners found themselves at the beck and call of the very men who they employed. Not so with Don Francisco.

From the very first day that the Don returned from school in Rome he showed everyone that he was not to be trifled with and more important he was adamant to prove to everyone especially the workers that his word was the law. He was quick with his fists and usually could back up any and all complaints with a hard punch or slap. Either way his opponents got the message that the Jannace family had a new boss, and a very tough leader.

The Don, since the day he officially took over the reins of the estate, ruled with an iron hand. He was different than his fellow land owners many being the privileged offspring of the rich. The Don, well educated, saw his role differently that what was originally planned for him by his parents. Traditionally the only son of such wealthy land owners, and politically well healed people, all that would be needed was a rubber stamp of approval. But this son was different. He never listened to the advisors his parents put in place to run the estate. Secondly he fired everyone politically connected to his parents and replaced them with people whose sole loyalty was to him. At the ripe age of twenty-nine the Don became the most powerful man in Naples.

The Don was brusque and ill-mannered even though educated in Rome and Paris. His parents had both died in a hunting accident before they were fifty years of age and their death allowed the new Don impetus to create a different yet stronger Jannace dynasty. The day after the funeral he demanded that the servants rip the portraits of his parents down from the main hallways of the mansion and put them in storage. As time passed he patiently chose what portraits he wanted hung. In the end the replacements were all showing him in various battles with him always victorious.

There were many things the Don had always disapproved of concerning his parents and their life style. But the one trait they possessed that appalled him the most was their penchant for reckless spending. After he officially took over the estate the servants would call him The Miser, of course, behind his back. In two short years the Don relieved all of the bankers who were put in charge of his family's fortune. He fired everyone even remotely connected to his parents.

The Don, now firmly encased as lord of his domain, needed the trappings of a family in order to be seen as the complete ruler. The first act was for him to get married. He chose a woman from aristocracy and promptly had two children. A boy and a girl. To the Don having children was much akin to having livestock. If the children measured up to his standards, then they would be tolerated and rewarded. That was the way the Don treated everyone around him, including his wife.

It did take a while but Mrs Jannace soon found out that besides the occasional sex, and that had become far and few as the years passed, the Don kept to himself and in the end practically ignored her. Soon revulsion and shame covered his wife and in the true aristocratic Italian tradition all that was left was an honorable death. The children both away at private school were, in effect raised by strangers, and not saddened upon hearing of her death. In the end the two children emulated their father, when he showed no remorse they followed.

As the children grew into young adults they were exhibiting individual characteristics that both elated and distressed the Don at the same time.

By the age of twenty-one Rudolfo had built quite a reputation as a lady's man and reckless spender. His sister Valentina was a carbon copy of her father except when it came to the men in her life.

Rudolfo was an extrovert to the extreme. It seemed to all the people who worked at the estate that Rudolfo was constantly desiring his father's attention. The escapades he got involved in, seemed to all who were part of the Jannace work force that it, was Rodolfo's attempt to get his father to notice him and perhaps care about what he was about. The help, especially the women, who had both tended to the Don's parents and eventually the Don himself realized early on that Rudolfo unlike his sister needed his mother not his father.

There were many occasions where the eldest of the help named Claudia was given the task to tend to Rudolfo's needs. Besides cooking and sewing Claudia was one of the few in house help that pleased the Don. Claudia, at thirty-three, had not been married and according to many of the help had kept herself available if the Don ever had any thoughts of associating with her outside of the estate. To Claudia's dismay the Don's affection was concentrated in one area when it concerned Claudia.

"Claudia, I need your help. Now that my wife has passed there is really no one that has the kind of gentle magic I need to help my son straighten out. Rodolfo needs a woman like you to put him on a better road in this life!"

Claudia knowing that the Don needed her thought this might be a good opportunity to try and ingratiate herself to him.

"Sir, I realize how important this is to you and I do want to help but..."

The Don stopped her in mid speech and seeing that she blushed as she spoke gave him the idea that perhaps Claudia wanted more from him than just guidance.

"Speak up child, don't be shy around me" The Don put his arm around her and as he did he could feel her tremble upon feeling his touch. The Don was slowly getting aroused and knowing that Claudia was a virgin excited him even more. The Don, sensing that Claudia was probably hoping the same, made his initial move by slowly getting behind her and she feeling his hardness began to push against him. She instinctively reached around without ever looking up and caressed him. In minutes the Don had mounted her and her moans and screams of ecstasy could be heard throughout the entire house. When they had finished the Don caressed her cheek.

"Claudia, you were sweet and wonderful, now will you go upstairs and tend to Rudolfo and his studies, ok?"

"Will you come to my room later Don Francisco?' She whispered knowing full well he had climaxed into her with such loving force and loving seeing how she reacted perhaps would prompt him to do it again.

"Yes Claudia I will visit you tonight"

Their household romance lasted for over a year but the Don strongly advised her that if she suddenly became pregnant it would be the end of the affair, she agreed.

Their relationship began to sour almost a year later when Claudia caught the Don fondling the daughter of neighbor who had sold the Don some prize cattle, as the dinner had ended and all were ready to depart the Don asked the neighbor could his daughter stay as they were all having such a great time together. Her father granted his permission. In that setting the father of the girl would have welcomed any advances the Don would have made because the class structure dictated it. A bachelor or widower who just happened to be the richest man in the country would be welcomed by most of the middle class citizenry. The end result might be a proposal and if that happened the girl's family would suddenly be elevated to upper class status.

Late that evening Claudia expected the Don to visit her as usual but when he didn't come she ventured from her quarters to the main part of the mansion. Hearing voices, she tiptoed to the library to which she witnessed the wild scene that ended her fairy tale thoughts that the Don might someday marry her. There in the library the Don had his neighbor's daughter all of sixteen practically prone face down over the large burgundy sofa having sex with her. It had occurred to Claudia that the Don liked having sex that way, she assumed that it probably did away with any emotional ties not having to look at the person while it was happening.

The Don, always knowing that his relationship with Claudia would never amount to anything, still demanded and expected her to take care of Rodolfo, and she did until he went away to school. The Don continued to visit Claudia late at night whenever he fancied until she suddenly took ill with some mysterious ailment. She left for the hospital and no one at the estate ever saw her again.

Valentina, in many ways, resembled the Don in mannerisms and demeanor. No gentleman caller ever had the upper hand. She was seen, by all who worked for the estate, as the mirror image of her father. And she made sure to uphold everything that was sacred to the Don.

Suitor after suitor would come to call for her hand and in the end they all went away wondering what had happened. What had transpired that made Valentina turn her back on all of them. There were so many men from prominent families all asking for her hand yet one by one they were spurned. The wagging women of Benevento spinning tales about Valentina and her exploits seemed to always center on the fact that in so many occasions they witnessed the Don acting as if his daughter was the apple of his eye in so many unsavory ways their actions were as lovers not father and daughter.

Much like the Don Valentina always held herself as an aristocrat with a vision. That made her actions odd and complicated seeing that the world she lived in was dominated by men.

She fancied herself a child of aristocracy. At social functions amongst the elite of Naples she would demonstrate her varied social and language skills that only the best Italian and French finishing schools could offer. She often purported herself as a sweet and decent woman only caring for the welfare of her father and the many who relied on his help and generosity but to the many who really knew Valentina she was seen as the most devious and cunningly cruel person. To the workers who worked and lived on the estate she was, behind her back of course, vilified as a vulture first and a lady second. Whenever Valentina was called upon to carry out her duties as the matriarch of the estate her true talent for offending came full circle. Berating the poor and helpless was an everyday affair with her.

Whenever anyone involved with the Francisco Estate tried to approach Valentine to intercede with the Don it was always a tragic conversation. It became evident, almost instantly, that this daughter of Don Francisco should never be taken lightly. Favors were granted but not without a price to pay.

On one such occasion the son of one of the long term gardeners, a man who started working for the Don at age 19 and at the ripe old age of 45 was still having to ask for intersession when trying to get a favor from the potentate.

Michelangelo was the main gardener on the estate.

"Senora Valentina voglio sapera si puy audar mio figlio Mario, nue volemo ga he podesa a la scola a Napoli,"

Michelangelo wanted to ask if Valentine would intercede with the Don in allowing his son Mario to go to school in Naples and of course be sponsored by the Don.

This was a big request. Valentina had not seen Mario in years. The day of the big meeting was set and Mario at 5 foot 11" tall was young, strong and attractive. His olive skin burned to a deep tan by the Italian sun and his long dark and rugged features made him a talking point amongst all of the available young girls within the Benevento area. Mario arrived right on time expecting to meet the Don instead he was greeted by a scantily clad Valentina.

Mario was surprised to say the least. In a matter of minutes Valentina had manipulated the situation and after an hour of satiation he was dismissed as one would a hand towel.

"Valentina! Oh Valentina, that was unbelievable!"

A panting and exhausted Mario loudly expressing his emotional state as he explored the ornate woodwork that adorned Valentina's bedroom ceiling.

Looking at her image through the ornate wall mirror that hung near her bed Valentina, completely dismissing Mario's obvious compliment

"What?" In an exasperated tone "What are you babbling about?"

Unable to grasp just what did occur he beckoned "Valentina! Why are you acting so annoyed, I thought you rather enjoyed what just happened between us! well! Did you?"

Valentina finished combing her hair and in one fell swoop dismissed the young stud.

"All right just get out! I said get out now!" Mario, stunned, begged for an answer

"Valentina I" But before he could utter another word Valentina walked out in a huff and yelled back as she passed the first of 5 bedrooms "Don't come back"

It was that quick and Mario stunned was gone. This scene had played out many times and the end result was always the same, Valentina had gotten exactly what she wanted.

Valentina used her power fiercely never minding who would be flattened by it. She inevitably, by the ripe old age of 21, commanded reverence from everyone no matter who.

The servants of the estate, knowing Valentina since childhood, observed that the Don favored his daughter to a fault. Sometimes the servants couldn't help but see the more than affectionate game being played by father and daughter that made them all uneasy.

As Father and daughter played out their childish games with their constant touching, teasing and kissing made all of the servants uneasy. These displays that seemed to occur more frequently as Valentina got older created a buzz that echoed, according to the gossip from Benevento, that the relationship bordered on being illicit. As both children grew into young adults their character was seen as distinctly different from each other.

Rudolfo strayed far from the duties of what a great land baron's son was supposed to do. Whereas Valentina took a more hands on approach to matters concerning the Don's estate and her eventual stewardship of the Jannace name.

Rudolfo, often referred to as a mama's boy by his father, retaliated to his father's remarks by spending as much of his allowance as possible. Gambling, womanizing, staying late and usually being brought home by cohorts, who the Don referred to as leeches, at the end of the night.

In the end the Don's tirades would subside until the next episode. Realizing that reasoning with his father was futile Rudolfo played the childish games that most children play in the hopes that tomorrow the authoritative one, being the Don, would forget it and chalk it up to youthful exuberance. In the end Rudolfo would have probably settled for a hug and fatherly embrace.

Valentina, on the other hand, was just the opposite. In the presence of her father and guests of the estate she was always on best behavior.

Valentina, knowing that everyone watched her every move when she was around the Don, would act as if the Don were the only person on earth. She would be kind and gentle with the servants and whenever visiting guests were around she was courteous to a fault. She was perceived by all in Benevento as the standard bearer of the Jannace future. The Don spoke about her as if he were speaking of a house mate and not a daughter. He talked of her as a treasure to be enjoyed by all. Behind the scenes it was a different story. She was in fact the devil in disguise. She was vile, crude and demanding. This acute attitude usually manifested itself whenever the Don was away. She accepted nothing less than what she ordered and hell would be paid if it didn't happen. The extreme differences between both children drove a wedge between them and Valentina's attitude was like it or leave it, brotherly love was lost on her.

After an all nigh binge with his friends in Rome causing much embarrassment to his father and sporting a mild hangover, Rudolfo was summoned to a meeting with the Don the following morning

"Father why did you belittle me, in front of all my friends?"

Rodolfo begged his father.

The Don took his time before answering. His handsomely coiffured hair and impeccable tailored suit mirrored aristocracy. The Don paced in front of the large bookshelf seemingly ignoring the rant by his son.

Nothing but silence from the Don.

"Father! Can you stop pacing and face me like a man! You humiliate...."

Before he could finish the word the Don turned and slapped him hard on the face.

"Do you think you're the first young fool the gambling halls have plucked?!

Are you even aware what monies you've gambled away?"

Rodolfo stood there dumbfounded. The shock of being hit took him back a bit. A small tear trickled down his cheek and the revulsion he felt at having his father hit him as if he were a commoner shook him even more.

Traditionally, as the Don and Rudolfo had repeated this scene in the past, this talk would have lasted a few minutes and it would be over. But not this morning. Not only did the Don yank him out of his luxurious surroundings in the gambling casino the previous evening but the Don's henchman, led by Philp Testa, embarrassed him in front of all of his gambling cohorts in doing so as they rudely pulled him physically away from his friends.

"Papa! Why would you humiliate me like that sending that animal Testa to do your bidding?"

Rudolfo was tall for an Italian but his white skin and facial acne matched the dullness of his teeth which when added together proved to his father that although Rudolfo was in his early twenties he still acted impetuously like a stupid schoolboy. Seeing that his father had not changed his customary demeanor Rodolfo began to tremble knowing that the Don was about to erupt even more. The Don seemingly discarding the fact that Rudolfo was his only son and eventual heir to the Jannace fortune continued his bellowing. To the servants who had observed this demeanor many times over hoped that perhaps in the end that this particular outburst might finally in some way shake this boy into realizing how badly he had failed his father. Although the help hated the Don with passion they still knew their place.

But something else was happening within the tirade. The Don, for the first time in Rudolfo's life, actually acted as if he truly didn't care about the boy. Seeing Rudolfo cringe at the tongue lashing actually heightened the Don's outrage.

"Don't you dare cry; do you hear me! Ever since you were a child your late mother spoiled you. Since you were a child you were always doing everything to please your and upset me. When I asked you numerous times to come hunting with me your mother said no! She said you were too delicate so! I took your sister. In so many ways she is the heir not you, and more of a man than you'll ever be. Now get out of my sight!"

This last outburst caused Rodolfo to run out of the stateroom cursing his father with every step.

Valentina entered the room brushing against Rodolfo who leered at her as she triumphantly stared back at him like a conqueror would his defeated enemies.

Rudolfo stopped abruptly and turned to face his sister.

"Why do you smirk sister?"

"I am not smirking brother, I am seeing that everything Father is saying is true, you're not the heir in this estate, you act as if you're a boarder, I haven't seen you for more than five minutes in six months. Of course he's right! Isn't he!" her cold stare made Rudolfo stiffen.

Valentina knew just how to turn the screws this last line was said with just the right touch of anger and victory as if it had always been a contest between them, to Rudolfo they had stopped becoming brother and sister right after Valentina's sixteenth birthday. The question that arose in Rudolfo's thought process in that instant was that he had lost and Valentina had won, it was as simple as that. The Italian tradition had always dictated the men not women ruled the earth. But not in Valentina's world.

"Valentina, I don't know what happened to you but if all of this is what you want then you can have it> But remember the reward will be that you will end up just like him, obviously that is truly all you ever wanted!"

Valentina tilted her head to the side and smirked.

"Yes brother that is exactly what I want!"

The division between brother and sister was finally apparent to everyone in the estate but for years preceding this final flare up the consensus was that after Rudolfo turned twenty-one years of age that the Don would relent and allow him his rightful place in the Jannace heir achy.

But now after what had just happened it was the defining moment in their relationship. Since Rudolfo was a child he always looked up to his older sister especially when their father had been unusually hard on him. But now the division was obviously unrepairable as Rudolfo in an instant saw that his sister claimed her right as the future Don. This signified that his time at the estate might be short lived.

"Father, you were a little hard on him weren't you" She said this in her most quietly facetious manner.

With her back turned to her father she began speaking in a shy almost childlike seductive manner eliciting just the right response from the Don.

As she spoke she slowly ran her finger across the marble encased book shelves mindlessly touching each and every book on all of the shelves as she spoke.

All this while having her back turned to her father as she spoke.

The Don watched this scene play out ever so slowly. He addressed his daughter.

"Well I can see that you finally woke up this morning and why are you now so concerned with Rudolfo's status in my house"

As he spoke he moved slowly towards her. She was still perusing the books contained within the bookshelf. She was extremely under dressed standing there wearing only a sheer nightgown. She was also well aware that her father had all his attention on her and that is exactly effect she obviously appeared to desire. The Don came behind her and immediately caught her fragrance, a mixture of lavender and fresh flowers.

"Are you really interested in those books you're touching? He was now standing directly behind her.

In an instant he signaled the servants to leave the room.

"All of you get out now!"

The servants quickly exited the main room as the Don put his hands on Valentina's hips. He pressed against her and as he did so she tilted her head backward as his hands reached around her arms touching her breasts.

CHAPTER 3

The Gabelotos on most estates were traditionally retired policemen who, for one reason or another, decided that working for the rich landowner would be better than waiting for a pension that might or might not materialize at the time of retirement. The history behind the Italian currency scenario was chaotic at best, not until years later under the guidance of Benito Mussolini did the Italian Lira stand for a little more that toilet paper.

For the Gabelotto of such an estate, like the Jannace estate, he needed many men to help him police the land and its farmers.

Anna was nineteen and judged one of the most beautiful young women of the province by many of the eligible bachelors. Many a young laborer within the confines of the Jannace estate, the province of the region, had eyes for her but Benito's reputation as the leader of Camorra superseded any thoughts any young man had concerning Anna.

The Gabelotto who supervised the Jannace estate was Giuseppe Testa. Testa was much older than many of the people he supervised. He was stout at five foot eight and his typical uniform each day consisted of his long sleeve white cotton shirt loose fitting vest and tight cotton form fitting pants, he'd wear the long sleeves even on the hottest days. The Don prided himself that his strong appearance and firm attitude towards everyone connected with him be tempered with calculating determination. The Don felt he could never afford to drop his guard with anyone especially family and close friends.

Testa, with the Don's blessing, ran the estate with an iron fist. His traits were punctuality and consistency. He never socialized with the help and the class division rampant throughout Italy for centuries was not lost on him.

Testa's approach to every farmer was that the farmer's job was to till the land and produce the crop and that to be divided on a sixty forty split was all they should worry about.

Testa, with his policeman's background and general gruff demeanor created a lot of respect from both the Don and the farmers. His constant intimidation and barrage of questions to everyone on the estate made one and all uneasy the moment he approached.

Throughout all of this it was evident that Testa had eyes for Anna as more than once was seen watching her as she walked to and from work to her home. Also present in Testa's mind was the ever present danger emanating from the man who brought Anna into the world her father Benito.

Benito besides being the most feared man in the region his legions were many and Testa, although rough and proud of his policeman's skills, was no match for a group of men hell bent on killing him.

Testa, on numerous occasions, carried on a dialog with Amalia Crespi about her daughter. Amalia tried with as much grace and diplomacy as she could muster to try and dissuade Testa from any advances to her daughter. Testa continued to badger Amalia knowing full well that her husband, although the most dangerous man in Southern Italy, was still incarcerated. The fact that Crespi was incarcerated would have given other men hope and confidence but Testa, not a fool, knew that in the end Anna was still Benito's daughter and that made him a little uneasy.

To everyone else on the estate a word in either direction from Testa meant an easy or really hard day on the farm. Testa had been handpicked by Don Jannace and owed his loyalty to the Don. The Don was not a man to be trifled with so whenever the Don commanded anything from Testa it was as sure as done. The commingling and socializing between people directly employed by Don Francisco Jannace and farm people was frowned upon by the Don unless he gave his blessing. The Don's law was that everything, even marriage, had to get his blessing first. If any young man wanted to wed he had to ask permission not only from the girl's father but from the Don because in the end the estate controlled everyone's life and the Don pulled the strings. Testa had asked the Don for the hand of Anna Crespi to which the Don answered that there was an age difference between them but Testa asked the ultimate of the Don.

"Don Jannace I have been loyal to you for years and there is nothing I wouldn't do for you agree?"

"Yes you have been loyal, so what do you want!"

"If It can be arranged, and of course with your blessing, I am fixated with the young Crespi girl, the one they call Anna, can you help?"

The Don studied his Gabellotto to see if it would be in his favor to grant such a favor. Knowing Testa's background and his obvious lack of both hygiene and sartorial awareness he took his request with serious consideration. The Don knew full well that after weighing all the facts that there would be considerable rage within the ranks of Crespi Neapolitan working class followers but then again the Don always loved challenges. The Don decided, strictly for selfish reasons, to grant Testa's request.

"If that's what you want, it's done!"

The strange irony here was that the Don never needed Testa's loyalty to prove to all that he was a strong leader but it was testing Crespi's influence that piqued the Don's inquisitiveness. And for that reason alone the Don relented to Testa's needs.

There were many families that share cropped the Jannace estate and for most of them survival, as hard as it was, was accepted as their fate. One such family was the Giancarlo Family. Salvatore and Carmella had two children a boy names Antonio and a daughter named after the mother. Antonio was a strapping boy of nineteen and the parents had saved money for years in the hopes that their only son might one day leave the farming life and with his education would strike out on his own and conquer the world. Antonio, after having his parents scrimp and save every available penny to send him away, was finally coming home after five long years studying at the monastery in Naples. Antonio had in effect had his fill of confinement and longed for the countryside he missed so much and the family he left behind.

Coming home to Benevento, Antonio, after his time away became alarmingly aware of how much his parents had sacrificed so he could be at school. His father, with his weather-beaten hands and his mother who seemed to have aged right before his very eyes made him realize how difficult it was for his parents to not only work the land but still manage to keep in in school.

"Mother I am not going back to Naples to study I can see that I am needed here."

Carmella looked at her son in awe, both pride and love combined brought tears to her eyes.

"My most beautiful son, I am so proud that you feel the way you do, but you coming back is not what is going to happen. Your father and I haven't struggled all these years for you to come back here!"

Antonio, only half listening to what his mother was saying had his attention span interrupted by what was occurring practically in front of his home. Only half listening to his mother he couldn't help but be mesmerized as he was awestruck by the beautiful parade of young girls walking up the hill.

There walking up the hill were roughly 15 young women coming home from a day's work in the fields.

They were laughing and giggling knowing full well they were being watched by the salivating hordes of young laborers standing idle by as this bevy of beauty paraded in front of them. As if in slow motion the young women slow walked passed sweating young males working the land who were just happy to take a break from the hot mid-day sun. The young women, in their glory, walked so seductively up the hill. This ritual was repeated every day at exactly the same time. One by one the young males whistled and cat called to the girls and so did their brethren who were both above and below the hill.

Captivated by the mere hint of young virginal femininity all hands, even the much older men, stopped working as they viewed the assembly of young beauties as they passed.

Antonio was no different than any of the young males. He too was fixated. He couldn't keep his eyes off one of the girls in the group. He swore to himself that he indeed had seen this girl before. Perhaps years earlier as many of the worker offspring were group home schooled. Perhaps he had seen her even years before on the picnic outings sponsored by the Jannace clan. But no matter he was fixed on her now.

He tried to get a better look at her. The rather hilly portion of the walk made it difficult for all the girls to actually walk in a straight line. The uneven steps had the girls bumping into each other and as each girl tried to get a better footing, heaven forbid they should accidentally fall, the embarrassment to say the least would be horrible.

But then in an instant he saw her. Although her full profile was, at times partially hidden, he saw that she was clearly the diamond in the bunch.

His best estimate was that she stood about five foot seven. Her olive skin highlighted by her long black hair made her visual seem more angelic than farm girl. But one glance from her revealed a look that rivaled every delirious erotic dreams he ever had at the monastery in Naples.

He finally figured it out. She epitomized every thought about the opposite sex that he, as the schoolboy, could ever fantasize at boarding school.

His mind stood racing. He took mental snapshots of her with every step she took. To his way of thinking she appeared as if in a slow motion only for his eyes to see.

He knew in that instant, even though he had been cloistered and hadn't really interacted with females in general, that he needed to speak to her.

The young girls, knowing full well they were being ogled, put on a show for the hot and sweaty laborers. The girls exaggerated each and every step knowing full well that their time tantalizing the young men would be short at best.

Antonio's heart began to race and instinctively he acted knowing what he needed to do. His palms were wet with perspiration and he began to fear that perhaps she might disappear over the mountain and he might never see her again.

He wondered what family she belonged to and how far away she lived. What fields was she assigned to? He questioned himself, was she promised to anyone? Was she married? All these thoughts ran through his brain. The questions began mounting until he couldn't stand it any longer.

In an instant he knew what he had to do.

At that very moment he began to walk out of the house towards her. At first his gait was slow and deliberate then quickly so as to catch the group before they made the last 25 feet or so walk up the hill to the other side of the mountain.

As the girls, still giggling and talking under their breath, deliberately slowed their walk up the steep hill. Just so everyone could get a closer look at them and knowing that fraternizing with the male workers was strongly looked upon as demeaning and classless by both the land owner and the parents. the girls had to literally walk that fine line.

The girls although engaged in conversation with each other were always cognizant that every able bodied man along both sides of the mountain stopped working just to admire the beauty put before them.

Seeing Antonio dart out like a crazy person his mother yelled.

"Antonio! come back" she beckoned knowing full well that any confrontation with anyone other than their fellow workers would result in punishment from the Gabbelotto and that would in the end cause trouble for her and the rest of the family.

In a few seconds he had reached the group of women and in that moment had made eye contact with this young angel.

He looked at her and instinctively he knew that in that instant he needed to form the words that would stop her and not make her afraid of her.

"Who are you? What is your name?" the oddity of the situation and Antonio's outburst suddenly positioned both

Antonio and Anna in what philosophers have called "a moment"

There was a pause in his speech and instinctively reached for her arm, pulling her out of the group of girls that were walking up the hill.

Startled and almost losing her balance, Anna allowed herself to be pulled out of line, she was startled yet calm.

Anna was rendered speechless.

The oddity was that aside from family members and a few young boys that had grown up around her Anna had actually never engaged in continuous conversations that are traditional between boys and girls.

Anna was full of life yet protected as were so many young girls her age.

She hadn't spoken to many of the young men much less have any physical contact. So when he grabbed her wrist she didn't know if she should scream, laugh or just stay mum.

After straightening out her dress and gaining her balance she looked up at this impetuous young man who still had her wrist in his hand.

Looking down at her wrist then back at Antonio half smiling and again she looked down at her wrist that by now had started turning red from Antonio's grip.

"Please let go of my wrist your hurting me!"

Antonio, in what seemed like a dream moment reminiscent to floating in time with Anna's face in his emotional view quickly awoke

Noticing what was happening he quickly let her go.

"Oh God please!" he apologetically asked of this rare beauty

"Please forgive me, I don't know what got over me"

She looked at this rather frail yet disarmingly handsome brown eyed young man. She noticed that unlike the other boys of the village his hands weren't rough or coarse. His skin was deep olive and his black hair hung on his head as an ornament to those deep piercing eyes, but his smile was what captivated her from the instant they met.

"My name is Antonio Giancarlo and I live with my family there" Pointing to the brown weather-beaten stucco home perched a few hundred feet away up the hill.

By now the path was deserted as all the girls had made their way over the mountain.

As Antonio pointed to the small house she quietly got lost in his exuberance and in that instant she, like Antonio, felt that their encounter was magical.

In the next five minutes he recounted to her what he had seen from his mother's window and again pointed to it.

There was an awkward silence between them Antonio spoke first

"Where do you live and what is your name"

Anna was still studying his face and like an echo she suddenly realized that he was speaking to her.

"What is your name, how old are you and where do you live"

For some reason the silence between them brought out a smile on both their faces as the nervousness had disappeared and only curiosity remained. She instinctively knew that this rather charming and handsome young man meant her no harm and she was actually happy that he stopped her.

He was proper in his manners and his disarming attitude allowed her the time so that the warmth of the sun could reach way down into her soul and comfort her.

The silence between them became deafening.

Realizing that neither one of them had uttered a word in what seemed like an eternity they both attempted to talk again only at the same time. Then silence again and in an instant there was laughter then more laughter and more laughter, bending over in comedic pain he held up his hand trying to catch his breath after laughing so hard that his eyes were filled with tears. She was in the same condition.

Antonio finally caught his breath raised his hand as if to declare that he would talk first. He could see that as he spoke her eyes followed every line of his face creating an invisible connection between them. He silently thanked God that this chance meeting was the luckiest day in his young life. He spoke first.

"All right we both just discovered that socially we need help correct?"

The belly laughs started again and again Antonio tried to make some sense and connect with this beauty before anyone could interrupt them.

"Ok, stop! What is your name?"

Her voice was music to his ears.

"Anna, my name is Anna Crespi"

He couldn't remember if he had ever heard a more beautiful name.

"Anna the moment I saw you I knew I had to talk to you"

It appeared to him that Anna hung on every word he uttered.

He also noticed that as he spoke Anna, like an innocent child of the world, seemed to hang on every word that he spoke.

He noticed her eyes moving from his mouth to his eyes and back again to his mouth Antonio sensed a sensuality that he too had never felt before it was as if this was the first time he had ever laid eyes on the opposite sex.

He assumed that his education and especially his historical Italian studies opened up a word that Anna had only dreamed about.

The fact that education was so vital to Anna made Antonio crave her innocence even more.

In the next two months the two of them met at the same spot at the foot of the mountain after their day's work was done. Being Catholic made it practically impossible for young people to socialize within the confines of the estate without the elders characterizing each and every gesture.

The class structure was such that many young girls, some of them barely into their teens, were promised to more wealthy and affluent families by their families. This did two things it elevated the families to a higher order in the community and secondly it made sure that a virgin daughter especially a beautiful one like Anna would carry into the marriage her prized possession, her virginity.

That was the main reason that unsupervised young people getting together on any occasion was frowned upon, pregnancy being the by word.

To both Antonio and Anna verbalizing was akin to kissing and laughter was akin to mischievous conduct. Anna loved to listen to Antonio's ideas on life and especially traveling to see what the world outside of Benevento was all about. Antonio was also so kind to her in fully understanding that her limited education would never stop him from caring deeply about her.

It was one of the nicest Saturdays with sunshine and low humidity. All the Saturday day workers had finally said well by to their chores, everyone had to work half days on Saturday, and mostly started to look forward to the one and a half days of rest accorded them by the Don's edict.

To the both of them what started out as pure friendship was slowly developing into much more?

Lately they had been meeting on the south side of the estate. This portion of the entire property line was only partially seen by most from whatever vantage point chosen. The reason they chose that particular portion of Jannace estate was privacy.

There was an artificial waterfall that the Don had created that fell into the lake. The scene was out of an ancient travelogue depicting trees and flowers all in their rightful glory and all pointed up to the sun.

The gigantic hillsides that bordered and surrounded the Jannace Lake made one wonder how could all the stories about the Don be true, any man that could create this beautiful landscape could never be as bad as they portrayed him to be.

Anna and Antonio needed privacy as their relationship had slowly gone from frivolous laughter and innocent role playing to touching and kissing with both knowing that perhaps sometimes soon they might need to be private as everything could get out of hand even in the most innocent way.

And although the farming families on the estate frowned on their teenage children fraternizing with the opposite sex the temptation was present.

As they lay on the hillside together gazing at the bright blue sky they both knew that sooner or later their relationship would be found out and every thought imaginable was spoken about by the two of them.

"If you had the opportunity to travel where would you go" he beckoned

She lay there with arms outstretched and pointed them straight to the sky, and in an almost dejected and pouting manner decried

"Oh Antonio how can I talk about traveling I've never left Benevento!"

The mere fact that Antonio, in a few short hours, illuminated Anna's mind giving her a geographical experience that could only be described as spellbinding. Anna had always known that there was a world outside of Benevento but to actually hear someone describe the vastness of the outside world in such a graphic yet beautiful way actually made emotionally jump for joy.

"Oh Antonio you describe those places so romantically! You are an artist!" She exclaimed!

When Antonio had finished describing how the great palaces of the Far East catered to explorers like Marco Polo Anna was all ears. Anna suddenly got up

"Antonio watch me dance for the King of Siam!"

She exclaimed and she twirled herself as if her imaginary partner was indeed the King.

He hoped that the most important aspect of this encounter, as he skillfully blended beautiful lines of poetry and prose, would illuminate the fact that he was different than most of the young men of the province. She being only slightly educated could in fact learn from him and the blending of his fondness for her and her wanting to soak up everything he had to offer made them an ideal couple.

He sat up on one elbow gazing into her beauty lovingly smiling at her wanting her to know that it really didn't matter to him what little knowledge she had about the outside world.

"Hey young lady it really doesn't matter" he could see that she was embarrassed at not having had any knowledge of what lie outside the estate. He took her hand in his and just held it tightly, wanting her to know that he simply cared.

"What does matter to me at least is that we feel good about each other and perhaps in the future we can plan on something a little more than working the fields. Sound ok? With you?"

Six months had passed and Anna and Antonio's friendship had blossomed into something more. They both agreed that clandestine meeting only heightened the anxiety between them. And as always the thought that anyone connected to the Jannace clan would discover their romance and ultimately disapprove. They were both warned by their respective mothers about the perils that young people full of exuberance and a healthy need for compassion need be careful because the worst thing that could ever happen to all concerned was pregnancy.

The Jannace people would never tolerate such a condition. It would rob the estate of an able worker being the girl and distract the potential father in not doing his fair amount of work. The stupidity of such thinking by everyone connected with the estate proved how backward they truly were. In the end Jannace law was the law of the land it governed with an iron hand.

CHAPTER 4

The makeshift beautifully sculptured grassy area situated acres away from the large Jannace mansion yet part of the Jannace estate was only used on special occasions and by invitation only. Some days, whenever the Don permitted, certain trusted members of the household staff who, according to the Don, who had earned the right would be allowed to celebrate here as to whatever the occasion demanded.

Centered directly in the middle of this beautiful setting stood a well-built carriage house. The house was used to house and take care of the Don's prize white stallions.

Throughout the years the carriage house was used as a meeting center, celebration hall and sometimes a makeshift court house. Being that the Don was the law of the land occasionally he was asked to adjudicate matters pertaining to the land or the estate.

Most of the time the house was used for weddings. Besides the occasional wedding and other festive occasions, the white stallions roamed the parcel as free as any man in the village.

No matter what the occasion or reason for usage on or surrounding the property it was never out of eye control of the Jannace caretaker Philip Testa. Many times one of his lieutenants would peruse the property just to make sure that Testa's orders were followed. The land so beautiful and pristine was obviously more important to the Don than the people who were allowed to enjoy it.

And so it was but this particular day was going to be unlike most other days because this rural setting was, as it had always been on occasion, to be turned into a court of law.

And as other days like it had shown marshal law and punitive justice dispensed by the Don was a serious matter. The Don had made it a habit of enforcing all of his rulings no matter how unjust they appeared to all. The carriage house was structured as a two floor structure. The bottom floor was Hugh and as needed a large platform was installed mirroring a judge's bench. Tables were placed on either side for both plaintive and defendant. The Judge's bench was, of course, higher that the other two tables. The back of the house had row after row of wooden yet polished seating for whatever audience was permitted to view the proceedings.

Whenever these types of proceedings were called but a few spectators were allowed to sit in the audience. As in the past on some of the Don's rulings the outcome was not favorable and stronger than any court the Don's ultimate ruling would stand.

17 Phip Testa and 6 of his men together with the few field hands were the only people in the building.

The Judge in this case was one of the Don's closest advisors, Don Claudio Bacca. Don Bacca owned one of the finest vineyards in Benevento and on many an occasion was asked to adjudicate matters for his fellow land owners. Don Bacca, a widower, had expressed his feelings for Don Francisco's daughter Valentina but the Don graciously declined for his daughter saying that she still had a lot of the world to see before she would decide to settle down. Bacca was sixty years of age. Good living had brought about a few ailments including the gout and arthritis that could readily be seen as he laboriously ambled his way into the small room adjacent to the court room so he could brief himself on the case before him.

It was a hot Saturday afternoon. Philip Testa, surrounded by his 6 lieutenants, slowly began to take their customary positions in the makeshift courtroom.

This day Testa was observed by the few in the courthouse as unusually sartorial. No matter how much cologne he managed to douse himself with his swarmy at best appearance highlighted by his crooked two front teeth presented a rather comical figure. In what could only be called an Oliver Hardy moment Testa made no bones that this day might very well be a memorable day in his life. In his best manner Testa wanted so much for everyone who looked at him or made contact with him to realize exactly what he had become as overseer for the Don. Testa wanted all to realize that he had evolved into a little more than a Gabellotto.

Testa wanted recognition as a man of respect but in the southern portion of Italy only Don Francisco could command that. But in the Don's shadow Testa campaigned as a man who not only worked for the most powerful man in Italy but he, in his own right, was a man to be reckoned with, a man of respect. But this day amongst the few in attendance he was unusually jovial he was acting like an expectant father. To the few who watch with humor as he continually kept looking at his reflection through the only mirror available that hung by the back door to the building.

Testa's appearance, with his traditional high to the knee cap fascist leather boots, in many ways resembled the ruling fascist regime gaining momentum in the country. He wore a soiled brown corduroy coat under which he had a light tan vest that barely covered his gravy stained white shirt. To the few who watched, as he ceremoniously inspected every nook and cranny of the make shift courthouse while inspecting his appearance through the small mirror on the back wall, appeared to be happy to a fault.

"Great day for a hearing eh paisan"

Testa bellowed to the bewildered farmer who was sitting in the front row. The oddity here was that the farmer had not uttered but a single word to this man who ran roughshod over everyone on the Don's property in over 10 years. With the exception to the few times Testa and not his handlers came around to collect the 60-40 split on fruits and vegetables there had never been a single word between them.

A few minutes had passed and a Crespi family made their way inside the courthouse followed by the Giancarlo family. As both families sat in the same row their mood unlike Testa was somber at best.

Mrs. Giancarlo took her hand kerchief and began to dab her eyes that were partially swollen from crying.

"I can't believe what happened, how this could happen he is such a good boy!"

Anna Crespi, also crying, looked at her mother as if to ask the same question, how something could so bad happen to the boy she had fallen in love with.

CHAPTER 5

Anna couldn't wait for her chores to be finished. Her mother seeing that her daughter had absentmindedly placed the eggs on the table and placed the bread where the eggs should have been had to stop her.

"Daughter! Can you see what you're doing? Look!"

As she pointed to the eggs and bread.

"What's on your mind, these last few days you've been acting so strange it's as if you're living with us yet your mind and your thoughts are a million miles away!"

Anna smiled and hugged her mother as strong as when she had been a child and her father and mother had rewarded her and her sister with sweet treats from Benevento.

"Oh mother1 I think I'm in love!"

Amalia knew this someday this day would come only she didn't expect it so soon. The biggest fear any Benevento mother has of her daughters is that once puberty set in that the normal chain reactions that follow are boys, discoveries and boys.

"Anna you need to hear this please sit down"

Amalia took her daughter by the shoulders and gently made her sit.

Anna still with a smile on her face couldn't keep it in.

"Oh mama, are you going to tell me the same story that Adeline's mom told her about the birds and the bees?"

Amalia needed to be firm yet caring.

"No daughter, you realize that your father is in jail and that to lose a daughter at this time would destroy us I don't need you to do anything that would jeopardize our position here until your father is released"

Anna still smiling tried to reassure her mother.

"I love Antonio Giancarlo, I think you know that and no we're not planning to elope or leave Benevento. He is so sweet and a gentleman. Mama he reads me poetry and tells me about faraway places and when he speaks he's so kind and gentle knowing that my home schooling has limited me it hasn't stopped him from teaching me about the world he knows so much about."

Amalia could see that nothing she could say would sway her daughter's opinion or her obvious happiness.

"I'm meeting him today and he's promised to read from Dante, oh I'm so excited, Mama your happy for me right?"

Seeing her daughter so happy all she could say was.

"Yes, I am"

Antonio was lying down on the grassy hillside letting the sun cascade upon his already tanned features.

"A penny for your thoughts?"

Anna had made her way to their favorite spot and like every other day these past three months there was her Antonio. As he lifted his head and as his black hair jostled to the side of his head she saw that smile that had, months ago, instantaneously won her heart.

"Hey there, I was waiting for someone perhaps you know her, her name is Anna Crespi, know her?"

"Well, let me see do I know her?"

She stood there in what was another game they both played. Questions than answers as each one of them listened so attentively to the sounds emanating from their mouths.

"Anna Crespi you say! Yes, I do know her but I do know something else! I am waiting for a young man who is so full of himself and his name is Antonio Giancarlo do you know this fellow?"

Anna playfully looked to her left and right as if to find her Antonio.

In one fell swoop Antonio pulled her down to the ground and in an instant they were laughing hysterically as he grabbed her and they both began to roll on the ground as young children would do. After a minute of hilarity, they both stared straight up to the sky trying to catch their breath.

"I am so happy you came "

Antonio rolled over on top of her and just stood there with his arms outstretched above her, their eyes met and slowly he lowered himself onto her.

Unlike every other time they had played this game the mood turned somber and serious. For the first time in months their bodies were together as one. He was on top of her and as their usual custom both would either change the subject or make a joke just to break the tension. As he lay on top of her she could feel him grow beneath her stomach and the fire that had been building for months erupted as he passionately kissed her. The clothes they were wearing were discarded in the blink of an eye and both of them delighted in each other's mysteries. Anna although thin had firm breasts and Antonio, also thin, was endowed delighting both of them as they probed and explored through continuous lovemaking.

There for that one magic moment everything their parents warned them about was forgotten. Passion that had been released and everything within the realm of lusting for one another was on for the taking.

This type of dynamic connection was not unusual when it involved young people who for the most part were always being told to stay with your own gender until they were married.

What was unusual about Antonio and Anna was why it took so long to happen. Like beginners in any endeavor passion is many times confused with whatever literature had described it to be. It is only when the real thing is upon the participants that true joy and in many cases happiness and togetherness would follow. The key to Anna's erotic feelings lay in the fact that she loved being held by this wonderful boy. Call it because she was fatherless and Antonio's strong grasp symbolized her jailed father's strength or just the presence of a man's emotional state when delivering ecstatic movements surrounded by bodies writing in passion.

Antonio, although schooled in Naples, was just as naive sexually as Anna. Their respective experiences meshed perfectly. He having read countless books from the Kama Sutra to the elicit poems of Italian Lotharios that magically found their way into that strict Catholic dormitory. And she having spoken with a few girls her age that had actually experienced kissing and petting not to mention what she remembered from her own parents. At night when her parents thought it was safe the two young sisters would listen to their mother moan with ecstasy as she made love to Benito their father. In their minds they tried to imagine what was happening and how did that act make her mother sound so different, confusing to say the least.

But no matter what horrors they were told by the elders of the village about sex and the work of the devil, the girls knew that the joys of togetherness and marriage were tightly interwoven in sex. The girls were not stupid they remembered how fondly a strong man like Benito viewed his wife he truly loved her and that was all the girls needed to know.

When a man and a woman like Benito and Amalia marry then whatever happens between them was only viewed as good and natural. The two sisters knew that from the outset. For Anna and Antonio their mutual love of their family and themselves created the bond that would eventually hold them together.

Antonio took his time and Anna trusting him yet wanting, at the same time, to speed up the path that his worn out book on positions and lovemaking, that had been read and reread a million times, allowed. He had memorized every page and photograph while pretending to sleep at school in Naples. But what he had never counted on was the passion that overtaken him and Anna and in an instant they both were part of the book creating their own chapters.

This combination of pent up emotions meshed with curiosity and joy actually started months before. Innocently at first with Anna trying to depict in her mind the characters Antonio was speaking about. When Antonio recited some of Dante's poems Anna would be filled with passion and conversely after Antonio read the poems and said his good byes his loins would subsequently ache for hours.

It was done and as they both lay exhausted they knew that there was no turning back. They were not only lovers but in love. As days turned into weeks and as they both continued in their everyday lives the thoughts of their first magical day together spurred them to do it over and over again.

Every day Amalia couldn't help but notice the look on her daughter's face. With every movement and gesture coupled with Anna's expression as she looked at everything in her everyday life as Cinderella looked and acted after she met the prince.

It was Saturday afternoon and the scene was reminiscent of the past three months. Antonio and Anna would secretly meet by the willow groves on the east end of the hillside adoringly named the Love Grove by Anna.

"I haven't thought about anything but you this past week"

Anna smiled but behind the smile her body ached for her lover and as the previous Saturdays had brought them together all they both needed was each other immediate and now! There was no foreplay only want. In seconds they were on the blanket that Anna had brought intertwined in each other's embrace. Without any fanfare or dialog their role playing followed the same script. As the cool summer winds rustled the tree branches above them as if in concert Antonio made love to he and her loud half crazed moan of Ecstasy echoed throughout the treetop branches that swayed and rustled answering Anna's calls like gulps of joy echoing over and over.

This scene played out again and again until both of them lay exhausted on the blanket.

Antonio propped himself on one elbow to look at this creature that captivated his heart. With his right hand he deftly followed the small lines and contour of, what appeared to him as angelic. Her eyes were wide and her greenish blue coloring reminded him of the multi colored Easter eggs he had loved as a child. Her lips partly split in the most seductive manner prompted him to perhaps muster up enough energy but thought better about it.

"Antonio! Your smiling what is so funny?"

As he tried to contain himself he couldn't get the words out.

"I thought for a second, mind you, that I might try to make love to you again but my body said no! So you see what you've done to me"

In an instant they were rolling on the ground holding their sides in laughter and as the tears started rolling down Anna's cheeks she suddenly stopped laughing and her demeanor turned serious into white stark terror.

Seeing this sudden expression Antonio exclaimed.

"Anna what is it, you turned white! Did I do something?"

Anna suddenly pointed to the hollowed out passageway separating one grassy hillside from another. The trees acted as a barrier but the opening had been used by the people working the land making it easier to access the other side.

"There!"

She pointed to the opening.

"There was a man watching us, oh God it looked like Testa Antonio he is the Gabbelotto here! I told you this was not a great idea remember!"

"Stay calm I'll go have a look"

In a minute Antonio was back and smiling.

"There is no one there, you're imagining things, and could you have made a mistake?"

Anna still shaking.

"No it was him, oh God do you think he watching us while we ……?"

"No now stop, if it was him don't you think he would have said something, after all he is responsible for all of Don Francisco's property, right?"

Anna had calmed down a bit.

"We had better go"

That was to be the last time they would ever be together.

Sunday am.

Philip Testa knocked on the door of the Giancarlo house with ten of his men behind him.

"We are here for Antonio Giancarlo, is he here."

Antonio's father, in shock at what he heard, stood back gathering his strength as his nerves had gotten the best of him.

"What do you want him for?'

"Your son is accused by Don Francisco for stealing provisions from the East end stockade where Don Francisco houses much of his imported artifacts and some of them are missing, your son was seen near there and until an official investigation is conducted he has to come with us, now! Send him out!"

It was that fast and in two hours Antonio, although pleading innocent every step of the way, was arraigned in the Jannace compound adjacent to the grassy hillside where he and Anna made passionate love together. He was jailed with no visitors not even his parents to visit or even see him. The compound was used primarily for workers who had a little too much to drink and the gabbelloto would lock them up there until they sobered up. Antonio pleaded with one of the guards but to no avail. It would be three days before his parents were allowed to visit him.

CHAPTER 6

The few workers that were allowed to stay and observe the courtroom proceedings made sure to be as inconspicuous as possible and to make sure not to make eye contact with anyone connected to the Jannace estate.

The rear door opened and there standing between two of the Jannace foremen was Antonio. To the onlookers he appeared pale and disoriented. He wore the same clothes he had on the day the Jannace guards took him from his family. As he stepped into the large room, with hands and feet manacled, his dazed expression only heightened the sorrow his family felt.

Within seconds of his appearance agonizing cried erupted from the aisle his parents were seated in. Upon hearing their cries Antonio too started to cry as a young child does when separated from his love ones.

Antonio's fate was now in the hands of the Jannace governing system.

Life, after today, would never be the same. The people who were closest to him were all sitting in the same pew together. His father sitting on the end of the bench had his head down and one could see that he was crying. The two women, Antonio's mother and Benito Crespi's wife Amalia, were holding each other hand giving comfort and support to each other as only mothers can do.

Anna was seated in the middle and as Antonio was ushered into the defendant's chair she tried to reach over and touch the man who had won her heart but to no avail. In seconds the courtroom became silent. There was an eerie calm in the courtroom as if some ominous force was about to do damage on all attending.

Antonio's mother in her most reverent tone pleaded with God for his intervention.

With a hush and quivering voice meekly lamented.

"Dear God please! Let my child go!"

It was not to happen.

Everyone waited for Don Bacca's entrance.

The large oak door directly in back of the raised judicial bench opened and out came Don Bacca.

To everyone in the court he represented the government and his decision was the law.

As Don Bacca, with his granny glasses drooped down on his nose and strands of unruly white hair hung loosely across his left eye, began shuffling papers in front of him and it seemed to those watching that he had no idea of who was being tried much less what the charges were.

"Order in my court" he suddenly bellowed wanting everyone to know that in the end it would be his decision as to who or what would be tried in front of him still, he seemed as if in a fog as to why he was there in the first place. His statement was odd being that the silence within the courtroom was deafening.

'As Don Bacca again began shuffling the few papers in front of him and nervously looking to the back door as if reinforcements were coming he suddenly stopped and looked directly at the one person who was standing up ready to speak.

"Don Bacca, I am sure that everyone is glad that you are here to adjudicate the proceedings."

Phip Testa stood in front of the bench addressing the Don in his most adamant way.

"The documents are there in front of you, Antonio Giancarlo is accused of stealing precious wine from Don Jannace's storeroom here in the East Meadow."

The judge looked at the thin young man with manacles on his hands and feet.

"This is a boy is it not? He can't be more than 18 years of age are we sure that this child is a criminal?!"

As Bacca uttered his statement Testa uneasily shifted his weight from one side to another. And then in a most animal like way Testa growled and in that instant he revealed to everyone in the court exactly what he was made of. In a roar reminiscent of circus lions ready for supper he reached over to Don Bacca's bench and banged his fist against the oak bench. It was obvious that Don Bacca's rather lax attitude toward the defendant was not what Testa intended to have happened.

In an obvious attempt to snap Bacca out of his reverie and make him understand exactly what Testa needed he snapped.

"You're Honor!'

Suddenly there was an eerie silence in the room.

Again Testa implored the judge in his most intimidating tone possible.

"Perhaps you hadn't looked at the court order in front of you, his tone was a bit calmer this time and in an instant he saw that Bacca finally got the drift of what he was implying.

Bacca, finally acting as impartial and judicious got serious, straightened his glasses and read the charges at first to himself concurring with Testa by eye sight, put the paper and his glasses down looked at Antonio who by now was shivering from freight.

"It is the order of this court that you Antonio Giancarlo be sentenced to three years in the Castel De Mare, take him away."

CHAPTER 7

"Are you happy with the verdict?"

Testa smiled and drank his glass of sherry.

"I am and I thank you for that Don Francisco"

The Don, with his back facing Testa, stood in front of his huge picture window that overlooked his most precious manicured gardens. There, with his arms folded behind his back like a king surveying all he possessed, chuckled out loud.

"Testa, you're so easy to figure out. How long do you think that young thing will take before she finds out that it was you who sent her lover to prison?"

Testa put his drink down and forgetting his place attempted to address the Don as two friends would after they had both been conspiring together. He casually grabbed an orange from one of the marbled tables next to where the Don was standing. Seeing Testa's reflection as it shone through the clear glass the Don simply allowed Testa to ramble on. Testa, now totally consumed with the juicy orange he had begun to peel, couldn't possibly have noticed that the Don was slowly getting upset. In an attempt at being gallant and a bit familiar in his tone Testa began pacing back and forth while eating his orange and almost cartoon in fashion discussing his dilemma like an orator in high court.

"I think that after a certain amount of time has passed she will see that her only opportunity to get out of the everyday work load is to be kind to me, I am her only salvation and then...."

Like a cat pouncing upon a helpless mouse Don Jannace, with as vicious a snarl that a man of his stature could muster, turned and screamed in Testa's face forcing him to drop the orange onto the waxed marble floor. Standing inches from Testa's face the ashen terrified Gabelotto stood frozen.

"Who do you think you're talking to!! We're not friends! You work for me, don't ever forget that!"

Testa was fear struck seeing the aggressive manner in which Don Jannace came at him.

"You survive! By the grace of me! Do you understand, and who the hell gave you permission to eat fruit off my table! And slobber on my marble floor with your unkempt presence! What you do with the girl is not my business what is my business is you knowing your place, YOU UNDERSTAND! Now get out!"

Testa hurriedly left hat in hand, not to mention what was left of the half eaten orange.

CHAPTER 8

Castel De Mare had not changed in over one hundred and fifty years.

It had been a year since that fretful day in Don Jannace's court.

Antonio Giancarlo was officially a felon.

"Antonio, why do you ponder the inevitable? I must have told you a thousand times you are here for the three years not thirty! I will help you, you'll make the best of it!"

Benito sat in one corner of the eight by ten-foot cell. Antonio, although truly in debt to Crespi for his very survival was still adamant that he had done nothing wrong to deserve his punishment!"

Crespi smiled and kind lines crossed his face as he marveled at the boy.

"You are a wonder! Hey Phillippo do you hear this lad! He still doesn't understand the garbage that did this to him"

Phillippo Cantalupo, Crespi's most trusted confidant inhabiting the cell directly across from him, benevolently rustled Antonio's hair as he took his noontime break. For two hours each day the inmates on the South wall were allowed to walk the length of the cell block hopefully getting a glimpse of the blue majestic Mediterranean a mere three floors below.

"Benito, the boys been here a year, do you think he will ever change and accept his fate?"

Benito, as if thinking about his life and family that he so missed was brought out of his revere, "Change? Perhaps, remember Italy always needs philosophers and teachers and Antonio here fits the bill, why after he marries Anna he'll probably set up teaching in Benevento eh Antonio"

"I guess so, hopefully I will still remember the knowledge that the priests beat into me. The great Italian thinkers who took years to write all those books, wow I hope that I can be that lucky to still retain whatever I learned from the priests. But I still marvel at what has happened to me in the end I hope those thoughts come back to me and with Anna we can make a beautiful life together"

Antonio kept looking out his window that faced the front of the prison and it was the first of the month which meant visitors.

The prison had three floors. The stairs leading to the second and third floors were made of wood. The steps had, for the most part, seen better days. Occasionally whenever officials from Benevento had announced they were coming for an inspection inmates were summarily told to shore up the steps so no mishaps could arise.

The Castel De Mare prison was not the friendliest place for law breakers least of all political prisoners whose only crime was that they disagreed with the majority. On the lower level the most hardened criminals were housed. It was there that Benito Crespi and Antonio Giancarlo forget a friendship that would last for over fifty years.

Many months had passed and Antonio's expression had not changed since the day he was forcibly thrown in with the common rabble that inhabited the lower level of the prison.

Most of the political prisoners were housed on the same floor and all to a man gave Antonio all the leeway and respect that any man could ever hope to have. Benito had paved the way for his future son in law and in the most eerie way Antonio didn't seem to care obviously still wondering why Testa had done this to him.

"You sit and ponder, what you think about!"

Benito slid down the wooden bench to where Antonio was sitting. In the last year he had grown fond of the boy and in his heart he felt that Antonio's motives were always with Anna's best interest at heart.

"Come on let's play briske (An Italian Card Game) I bet I can scoop you, Antonio!" Benito implored.

"Get the cards you deal"

ANTONIO WITH A SHEEPISH GRIN SLOWLY WALKED TO THE FAR SIDE OF THE CRAMPED QUARTERS AND THERE ON THE SMALL BENCH WERE THE FADED YET STILL IN GOOD CONDITION PLAYING CARDS.

"Benito, I need you to explain something to me OK?"

Benito pulled the two chairs and small card table together and motioned for Antonio to sit down.

"Will you stop pacing and come and play cards!"

Antonio had waited all month for his visit from Anna. It had never occurred to him that Benito had the same feelings for both his daughter and his wife.

"You don't understand; I love your daughter Benito! I truly do and I would be the best son in law you'd ever want, but this waiting is killing me, where are they?"

Benito had seen the anguish and despair from others incarcerated with him. The monthly visit from family and friends was looked upon as one would await the coming of Christmas. Other than playing cards and reading the hours passed slowly and the most crippling thing about prison was the thought process it put the individual in. Apprehension, fear and despair these three words were on everyone's mind within the Castel DeMare walls, all except one man. That was Benito Crespi. Day in and day out he kept his composure. Not a day passed that every prisoner didn't look to him for strength and guidance. Benito felt that some way somehow he'd eventually get out and when he did he would annihilate everyone connected with his imprisonment, but for now he stood pat.

"Antonio! I implore you please let's play cards! When they arrive they will call us I promise.

This day had marked the one-year anniversary for Antonio but just the thought he'd be a fee man in less than two years and he'd be with Anna made him smile.

"You smile my young friend, how about sharing your thoughts with your future father in law",

"Pappa, I hope you don't mind me call you that, the only thing I constantly think about is Anna, and I do apologize in not talking more to you about why your here and less about the troubles I've gotten myself into, again I am sorry"

Benito upon hearing young Antonio speak with his heart as well as his mind felt great that his daughter had found such a beautiful young man.

There were many times in the prison where Antonio carried on long conversations with other politically labeled prisoners but never out of earshot or eyesight of Benito's benevolent manner.

On more than one occasion whenever the subject of "The Camorra" was mentioned every man to a one would check with Benito to see if it was all right to speak to Antonio about the secret organization. Each and every time Benito said no.

"Benito, why won't you tell me what the cross on your hand stands for? Do you think I would betray you to anyone once I am released?"

Benito thought long then answered.

"My young Antonio, soon to be inducted into my family, no it was never about that. Rather I want your mind clear and your decisions above the law whenever concerning my daughter. I don't want the life for you! Let's just stay like that and perhaps in the future we'll discuss it ok? But for now concentrate on our card game, you won last time I don't want any excuses after I beat you"

In an instant both of them burst into laughter. They laughed so hard Antonio accidentally knocked the card table over, and that again brought a roar from both of them.

CHAPTER 9

"Crespi!, Crespi! Your visitors are here! Giancarlo your visitors are here!"

Benito, walked out passed the guards and into the area that occupied the few family and friends allowed for the once a month meeting. In an instant his face lit like a Christmas tree upon seeing his two daughters and his lovely adoring wife Amalia. As Benito sat down he noticed at the next table the Giancarlo family. He acknowledged both Antonio's father and mother and his sister. In an instant he noticed something different about everyone seated both his family and Antonio's.

"What is it woman, why so glum?" This he directed to Amalia.

"Are you or you girls ill or something!"

Within seconds and with a Father's eye on one of the three most precious things in his life, he saw it. Anna, although smiling, had her face half covered with a brown moth eaten scarf. Benito noticed that her face was scarred and her left eye was swollen. Her eyes seemed puffy like when a person hasn't had the required sleep.

Anna's complexion was pale at best. She avoided her father's glare. He took his hand and slowly moved the scarf away from her face. For the first time in months the anger that he had so skillfully hidden against his enemies erupted.

Looking at his wife he bellowed in a voice that had the guards quaking in their boots.

"Who did this to her woman!!!"

Amalie with both her hands and body shaking vehemently stood up and motioned Benito to come as close as the guards would allow. She whispered into his ear. Benito sat down, it was as if the anger that he had demonstrated seconds ago had suddenly gone back inside his body and only that stare, the stare that could kill another human being was left. Just then Antonio came into the room and immediately ran to his mother and father where they embraced and kissed him. Then he turned to the woman that captivated every waking moment this past year.

"Anna"

He joyously called to her across the long table where she was seated with her head down.

Anna slowly raised her head and eyes looking at Antonio as tears began to fall from her face.

What Benito saw was now evident to Antonio. He turned to Benito for some encouragement but there was none. All he saw was that Benito was not smiling. Antonio then turned to Anna who appeared to have gone through some sort of physical ordeal. It looked to him that her eyes, puffy and bloodshot, could possibly carry pain and suffering.

Antonio looked hard questioning Anna's obvious appearance. He implored Anna to tell him.

"What is going on Anna, your eyes and your face is swollen and scratched! Did you get attacked by some animal?"

Antonio looked at Benito, hoping for some explanation. Looking back at Anna he could see the tears welling up in her eyes and his heart began pounding as the combination of concern and want mingled together made him shudder. He wanted so much to hold her and caress her and tell her what she meant to him but prison rules said no.

He implored her again.

"Anna, did something happen that you're not telling me?!"

Anna stayed silent as she tried to compose herself.

The guard in charge of the meeting room cleared his throat as if to announce that visiting hours would be over soon, Benito looked back at him with as menacing a look as Antonio had ever seen.

"I will let you know when my family is ready to leave ok, Fredo!"

The guard swallowed hard as he gently acknowledged Benito's statement and benignly uttered.

"No problem!"

Antonio held Anna's hand in his and they were so emotional that all the women in the room were crying just seeing the two of them and how attached to each other they were yet her appearance had Antonio bewildered.

"Anna my love, I know something is wrong! Did something or someone hurt you?"

Anna wiped her eyes and half smiled.

"Oh God here I am looking terrible, no! It's just a bad cold that's all, don't worry. Just think that in a short time we'll all be together."

Antonio didn't buy it.

"There's something wrong I can feel it"

Just then Benito reached over and grabbed Antonio's wrist so hard he almost broke it. Then in his most forceful yet quiet way Benito leaned over and half whispered in Antonio's ear.

"Son, I love you and I know you mean well but leave this alone for now we'll speak inside remember the walls have ears"

The two lovers said their good buys and a bewildered Antonio went back to his cell and waited for Benito to come and explain to him exactly what had just happened.

Antonio heard some commotion outside the cell and then the cell door half opened, couldn't help but overhear Benito berating one of the guards.

"Justo, this is the last time I'm telling you! When I'm with my family I don't want that piece of shit Fredo standing watching me and my family!"

"What was that all about?"

Antonio surmised that Benito's bellowing had something to do with the visit but he needed Benito to elaborate.

Benito walked to the back of the cell then began to pace without saying a word. His demeanor was of a man thinking and contemplating his thoughts as if he were the only one in the room.

"Benito! Can you stop pacing and tell me what the fuss was about outside a moment ago? And something else! You said that you would explain something to me when we were in the visitor's room, remember?"

Benito just looked at Antonio then shook his head as he slowly put his head down to his lap where he covered his face with his huge hands. Seeing this almost childlike gesture made Antonio realize that what Benito was about to tell him would probably shake him to his very core. The silence within the tiny cell was deafening. Antonio, scared to even utter a sound, waited for his future father in law to give him the answer he had begun to dread hearing.

In one fell swoop Benito got up and stood before Antonio. He reached down and picked the boy up holding Antonio's shoulders as he gently lifted him up to where Antonio, although shorter, looked directly into the big man's tearing eyes. Benito began to choke up but Antonio could see that the big man's inner strength had begun to take over and as any father would do he pulled Antonio close and hugged him as if to say good bye.

"Sit down my son, we need to talk"

As the guards began to take their rounds they heard a shrill roar coming from the east end, the political wing. Knowing full well the cell it was emanating from they feared going there to reprimand anyone making a disturbance. From the loud cries everyone knew to stay away.

CHAPTER 10

Time passes ever so slowly at the Castel De Mare and for each man about to be released the knowing reward is freedom but the wait for that freedom in many cases is a nightmare of anticipation, and hoping that the authorities don't change their mind.

But for one prisoner freedom finally comes and with it a heavy price.

Two years and eleven months had passed since that fateful day when Antonio first began noticing that there was something happening to Anna. At first he chalked it up to anxiety what with her eyes bloodshot and her skin had somehow lost that glow every time they had the occasion to meet. Her speech, which was almost staccato in rhythm had disappeared and in its place was a plain and not so happy teenager who was resigned to her fate.

The mood within Benito's cell was somber at best. The days were long and to Antonio each day's passing held nothing but for the monthly appearance of the one he loved.

The guards who were responsible for the everyday activities of each prisoner knew better than to interfere and speak abruptly to either Antonio or Benito about anything except when dinner would be served. In the past two years Antonio had slowly developed an aura of a man not to be trifled with. A stark contrast to the young and naive fellow who was incarcerated unjustly almost three years prior.

Being that Benito and his band of Camorra followers were both feared and respected by the guards, approaching any of the group by any guard in a confrontational way would result in grave consequences for that guard and anyone connected to him on the outside.

Camorra was the by word on the wing and its leader held court each day. This day Benito addressed Antonio directly.

"I think we've gone over everything you need to know. The names of the people you need to see and the days in which those meetings are to take place, do you want me to go over it again with you"

There was a deafening silence. The few men, all Camorra, who were allowed to converse in the Crespi cell for the only hour of the day permitted by the prison listened as Crespi was about to issue his order of the day. Each day Benito Crespi reinforced the Camorra way of life to each and every prisoner. To the newest inmates the ritual was the same. A one on one with Crespi whereby his rules within the prison walls were detailed and explained. The rules of Camorra were equally explained. The men who were in Crespi's inner circle, some, like Crespi, were there for a long time and others whose sentences were less all listened intently. For the newer members, noticing that most of Crespi's followers were tattooed, stayed both silent and reverent.

As each member took his turn speaking privately to Benito and asking for his council Benito would occasionally glance to his left and there gazing out through the small window overlooking the blue Mediterranean Sea was Antonio. Lately it was Antonio's modus operandi to gaze for hours at the ocean. To the few who were in the inner circle the slow methodical transformation of this once quiet boy to a most fearsome looking prisoner struck terror into even the most hardened criminals in the prison. Antonio stood there seemingly impassioned and totally introspective in his manner. In many ways, without ever uttering a syllable, he radiated danger and power to the rest of the inmates.

Antonio's metamorphosis had not been lost on the guards either, they feared him even more than Benito.

With his head shaved and now sporting a beard he resembled more a follower of Rasputin rather than an Italian who was unjustly incarcerated. With Benito they knew what they were going to get. With Antonio his intense and quiet demeanor created a pent up torment rarely seen by many of the guards at Castel De Mare.

Antonio demonstrated a man with bottled up torment hinging on a soul that tempted the devil himself. Antonio had changed and now because of Crespi's insistence his life was about to take an even more drastic turn than anyone could ever expect from this once innocent young man.

Antonio's transformation did take a lot of time but then again time can either help or heal whatever wounds an individual has or the opposite can occur. In Antonio's case time worked against him like twine wrapped tightly around an object until the original object is completely covered leaving only the twisted and tightly woven after affect.

To the many prisoner's men who made their daily visits a must to visit and speak with Benito the sight of this once slender and happy go lucky young boy now being replaced by a muscular tattooed member of Camorra resembled neither a young happy man or a man who looked to tomorrow for salvation. All they saw, all that was now left, was a man who now resembled a warrior ready for battle.

"You're unusually quiet this morning"

Benito casually addressed his young charge who had made a daily practice of systematically hitting the prison wall an hour each morning until his knuckles bled. Noticing that there was blood on Antonio's knuckles he turned his head away and waived the few faithful who were in the cell dismissing them.

Benito motioned for Antonio to come and sit by him.

"Antonio sit down we need to talk. We spoke about what has to happen and no matter how many times you strike the wall the situation will never change. Remember we spoke about this Antonio! I need you to be calm, stop torturing yourself, whatever happened deal with it! In a month you'll be out of here, there are things you need to do"

CHAPTER 11

Rudolfo under pressure from certain Camorra gang leaders in Naples who he owed serious gambling debts to was forced to make a surprise visit back to the mansion where he hadn't been in over a year.

The servants were happy to see him. They noticed that he had put on weight since his departure but his nervous attitude and questionable behavior secured in their minds that Rudolfo was still in some sort of trouble probably financial, only this time they knew that Rodolfo was not a welcomed guest at the estate, yet all his years as he grew and co-mingled with the help he was never judgmental. Rudolfo was actually liked by the staff.

It had been over a year since he left that fateful day in which he cursed both his father and sister. But now he needed help, any help to keep the mad men of Naples away from his door.

He looked for Valentina and he thought, even though they had their differences, she was still his sister. The main chambermaid, who had made her way back from the kitchen, smiled at him as she hugged him and greeted him.

"Master Rudolfo, good to see you I will bet that your father and sister will be glad to see you!"

Rudolfo looked at the trappings that adorned the walls of the estate.

"Doesn't look like anything changed, is my sister at home?"

She looked towards the bedrooms on the second floor.

"I do believe she's still in her room, although I haven't seen her since dinner last night. As far as your father is concerned we haven't seen him in a few days but he's probably in Naples on Business."

Rudolfo snapped.

"My father? I don't care if I ever see him again! But I will go up to see my sister"

As Rudolfo reached the top of the stairs he stopped and contemplated knocking on her door not knowing what her response was going to be but his need for money far outweighed whatever problems he might have had with his sister. In every way Rudolfo wanted to be anyplace but there but his needs far outweighed the hatred he bore with his family. He reached her door and knocked.

"Valentina! Valentina it's me open the door" Impatiently he tried to open the door but it was locked. Again he yelled "Valentina, dammit open the door"

Still no answer. Frustrated he tried a few of the other doors along the hallway and although they were opened, including his old room, they were all empty.

Questioning the staff to the point of hysteria Rudolfo hastily stormed into the library and immediately ran to the safe. He remembered the old combination as he tried to open it he surmised that the locks must have been changed. He needed money as his gambling debts had mounted to such an extent that only a man like Don Francisco could keep the wolves away. He searched around for anything of value. Instantly he saw what he believed would be a beginning.

The Don collected rare manuscripts and many an occasion he would regale the children with stories of how he managed to swindle some poor book store shop keeper in Naples browbeating the poor shop keeper that certain rare books on his shelf were better suited in the Don's library. With the Don's great wealth and power, he was never questioned so the shop keeper reluctantly had to let the rare manuscripts go.

There right before his eyes was a rare first edition of Dickens in great condition. Rudolfo thought that there had to be many people who would pay a lofty sum for the manuscript. He grabbed the book as well as some of the gold ornaments the Don had on both the coffee table and upon the long marble mantle. He remembered growing up how careful his father was in handling the rare porcelain figurines and small statues that adorned the library.

Rudolfo surmised that with all his current problems that he probably would never set eyes on this estate again, at least not in the near future, so with haste he began to gather whatever he thought was valuable.

The amount of booty he had collected would not be an easy task hiding it from the help. Besides the logistical problems he had the fact that so many items missing would certainly send an alarm and he would be in more hot water than he already was. He thought on his dilemma. In an instant he realized that this grouping together of so many valuables were a bad idea. He quickly put everything back. The fact that there was no one home didn't bother him a bit he rather liked the quiet of the library. As a child many times he had come down from bed hoping that his father the great Don would take him and rock him to sleep in his arms, the reality was a scolding and dismissal and off to bed again no, he like it quiet. The question beckoned, what could he take and not arose suspicion.

It came as a revelation. There had been in his family a throne. Yes, a throne that was originally used in the old

Garibaldi Family that his grandparents had gotten for their great service to Italy. It was priceless yet when his grandparents had died suddenly and his father had become potentate of the Jannace estate and all its holdings The Don, who despised his parents, ordered that everything connected to them be either destroyed or put away. He remembered that the great throne was bottled away in the carriage house annex, where the Don kept his vast Wine Collection as well as artifacts gathered on his yearly safari's.

CHAPTER 12

The carriage house on the southeastern part of the vast estate had always been a centerpiece for joy and celebration for many of the workers of the estate. Rudolfo remembered many an occasion that both he and his sister were taken to some of those festivities by the help. The Carriage house was also used on rare occasions as a makeshift courthouse where disputes amongst the help were settled, usually by the Don, and where both he and his sister did in fact have many fond memories of those occasions.

As swift as any rider in Benevento Rudolfo could ride a horse rather well as his father often remarked "Sitting on top of an animal and going fast sums up my son's calling in life"

Rudofo remembered all of that as he galloped towards the carriage house. He truly did not remember in which of the three houses the famous throne could have been stored away. He elected to open and inspect the smallest of the three and most obvious as a storage unit and because there were no windows made it perfect so that the elements would not harm the beautifully crafted and expensive piece of furniture as well as any other valuables.

Rudolfo was in shock as the room was empty. And so he proceeded to the next largest building where he remembered food stuffs and very expensive wines and cheeses had always been preserved there. The thought that any piece of furniture, especially something so valuable, would never be stored there with food. But none the less he opens the doors and again empty. It was as if there had never been anything ever stored there. The shelves were barren and the floors were swept clean, he asked himself "Where was all the wine and foodstuffs?"

That left the main building. Knowing that it had been used as a makeshift courthouse and meeting hall precluded it from being any sort of a storehouse facility. The door to the entrance was stuck and the jelly like substance around the wooden knob made it difficult at first to open. In an instant Rudolfo was hit with an odor that could blacken any man's senses. He stepped back and pulled out a handkerchief from his pocket and shielding the sun from his eyes he stepped inside the foul odorous smelling room.

Even as a boy Rudolfo had been fearless. He was a tough street smart aristocrat who loved women and gambling defying his father at every turn. What he saw revolted him to a frenzy that all he could do was scream and begin to shake uncontrollably. He screamed until the only sounds coming from his body was air.

There in the midst of the makeshift courthouse was carnage that he could have never imagined, the horror made him vomit right there on the spot.

Eight bodies were strewn around the entire front portion of the courtroom in front of the bench. Blood splattered in every direction on all four walls. The heads on all the eight bodies were severed.

There laying side by side were the fully clothed bodies of the mass massacre. As he stood there shaking to his very core the bright sunlight coming through the open door camouflaged for an instant the insanity he was witnessing.

Rudolfo gagged at the sight until there was nothing left to vomit.

He quickly thought of savagery that must have taken place the cries and pleas of the victims must have been horrible.

What he saw next made him sick all over again.

The first three heads he visibly recognized were of his father and sister.

He then recognized the head of Philip Testa as well as a most familiar face yet the contorted anguished look on the bug eyed person made the immediate identification difficult. Then in an instant it came to him it was his father's good friend Don Bacca.

Rudolfo, nauseated beyond control, began to slowly peruse the foul smelling and carnage laden building. He was finally able to concentrate on what had happened. He could see that the bodies were in various stages of decomposition and the stench was overwhelming. The dismembered bodies were all positioned in an odd array of angles within the building. The torsos were all beheaded and their heads were positioned left to right and strewn atop the blood splattered bench. Rudolfo surmised that whoever carried out this ghastly thing must have had the built up hatred of a thousand men to do such heinous carnage.

At first he squinted then slowly he fully opened his eyes, not wanting to see any more than he had to he again couldn't stop shaking. There was what was left of his family.

What truly frightened him putting him in a mental straightjacket was seeing his sister's astonished look of bewilderment. Her eyes were so big and wide open. It seemed to Rudolfo that her complete shock at what she perceived as her death made her look that much more bizarre. Macabre, to say the least the carnage was so savage. Rudolfo staggered outside the building. There was no vomit left inside of him. Who would be so savage as to do something like this? He again looked back inside at the horror and he knew that he would never be able forget what had happened here.

He looked back once more as he began to run, but he questioned himself as to where would he go?

It would take seven years but the advantage to the status quo ended as soon as Mussolini made himself "El Duce"

The Jannace estate was reduced to small farms all share cropping as before but under the new government the farmers would keep what they produced and a tax system was put in place. The wealthy land owners were all put on trial and the Fascist government was the last word.

Castel De Mare was abolished but the revolutionary leaders, who were imprisoned for years, were released and allowed to go back to their respective families.

The Camorra did go underground but would never again be the power it was before Mussolini.

Benito Crespi resigned himself to the life of a farmer with a broken family. He kept constant tabs on the whereabouts of the son he adopted in prison. There were no tears of joy when he heard about the massacre at the Jannace estate, all that was left was weeping for the daughter he would never see, the grandchildren he would never hold and hope that Antonio might somehow some way find his way back to Italy.

Antonio Giancarlo, with a wig and an invalid's cans made his way onto the train that would take him to Rome where passage had been booked for him to come to America.

CHAPTER 13

With a new name on his new passport Antonio set sail two days after the news had reached everyone in Benevento that the Jannace clan had all been murdered. Chaos had run amok in Naples as Don Jannace had either partially or in whole controlled everything from grain to livestock in the city. The political heads were all stunned at the fateful events of that night. The Camorra was still in power.

Hundreds of miles away the huge ship passed Genoa on its way to the mid-Atlantic and one of its passengers contemplated starting a new life in the new world called America.

NEW YORK

As he lay quietly on his bed in his cluttered dank and drab cold water flat, that just happened to look over a noisy and unusually busy Twentieth Street and Ninth Avenue in Manhattan, Antonio, whose last name was now Piccolo allowed himself to dream about the life he so hurriedly left back in Italy?

One of Benito Crespi's top lieutenants, named Giuseppe Piccolo, allowed Antonio to use his name. Being that Giuseppe had only girls in his family he felt it an honor when Benito asked if Antonio could now carry his last name.

As he lay his bed Antonio had visions of Benevento swirling in his conscious mind. He darted back to that life when beautiful Anna was his and his future was as bright as any star in the heavens. And again the torment of how fast that life was taken from him. His thoughts, lately, had always taken on the same pattern. Lying on his single spring mattress closing his eyes he would dream. The reoccurring dream would appear and play itself out so beautifully. In an instant he was transported to the beautiful hillsides of Benevento.

As he drifted into sleep he managed to drown out the blatant sounds from the teeming neighborhood. From the very first day that he settled into the overcrowded masses injected scenario where every day his gut sense told him there was not only poverty in his overly populated neighborhood but also the tremendous underlining pain and discontent associated with every immigrant that just happened to land there.

He attributed the tormented state of so many immigrants to the squalid conditions they were forced to live in. Jew, Gentile and alike all thrown together. Ethnic groups that had never seen so many different people speaking different languages and different mores, so confusing and many yearned for their homeland and away from these new surroundings.

The constant nightly emotional outcries from the neighborhood sent him mentally back to Italy.

The cries emanating from the masses created vibes that Antonio felt to his very core. The sounds and laments were the sounds from the many immigrants yearning for a better life.

It seemed to Antonio that many of the newly arrived from Europe immediately felt oppressed and put upon, especially the younger emerging breed of offspring of so many immigrants. Their furor ranged from hatred towards their real and imagined oppressors to loss of hope in God's mercy. As he lay and half listening to the laments of the poor and misguided he again was reminded that the stories depicting America's streets that were lined with gold was still an appealing thought but again as he had done these past six months he closed his eyes and force ably pushed the sounds of the tenement from his conscious mind.

What Antonio did not know at the time was that America's ethnic landscape was divided in triplicate.

The English were still the nobility, they controlled the banks and investment houses and because of that they controlled the money. The Irish, many social rungs below, represented the civil enactment of the law. Keeping the peace and making sure that Irish votes were used to the betterment of all concerned was the main objective of the sub ruling Irishman's world. The Irish used patronage to achieve success and the rest of the population had to fend for themselves.

Day after day Antonio came to realize that perhaps Castel De Mare might have been a better place to pass his life away.

The teeming tenements offered nothing to console him about his fate. Only his thoughts of what was. Each night repeated itself until the routine was as normal as breathing. He would close his eyes and be transported back to what had been the fairy tale and if God willed it this particular evening he might just sleep through and never wake up.

As sleep offered his only value in his rather tough realization that his life in America was not going to be a bed of roses.

In an instant he was transported back and there she was sitting on the side of the hill that bordered the woods and the grassy knoll in Benevento. The thought of her laughing, so spiritual yet real, made even his subconscious mind forget that he was again a prisoner sequestered in this building that he now called home. And within the damp and crowded conditions that suffocate the very life out of an ordinary person he was left to survive and forget the dark and terrible things done to him and what he had done in retaliation.

But for this moment sleep and dream about a time not so long ago where dreams actually could come true if the right people were involved.

He reminisced about their time together and truth be told nothing mattered except his time with her. The rest of his life was a fog laden gray that clouded everything he touched.

She stood there on one elbow looking into his eyes and smiling. He felt her warmth and soaked it in, that was love and he knew it would never be like that again.

His dream would always end there. The cold savage hatred for those who allowed her to be killed as well as those who killed her raised his blood pressure like a kettle filled with water at the boiling point.

He jumped up in bed, as he had done so many nights since coming to America.

His bed, soaked with perspiration, lay evidence as to his thoughts and emotional state every night that dream appeared. Yet the violence that engulfed him had not subsided. His blood curled at the thought.

Since he arrived in America he had been diligent. He ate alone and socialized with a few of the older Italian grandmothers who prayed each and every night that their sons and grandsons come home safe and sound and hopefully with some food to eat.

He never ventured any farther than the streets he used to traverse as he went to work each day.

He never frequented the many supposedly friendly Neapolitan bars and eating halls he was directed to by his sponsor, Jannaro Queli.

He was directed to report to Queli once he arrived in America. Queli was mentioned to be a top ranking "Cammorista" (a man in the Camorra), in other words a man of respect in the Naples arena that controlled that section of lower Manhattan.

The new groups of Neapolitan's fresh off the boat were told in advance who to pay their respects to but it had been quite a long time since the likes of man like Antonio Giancarlo, ne Piccolo had come to pass and paying respect to anyone was not in Antonio's make up.

He made sure to never go to any places in lower Manhattan where he might be recognized as a fugitive, he actually never realized that the authorities were light years behind in looking for a murderer from other countries. They lacked the sophistication and communications needed to succeed in that venture. It would be at least ten years before those records of felons coming here from other countries would be readable and accessible to all law enforcement.

The authorities had all they could handle with the American hoodlum and the scores of gangs that preyed upon the helpless and the weak.

Antonio, having no papers and not a legal citizen, needed to keep a low profile.

The authorities in America might have been on alert for one such a man wanted for crimes in Italy. He could not take that chance.

He continued to stay low key.

One years had passed and it was now 1926 the roaring twenties were happening and he was making two dollars a day as every day laborer.

He had been given an opportunity to work for a rather large construction company. The boss on the project was from Naples and not a kind man to say the least, this was surprising to Antonio as because Benito and his minions commanded great respect in and out of Italy. The word coming back to America was that Antonio was a man of respect and to be treated that way. The job market with or without Camorra was terrible for many young Italians coming off the boat. It was told to Antonio that if it hadn't been his benefactor, Mr. Queli, he wouldn't be working. Queli had been ordered by associates of Benito Crespi in Italy to make sure Antonio landed on his feet. But three thousand miles could make anyone forget their duty.

"Antonio Piccolo, is that your real name"

Antonio looked at this rather poorly dressed yet proud man and quietly tried to asses if he liked the man or not. In a raspy but solid tone he answered.

"Yes it is."

"You don't speak very much young man, in America you must learn respect and know who to talk to, in America I am that person. Oh yes I was told that you come from good stock in Italy, Benito sponsored you but that was there, thousands of miles away …. You're on my turf now!" This he said as if it were a threat yet Antonio continued to study his so called sponsor.

As the new boss walked around the room, with his two thumbs planted firmly in his vest, he appeared to be getting stronger in both attitude and speech as each word was spoken quite loud and actually menacing.

He was trying so desperately to convince his young friend that he was the boss not some Italian using a slogan like "Camorra" to issue threats of force that in actuality controlled nothing. All the while Antonio studied the man and convinced himself that in an instant he could choke the life out of that fat out of shape contemptuous blow hard. Antonio listened and thanked the man as he accepted a laborers job at the request of Mr. Queli.

For the next four months Antonio worked as hard as any laborer on the job. He kept to himself and mostly tried to wear gloves on the job so as not to alert anyone to his tattoo on his right hand.

Even though he kept to himself, allowing just a few hello's and good byes to the few Italians he actually spoke with, he was basically a loner.

On more than one occasion he had been asked to have dinner at one of his coworker's home but he kindly refused. Everyone chalked his quiet nature up to being in a strange country and without any social life basically without any friends. And it came to pass in the fourth month of his employment his fellow workers found out quickly that this quiet young man had a most frightening way of convincing others that he would not be trifled with.

Antonio was instructed by the foreman, a Sicilian, to wheel barrow mortar and bricks to the far end of the building under construction. Once there he was to unload the bricks go back and mix mortar and cement then return to the same spot and be the helper to the mason who would actually finish the job.

Upon returning to the spot Antonio discovered that half of the bricks he had dumped were gone. He looked around, assured that he did indeed bring the correct amount, to see if he happened to drop any along the way. As he stood there pondering he would quickly get acquainted with what Americans call "A Practical Joke"

The foreman, a Sicilian, and a burly man of 40 who professed to anyone who would listen that he distrusted many of his fellow Italians especially Neapolitans, didn't think Antonio's bewilderment was real.

"Is there something wrong with you paisan?" The burly foreman spouted using the word paisan in the most mocking way emphasizing the fact that Antonio couldn't have been more stupid than to fall for a joke like that.

Then in an almost exasperated gesture he spun around to what had become the main working force within the yard and said.

"Yes I do believe that this boy is as stupid as he looks" The guffaws were instantaneous and Antonio, still with the wheelbarrow in hand, listened to the catcalls and laughter coming from his countrymen.

But something else happened. Sometimes it's the moment and sometimes folklore push the story until the mortal man becomes a giant. In this case Antonio reacted differently than any Italian boy had acted in the past under those same circumstances.

Antonio attacked his boss, unheard of in 1926. And even more astounding was the fact that an Italian immigrant attacking his boss, even if he was Italian, was even more implausible.

Within the second by second framework of events the catcalls and laughter stopped and what was left was disbelief, shock and to some degree inner glee felt by many of the put upon Italians who they themselves just happened to have been the brunt of many jokes levied at them in recent months from that specific boss plus the other three upper level Irish bosses.

All eyes were focused at the center of the controversy with many of the onlookers secretly wishing they had the courage and nerves of steel to do what they were witnessing. The Neapolitans with all the weight of discrimination like 60 lb bags of granite secured neatly on their shoulders watched intently. The pure message being witnessed here was that each man represented generation upon generation of put upon Italians by their Irish fellow countrymen and also their own brethren, all of the onlookers stood in total disbelief.

It was as if a sacred covenant had been broken.

As any good Italian would tell you a man like Antonio, coming from a foreign country was supposed to take the ribbing and personal insults just to, in other words, pay his dues.

No field hand or laborer or any worker of any sort of Italian extraction would ever strike, attack or otherwise show up his boss especially when that boss was a non-Italian and even more an Irishman.

What everyone was witnessing had not been seen in this or any workplace environment in many a year after all it was New York in 1926.

Antonio had the foreman on the ground, one hand over his mouth and the other plunging a knife into his leg. The foreman was badly wounded and Antonio quietly walked off the job leaving the bleeding man holding onto his leg and screaming for help, while the bricks lay on the ground and the mortar became as hard as any rock could ever be.

To a man each one of the workers stood quietly but deep inside their souls had suddenly been lifted for here was a man who defied the laws set down by the Irish bosses saying that if the Irishman or anyone representing the Irishman spoke it was gospel. The men, who just minutes before were laughing at one of their own, looked down at their fallen boss and with silent admiration at one of their own who defied the process and showed that Italians had guts to fight for equality, many of the men secretly envied that brash and headstrong young man. The legend of Antonio Giancarlo (nee Piccolo) had begun.

That was the last time Antonio held and ordinary job, anywhere.

CHAPTER 14

The Streets

The fourteenth precinct lay just between the Bowery and Canal Street.

Antonio had been picked up by the police after one of the Irish bosses on the job made the complaint. Antonio was charged with felony assault with a weapon as well as attempted murder. The charges were grave and for most the fear of jail would be enough for any policeman to get any information they wanted from the offender as well as anything else that could make the arresting officer or officers be in greater stead with their superiors.

"Antonio Piccolo, that's your name right punk?"

The sergeant spoke never lifting his eyes off the arrest report.

"Did you hear what I said Dago? Is that your fucking name?"

Antonio slowly lifted his eyes towards the detective and calmly answered

"Yes it is"

"Listen WOP I don't have all day to wait for an answer from you understand!"

No sooner did the detective say his piece he quickly, in a fit of rage, raised his hand and swung it in an attempt to slap Antonio. His hand came at Antonio with rapid force yet Antonio's reflexes were faster. In one fell swoop Antonio caught his hand and with one quick move and twisting it hard brought the detective to his knees. The Detective screamed and in seconds the room was filled with plainclothesmen and Antonio was on the ground.

"What the fuck! What happened?"

Captain James, commander of the precinct, was flabbergasted at what he was witnessing.

"He threw me to the ground, the little punk!"

The Captain obviously aware that one of minions had, again, gone way too far.

Looking down at Antonio and seeing that there was at least 6 men in blue around him, uttered the final insult.

"What I see here is a dago obviously out of his element" The Captain began to chuckle and in seconds the rest of the men in blue followed suit.

The laughter subsided for a moment as the Captain cleared his throat to achieve an element of authority.

"All right let him up and sit him down, listen young man this is not professional wrestling if you don't want to spend the next week in the hole you'd have better cooperate and behave got it"

The Captain was about to leave the room when Antonio spoke.

"I make it a habit of not letting any man, no matter who he is, to attempt to hit me for no reason

Especially a man like him!"

"What does that mean like him"? The Captain retorted.

Antonio chose his words carefully as not to invoke the Sargent's ire again.

"A man who picks on the weak and truly enjoys being a bully"

The Captain always landing on the side of his men made his judgment.

"Take him to the hole maybe down there he can spout those words to the other scum and when he decides to talk and cooperate then maybe we'll let him sit and mingle with the good people of this world."

Antonio spoke.

"Captain what do you mean cooperate? with who about what!'

"The Black Hand, you're a part of that shit you Dago's believe in. I want to know who the number one guy is I know all you guys know the answer but somehow nobody wants to talk. Maybe a few days down below will change your mind eh?"

Antonio couldn't believe his ears. As he was being led out of the room he yelled back.

"Black Hand? Captain I work for a living, with my hands! Dam I'm not a boss or anything like that!"

The Captain got to within inches of Antonio's face and with the largest smirk reiterated.

"Oh and I guess that tattoo on your right hand doesn't mean anything right my Dago friend, take him the fuck downstairs and don't bring him up until he's ready to talk, you guys understand!"

And just as quickly Antonio was carted off.

The true irony of the entire situation was that the Captain knew very well who the leaders of organized crime were, his name was the first name on the weekly payoff that came directly to the stationhouse.

The tombs as they called it consisted of twenty cement block encased rooms situated two floors below the main building of the fourteenth precinct. Each cell had one window that led to neither the outside nor anything resembling humanity. On a decent spring day, the warm rays of the sun never got that far into the Toombs.

Some days when the police upstairs felt charitable they would open all the windows and doors of the precinct and some of the fresh spring and summer air would eventually filter down to the Toombs. This atmosphere together with the Indian summer winds made the day bearable at least. But this was not summer and the cold winds together with the cement enclosed structure made sitting in that environment for twenty-four hours unbearable that is for most men but not Antonio. Compared to Castel deMare the tombs were a pleasure.

The food was simply bread, stale at best, and many times water with lemon that one of the guards brought from his own home. Thomas Madden, a sergeant who was on the wrong team politically, was the official sergeant at arms for the tombs. In less than a week Antonio not only had a checkers partner but also a man who like himself put principal above politics.

"Well Tony that makes six games that I beat you, say how about I give you a handicap and play blindfolded maybe then you can win"

For the third time that week Antonio allowed himself to relax noting that perhaps he had found a friend in Madden. Many nights Madden would smuggle Chicken soup for Antonio which he brought from home.

"I truly appreciate your kindness"

"Stop it ok, are you just trying to butter me up so I'll let you win at checkers."

Their relationship had gone past guard and prisoner. Madden was stern with all the other prisoners knowing full well that mostly all of them were rightfully imprisoned but not with Antonio.

Although he sensed that Antonio did have both the mental and physical strength to survive he felt that perhaps in all of his time as curator of the cells down in the tombs he had finally found someone he could relate to.

Almost, as if by schedule, Captain James, would make his daily visit to the tombs and also on his daily visit he surely expected that on that day Antonio would finally give up the answers he wanted.

"How's he doing Madden giving you any shit?" As the Captain made his way passed the eighty percent filled cement cells and holding court as he walked.

"You know something Madden how many years has it been Six, I think six right? That you've kept vigil down here"

This last statement was said tongue and cheek as he and Madden had no love for each other.

Madden knowing full well that Captain James was part of the precinct payoff sheet yet he never alluded to it, that would be Emerald Society suicide.

It was 1921 and the dough boys were all home from the war. Thomas Madden had served his country well having fought in France in the Argonne having won a few meritorious citations for bravery. Actually to be an Irishman in New York being a cop was as natural as breathing. The unwritten police blotter that housed the Irish Bible was called the Emerald Society. It signified class and stature within the rank and file and everyone knew that nobody "Fucked Around with the Emerald Society" Once you were in it was for life.

Tom Madden knew the rules and tried to be the best cop on the force. Collar after collar he arrested muggers, pimps and thieves. So much fanfare that in two and a half years he was promoted to sergeant. That, sadly, is where the heroics and love affair between him and the NYC Police Dept. ended.

One of the biggest political fixers in Manhattan was Jimmy Hinds and behind him stood Tammany Hall the main political power that fueled the other two parties in the early 1900's to the late thirties.

Tammany hall was the center for political patronage in New York City. The mainstay of the party was Jimmy Hinds, an old world politician, who felt just at home with both the President of the United States and the leaders of the Underworld. His partner and cohort was Albert Marinelli, an Italian who handled the affairs of Tammany especially when it related to the Italian Underworld in connection with every department of New York politics. Hines, was what the politicians called the ultimate fixer. Shamus Caffery was the nephew of one of the oldest Irish Catholic families in the city. His father was alderman and was instrumental in getting Jimmy Hinds to where he was. So, it was a natural set of circumstances that when young Shamus became a man he would follow in his father's footsteps.

It came to pass that Shamus Caffery had paid his dues and his reward was holding the alderman's seat vacated by his father.

Tammany Hall wanted Shamus Caffery to get the position so that he could, with the blessing of all the powers in New York, control most of the hiring and firing within the Mayor's office.

On one such cold and rainy evening politics clashed with reality.

With Prohibition at full swing Mr Caffery and two women companions were out on the town. Drinking and eventually driving from one of New York's largest speakeasy at breakneck speed the three of them, having the time of their life, threw caution to the wind.

The roads, because of the cold and blustery conditions, were not suitable for fast driving as a snow storm caught the city by surprise that evening and the sanitation crews of the city had not had the chance to clean the streets properly. Caffery, drunk and at the wheel, simply ran red light after red light trying to get to the next speakeasy and see how much liquor he could consume that night. Unbeknown to him, crossing one of New York's largest intersection at the same time, was a woman with three children in tow. Caffery driving erratically and paying no heed to what was happening right before his eyes struck the woman and her children, killing two of the children.

Coming home after his shift Tom Madden witnessed the accident and subsequently saw the automobile stop for a moment then proceed as though nothing had happened. Madden jotted down the license number and quickly attended to the accident victims. In minutes the ambulance arrived pronouncing two of the children dead.

Madden called the accident in and asked the dispatcher about the ownership of the vehicle.

Angry beyond reason Madden vowed to catch the perpetrator and beat him within an inch of his life. Seeing the dead children lying there within the chaotic combination of lights sirens and inclement weather Madden became emotional. Seeing two children dead and he childless because his ex-wife was more interested in screwing other men rather than be a good wife and mother made him realize how precious life truly was and how valuable a gift it was to have a child. The thought of him someday becoming a father was always a calming ingredient whenever he would witness a tragedy like this.

CHAPTER 15

The Secret Society

It took two days but Thomas caught up with Shamus Caffery. He booked him and charged him with Murder, leaving the scene of a crime and avoiding arrest.

It was late Friday night when he and Antonio had their little checkers match.

"Tom you only told me half of the Caffery story, what happened after that, I mean although it happened a few years ago you still remember it right?"

Madden truly didn't want to rehash that story again but Antonio never asked for anything except friendship and liking Antonio was actually more important than his hurt feelings way back then.

"Only for you my Italian friend, only for you"

Tom recounted to tony how on that fateful night four years ago his life and attitude towards everything he held holy collided with his true self.

He had just finished his reports and was about to say good night when he noticed that the court blotter showing upcoming cases to be heard by the presiding judge failed to show even a hearing on the Caffery arrest.

It was a lesson he would never forget. Politics played a great hand in the Caffery Madden saga.

Tom was beside himself. He began by literally going straight up the chain of command demanding an answer. Why had an arresting officer with such high credentials in the department asked, by so many people of authority in so many ways, to simply look the other way? Summoning all the strength he could muster he went straight to the Police Commissioner. He walked out of the Commissioner's office with his head down and dejected. What was so important in this city that a man like Caffery, who killed two people, be allowed his freedom as if he were bulletproof? He decided that he needed to pursue this matter a little more aggressively even though everyone up and down the police hierarchy told him to back off and forget it but everything he ever believed in concerning the police department demanded that he take the next step.

It was cold and snowing as Tom approached the Caffery residence.

The front door of the big white Tudor opened and a Negro maid announced his name to the household in minutes Caffery appeared in dark blue silk pajamas and in his slippers. What Tom thought amusing were his slippers. Black velvet with gold medallions on each slipper. If that wasn't strange the cigarette holder measuring almost ten inches long dangled from his mouth. It was the largest cigarette holder Tom had ever seen. The almost cartoon like way Caffery appeared together with his Tallulah Bankhead demeanor actually gave Tom a chuckle.

"Can I help you, Mr. Madden Is it?"

"Yes that is my name but I'm Sergeant Madden to you, does that name mean anything to you?"

Caffery looked quizzically at this rather broad shouldered man standing in his doorway.

"At this moment no, it does not! Should it?"

"Well, a few weeks ago I arrested you because you killed those two little girls! Dammit do you remember that!"

At this point because of Tom's menacing tone Caffery quickly closed the door behind him.

"Sir those insinuations are without merit..."

Before he had finished his sentence Tom had him around the throat and in seconds he would have passed out had Tom not released him.

Frightened beyond his senses Caffery stood there shaking.

"Please I have a family and just hearing awful things like what you're saying will scare my family to bits, I don't want my family to get the wrong impression of me!"

Madden stepped away to actually look at this poor excuse of a human being.

"Politics aside, are you serious about that family stuff? You're worried that your family might get the wrong impression of you? I can't believe what I'm hearing, Dammit man you're a murderer!

You do have friends in high places and by now I know that but remember something they can't always protect you, every time you're on the public spotlight I'll be there to make sure you don't ever kill again, I will always, as long as I am a cop, wait to put you in jail where you belong!"

"Why are you prosecuting me, I've never done anything to you! Mr Madden I am sure that things can be worked out for you by some of my friends why I can even...."

Before the sentence was over.

"Don't even go there, I am an honest cop and I resent that implication, be forewarned"

Madden had already begun to walk back down the red and black brick steps when he turned around to say his final good byes to Caffery.

"You've done plenty of harm in such a short period of time my friend. Scum like you should never be allowed to represent anyone. I hope you realize that you killed two little girls!"

Caffery could see that Madden was getting angry all over again and decided to go inside and lock his front door.

Back in his cell Antonio listened intently to Tom Madden's story. He could see that Madden, as he was retelling the story he was actually reliving the events as they were unfolding.

"That was some story. So what happened after that?"

"The hammer came down on me from Tammany. Jimmy Hinds the big shot over there paid me a visit here at the station. It was him and Chief Reilly and they threw the book at me. They explained that sometimes a little bad can be overlooked when the end result benefits so many people.

"I actually had to laugh when I heard that fat tub of shit explains that crap to me! Chief, I said, are you two guys kidding? That maggot killed two kids and you're telling me for the greater good!!! go and fuck yourselves! And I walked out. The very next day I was assigned here and I've been here ever since"

CHAPTER 16

The Pact

It had never really dawned on anyone at the fourteenth that this prisoner names Antonio Piccolo was still in the tombs and no justice was in sight.

Two months had passed and a reckoning was about to happen.

On two separate occasions as Tom sat near Antonio's cell his conversation was interrupted by a few disruptive inmates to which Madden dispelled an attack that had many of the prisoners shuddering. He was brutal in his attack on the two unruly prisoners so much so that there, for the first time that evening, was peace and quiet. When he finally had the chance to talk to Antonio he found him smiling.

"So! What's so funny my friend?"

"You make me laugh. The prisoners are here because they did something bad on the outside well I bet that if given the chance knowing what they know about you and your brutal reputation down here they probably would be angels on the outside and never do another bad thing, that's why I'm laughing, so do you know what the motto to that is?"

"No! But you're going to tell me right?"

"Oh yes my Irish friend, what you've got to do is to continue kicking the shit out of everybody down here, every hour of the day! Think how much you'll be helping society!"

With tongue in cheek Tom, all stern in his demeanor and all, could only muster

"Oh yea!"

And on that note the both of them began to laugh at how preposterous that statement was.

Holding his side as he rolled over in laughter Antonio, barely audible above his screams.

"You're funnier than Eddie Cantor"

Madden holding onto the cell for fear of falling down from laughter.

"And I'm not even Jewish"

At which the howling started again. Madden began to walk away yelling back as he did.

"Don't go anywhere I'll be back got to take a piss"

A week had passed and Tom had something to talk to Antonio about, he said it was important,

He wanted to wait until the wee hours of the morning before his shift ended to discuss it with Antonio

It was Six am.

"For God's sake Tom what the hell was so important that we couldn't talk about it later?"

Tom looked up and down the cell block to make sure he wasn't overheard.

"Tony, there are so many ears in this place that if word got out about what I'm trying to do we're both fucked. I never told you about my uncle Owney did I?"

Owney Madden, nickname Killer" owner of the Cotton Club in Harlem was one of the most feared Irish Gangsters of the Twenties.

The Madden's all came from Leeds England and settled in the United States in the hopes for a better life. They settled in New York City and from the outset Owney was a troubled youth. He was strong and fearless and in no time had, at the age of fourteen, organized a gang of young toughs that terrorized the lower East Side neighborhoods. He was always in trouble with the law. Indicted for murder he served ten years and was given parole.

Besides being heavily involved in illegal liquor distribution and prostitution Owney joined other rival gangs in hijacking liquor shipments from his competitors and in all of this was considered one of the toughest and most feared hoodlum of the era.

He was, although, in awe of a few special young men that had, within the New York City landscape, literally carved out an enormous empire based on money and political influence. Two of those special individuals were Charles Lucania (Lucky Luciano) and Meyer Lansky. What these two individuals did that made them different than most was that they had the ability to align themselves with power brokers on both sides of the law. For Luciano, who Owney admired, his answer to class sophistication and street smarts was Arnold Rothstein, the mastermind behind the 1919 White Sox Baseball scandal. The small edge that Luciano and Lansky acquired was all they needed to both buy and influence everyone that was anyone in New York circa nineteen twenty-seven.

Owney finally aligned himself with Luciano and until Luciano's deportment back to Italy in 1946 they had become lifelong friends and investment partners in more than a few ventures both in and out of New York City.

CHAPTER 17

I NEED TO SEE HOW THE OTHER HALF LIVES.

It was late but seeing the amount of human traffic that stood outside of the Cotton Club Antonio's head, moving back and forth, reminded Tom of a bobble head doll moving side to side.

As they both observed the goings on the sight was right out of an opening night at any gala movie premier.

"Tom, please explain something to me. I realize that there are people that have money but are all these people I'm looking at millionaires, are they?"

Antonio looked at Tom for an answer and he could see that Madden was smiling benevolently,

"Oh my boy have you got a lot to learn, Tony! A lot of these people do have money but having money and acting like you have money are two different things, capire? (understand)!"

Tom's attempt at Italian had Antonio turn his head towards his friend and giving him the most quizzical look

"Since when did you start speaking Italian?"

"Antonio my friend before we go inside I want to share something with you, for the past 8 years whenever I put on my uniform in the morning before going to work I never thought that on that specific day I was going to arrest a so and so because he's Italian or Polish or whatever, no! Whoever broke the law was on my shit list, but since the very organization chose to throw me under the bus I've had a change of heart and you're at the center of it. I learned that word because I've come to realize that, perhaps after these years on the force, you are the only true friend that I really have, and I just wanted you to know that I care. The powers to be have decided to give both of us a hard time. Maybe together we can achieve something, what do you think paisan, eh? Capire?"

    They smiled at each other as they crossed the street and headed for the servants entrance to the Cotton Club

CHAPTER 18

HORIZONS

"How's your meal?"

Like a protective father watching his children eat, Owney surveyed these two young men and wondered out loud, what was next?

"Now that both of you have eaten, why are you here?"

Both Antonio and Tom looked at each other with a quizzical look.

"Well Uncle Owney I thought that since Antonio had no place to go without a home or job that maybe he could..."

Before he could finish the sentence Owney practically jumped down his throat.

"You thought!" Owney screamed, as patrons turned around but seeing who making noise was quickly knew better of it and turned around.

"You bring this smelly piece of carcass from your jail to my place and after 4 years of not hearing from you ask the biggest favor in the world of me your man here gets out of jail and then you come to me? I don't hear a word from you, thanks Uncle nothing. And now you show up and start asking more favors?"

As Owney was reprimanding his nephew Antonio slid his chair back and took the only money from his pocket and threw it on the table. There was suddenly silence amongst the three people but one thing was evident for sure, Owney took notice that Antonio, unlike his nephew, didn't fear him rather Antonio had a stare in his eyes that took Owney to task. In Owney Maddens life he knew three things. You're born, you pay taxes and you die. In Antonio's glare he saw himself a man who would die for his principal no matter right or wrong.

"This is all the money I have, I don't want your charity and I do appreciate what you did believe me, I will pay you back. Your nephew was just being kind to me that's all, Tom let's leave NOW!"

Antonio made himself clear and in any other situation his decision would have been all there was to it but Owney sensed something special in this rather rough looking character.

As the two of them approached the back door to leave they heard someone calling after them.

"What the fuck is it with you two, a man lets off some steam and you both walk out! Here Antonio, take this please, if you like call it a loan whatever! OK? Get a shave and a haircut and some new clothes and come back late Saturday night I need to talk to both of you OK? Now get the fuck out of here see you Saturday night"

"Wow" Antonio was taken aback by Owney's generosity,

"Tom he gave me $500 dollars! Here take half, we're officially partners now, right?"

As they walked across the street Madden was smiling knowing full well that Antonio had shown real balls inside and that Owney, who took a back seat to no one, realized it. He had to marvel that Antonio's not in the country but two years and already being courted, maybe there was something to the old adage that everything happens for a reason.

CHAPTER 19

Kings Row

Saturday night had arrived illegal booze was running rampant and money flowed like raindrops on a cloudy day.

It was twelve thirty pm when Antonio and Tom entered the Cotton Club. The music supplied by the world famous Cab Calloway and his orchestra, the pounding rhythmic sounds were so loud patrons had said that it could be heard for blocks around the club.

The world famous song called "Heidi Heidi Ho" was being performed by it's author singer and master entertainer Calloway and no sooner had he finished the crowd began asking for the other song he was famous for called "Minnie The Moocher" Calloway a High Yellow Negro (light skinned black person) drove the patrons wild, especially the women. But the times dictated that the race line was in triplicate and Owney held strong that there had to be a divided line between the entertainers, who were all black, and the audience.

That Color line a Black Person dare not cross. In the 1920s segregation was the word of the day.

For the resourceful few, especially the beautiful and virginals young light skinned black girls, the road to fame and fortune was at hand. If Owney Madden sanctioned it then any rich White Man could avail himself of whoever he wanted, as long as there was something on the back end for the female.

And not to be forgotten the young and handsome Black men, who worked in the orchestra and performed. There were many a socialite who, with the OK from Owney and company, availed herself while paying heavily for the services of a few of those handsomely endowed young men while their husbands looked the other way. The young black men like the showgirls all were discreet and professional.

The patrons were spending money as if the printing press of green backs would never stop coming their way. A few short years later many of those big spenders were at the door of organized crime asking for handouts, loans and partnerships, and many of them got it and in time lived to regret it.

There wasn't a table to be had, SRO as Tom and Antonio made their way to the bar.

While they waited various cocktail waitresses came by and gave these two young men a look as they peddled their drinks and cigarettes. Owney's law was they would have to be nice to each and every patron to a point. Owney tolerated no rough stuff and if a certain patron wanted the services of a certain girl it would have to go through him.

Within minutes Owney appeared and upon spotting his nephew and Antonio at the bar he broke out in a grin. Looking at Antonio's new clothes he was visibly happy.

"Now you look like a banker, so which is it a banker or lawyer? Guess what both professions steal with a pen and pencil, we sadly need a gun"

With that he broke out into laughter at his own sense of humor.

"Finish your drinks and come upstairs I want you two to meet a few friends of mine"

They followed Owney as he glad handed everyone from the bankers who were probably spending their customer's money to the high and low of organized crime all mingling together in this festive atmosphere. As the music played and Calloway warbled his favorite tunes Antonio couldn't keep his eyes off one of the chorus girls. She stood at least five foot six athletic and shapely. But Antonio looked at her angelic face more Island look that American Negro. Her features, although light tan in color, were definitely European. It struck Antonio as odd that a girl with that look would be in the chorus and not in front. Perhaps she couldn't sing. Whatever the case she was a great looking woman.

He asked Owney as they approached the upstairs off what her name was.

"What is going on Tom Tony here likes the dark meat eh?"

"Well Antonio do you?"

Antonio watched her cavort in the back of the chorus and for a few seconds lost himself in her mannerisms and smile, that smile took him back to Italy. It took him back to Anna and the life that was taken from him. As he looked at her she voluntarily waved at him smiling all the time. It warmed him knowing that perhaps this girl might fill the emptiness in his heart.

"Hey Tony snap out of it will you. You just stopped dead in your tracks can we please go into the office."

The three of them were now staring at the bevy of beauties tap dancing to the beat of the Calloway orchestra. Finally Owney snapped once he heard his nephew yell out over the blaring music..

"Uncle Owney, from the looks of my partner here he's got the hots for that girl in your chorus"

Owney spoke to the group but directed it to Antonio

"Antonio, a word of advice. Stay away from the Negro broads. Every one of them has at least eight boyfriends who would love to stick an eight-inch blade into any white man's stomach!

Antonio just smiled "Maybe that's what will happen maybe it won't but one thing for sure that's one girl I'd just love to get to know.

Owney's office was plush to say the least. Except for one large Mahogany desk in the center of the room the rest of the room emulated a living room more than any office. The large black pillowed sofa seating at least five people looked so soft and inviting that in Antonio's mind sleeping on it would be a pleasure.

The refrigerator as we know it hadn't been invented yet but Owney was ahead of the times in that department too. The large white box like structure had two shelves. One for a thick block of ice and the other for bottles of beer.

Antonio had actually never once tasted beer. Many of the working class Italians were more into wine than beer. Their ideas came from the old country where wine was as much a staple as bread and water. On more than a few occasions he was asked to drink with the men of the building where he lived but refused each time. What the men there did not know and could never comprehend was that drinking and intermixing with others was a social pleasure that Antonio found offensive simply because he lost the love of his life and anything else was senseless.

The potential of tasting warm beer did not initiate a want from Antonio to imbibe. But tonight when Owney offered him a cold one, as they say, he actually liked it. As Owney was speaking to him and Tom his thoughts drifted to the chorus line of the club. Perhaps it was the alcohol working on his senses but he couldn't get his head around the fact that since he had arrived in America he hardly ever thought about the opposite sex. He was all male and his sexual desires were no different than any red blooded Italian or American, for that matter. But not until now had some of those urges that had been dormant these past few years suddenly reappeared.

He remembered first seeing her on his first visit there and even then, with his shabby wardrobe, she still smiled at him. The smile, one of sweetness and kindness, gave him the idea that they could be friends. The fact that she was practically naked helped his thinking a lot but still he felt this girl was special.

CHAPTER 20

ONE CHAPTER ENDS
ANOTHER STARTS

The warehouse they used for rehearsing was located on Twenty-Eight Street and Eleventh Avenue in New York City. The building was partially rented to a phony real estate company controlled by Owney Madden.

The rehearsals had been going on for two days. Both Bo Weinberg and Red Levine thought the preparations were overkill.

"I mean it's not like we're choir boys and it's our first time, with all due respect to you Madden and your sidekick there the silent no comment about anything for two days' fellow, we've been there before Madden, God why all this fuss" The comment Weinberg hurled at the complacent Antonio phased him in the least.

Madden continued to clean and polish his revolver and looked at it for what seemed like an hour, then he looked up spoke.

"Before we came here I was told that you two were as professional as they come! The boss said I should use you and when he says that we follow, am I right so far?"

The two nodded.

"Ok, now he wanted this to go off without any fanfare no guns, only knives so even the smallest detail has to be done until its routine. We of course will also carry firearms but again we'll not use them, not unless we have to. The intended target is sharp and he's always on the lookout for something like this that could possibly happen. We have to be so professional, from the moment we enter the building to the time we exit. And as far as he is concerned"

Pointing directly to Antonio

"Don't worry he's as professional as they come!"

Assuring the two of them was what Tom needed to do. And although Antonio's demeanor was silent and stern he still wanted to assure them that he was more than capable.

The four of them sat and ate their final meal together at the warehouse, for tomorrow was soon to come.

The Wannamaker Building, situated on Eighth Avenue and Twenty Ninth Street in New York, housed many of the Garment Center Manufacturers offices. The fourth floor housed only two companies and they were both related. The first company Castle Incorporated, was an Import House selling and distributing Italian wools and linens. The second Company was a Customs Broker called S. Marra Inc. This company had as its largest customer Castle Inc. Both companies were fronts for the owner and intended target of the exercise Salvatore Marranzano.

No sooner had the elevator doors opened and the four uniformed officers appeared in the hallway they were met by two rather ominous and burley looking goons.

"Ok fellas stop right there what business do you policemen have up here"

Before he could utter another word Madden stepped out and introduced himself.

"My name is Sergeant Madden from the fourteenth, I have here a few legal papers that Don Salvatore Maranzano needs to sign and we're out of here" In an instant Madden fell into his old ways as a top flight police officer. In seconds he had complete control and in an odd yet comical way he actually forgot for the moment what his mission was. His years as a valued member of the force showed as his professionalism in assembling facts as to why they were there in the first place was carried out Asif he really was in charge.

"Are you waiting for something? You're just staring at me" The bigger of the two men asked Madden

As the bigger of the two men questioned Madden he suddenly remembered why they were all there and the plan began to go forward.

"Say, that bulge coming from your waistband wouldn't happen to be a gun would it? Because you know in this town you can't carry a weapon like that without a permit, do you have a permit for that if in fact it is a gun? And if it is and you don't have a permit I have to take both of you downtown now!"

The last few words uttered by Madden were not said in a friendly manner, rather they were actually uttered in a threatening manner. Madden had his hand on his own revolver as he spoke to the two bodyguards.

The larger man of the two spoke first. In an almost apologetic retreat from his stance just a few seconds ago he was submissive in his tone.

"Officer we just got hired and we're from out of town is there any way we can square this I mean so that we don't have to go downtown and of course keep our weapons?"

Madden looked at his cohorts and chuckled out loud.

"Are you two a pair? No you can't have your guns hand them over now!"

As the two were obeying orders Madden tempered his voice.

"All right hold on maybe I was a little rash, look, both of you get out of here now and tomorrow you can come to the precinct and pick up your guns, but for now you have to leave"

In an instant the two men turned over their weapons and ran out of the building. Madden had done his job well. The four of them proceeded to the office of S. Marra. They entered and this time they were met by another man only this fellow was different than the other two. He was extremely well dressed in a dark Grey double breasted suit and fancy diamond stick pin on his tie. He was obviously Italian from the deep accent as he spoke.

"Ah Le Carbiniere eno venuto(The Police Have Arrived)"

He stood five foot ten at least and two hundred pounds and unlike the other two they encountered in the hallway he not only was of a higher intellect but was fit and suntanned as well. At first he was gracious offering the four uniformed policemen some refreshments, Madden declined for all four.

"And who may I ask are you and what can I do for you"

"If you are Signor Maranzano I need you to sign some papers, are you that gentleman?"

Madden knew full well he was not Maranzano but appearances were utmost at this juncture. The slowness of this conversation was talked about at length by Madden in preparation for what was about to happen. He warned that something like this could happen, so he urged them to always stay calm and act as if it were the most ordinary thing to wait for the man to come out and act as if being a policeman was the most boring thing anyone could do. They did not anticipate this fellow and the question also beckoned was he alone?

"I am sorry but we have a few places to go to after here, is Mr Maranzano available now"

The man walked around his desk and now his face became sterner yet still friendly.

"Anything Mr. Maranzano needs to sign I can do it, you have to understand without an appointment well....'

At that point Madden turned detective and accuser all in one. His tone became clipped and hard.

"OK cut out the shit I'm Sergeant Madden, I'm no rookie now get the fuck out of the way or tell Maranzano to come out here we don't have all day!"

The man's face turned red in an instant.

"You talk to me like that I'm Ciro Terranova, they call me the Artichoke King I run everything from the Fulton Market to the ...."

His voice tailed off and as his speech slowed, in that instant he turned white as a ghost. He stepped back as if to assess the situation. He looked down at his suit as he staggered backwards and half falling on his desk. There directly in the middle of his body a large red stain slowly appeared, getting bigger and bigger by the second. The stain was blood caused by the ten-inch blade sticking directly out of his chest, Antonio stepped in front of Tom Madden and shoved it directly into his heart. In a second he was on his knees and just keeled over, he was dead instantly. Madden turned to Antonio but before he could say anything Antonio blurted out "let's go inside, there is nothing left to do here"

The other two men with Madden were not in shock at what they had just witnessed but in all honesty, they would later express to their fellow mobsters, witnessing the unemotional savage attack by Piccolo to Terranova told a whole other story about the man.

Levine would later describe Piccolo's attack as brutality with absolutely no emotion connection to anything human it was as if he was dead and killing another human made no difference.

The quartet needed something done quietly and dramatic so they could advance into Maranzano's office

As the four of them entered Maranzano's office they witnessed a rather large man, for an Italian, in many ways he resembled anything but a Mafioso so well known within the Sicilian community.

Maranzano stood six feet tall manicured and tailored much like the magazines of the day that portrayed what the elite businessman in nineteen thirty New York looked and dressed like.

Maranzano stood up and asked what the four officers wanted. He looked around the men to the office door seemingly wondering where his security was and why had they not alerted him as to the police arrivals.

"Gentlemen, how are you oh and by the way did mister Terranove see you before you came in here?"

In seconds the four uniformed killers approached Maranzano, only this time they were not pretending. Like wolves about to pounce on a cornered elk the foursome attacked he and world that Maranzano ruled would slowly create a black hole in his subconscious mind.

His attitude was lucid and calm as he noticed the knives that his tormentors were about to use on him. He also knew that screaming for help would be of no use as in all of the Sicilian rituals crying out for any help was unmanly even sickening, yet the thought raced through his mind that perhaps jumping out of the fourth floor window might not be a bad idea.

Maranzano instinctively knew that in seconds it would be kill or be killed. He reached down with every ounce of fortitude he thought he had and fought strongly warding off knife attacks as both Bo Weinberg and Red Levine attacked savagely at his torso, yet he was strong, so strong that both Levine and Weinberg knew that two men against him would not be enough.

As the savagery continued Madden and Antonio made sure that Maranzano had no outlet for escape. In seconds it was over as Levine ended it all with his signature, cutting his victims throat.

The four men knew what they needed to do, time was of the essence. Their uniforms were thrown into a basket they had placed inside the vestibule of the building. The clothes were set on fire and all four men exited in different directions as calm as could be.

CHAPTER 21

SHAKE HANDS WITH THE DEVIL

Owney's guests had just arrived. The head waiter informed Owney and the waiter was directed to send them up immediately. The door flew open and there stood what many people have since called the mastermind behind organized crime as we know of it today.

Walking into Owney's office was none other than Charles Lucania known as Lucky Luciano. He stood five feet eleven inches tall, very tall for an Italian, bespectacled and a smile ten feet long. He was dressed in a bone color double breasted overcoat. Madden thought that, even in the smallest of men's shops, had to have cost him a fortune. Tom also noticed the shoes. It looked as if there was fifty layers of polish on them. Impressive could not describe what his entrance was like, topped with a light tan fedora made by Borsalini, one of the finest hat makers in America. Accompanying him was a smaller gentleman also bespectacled, who simply waved at Owney, and took a chair on the opposite side of the room.

Owney, smiling like a brother would after not seeing his sibling in years, embraced Luciano.

"Charley it's too long between visits, what takes you away from my place that I only see you maybe once a month"

Luciano stepping away from Owney's embrace smiling all the while as he walked around the office looking at all the photos that Owney had on the walls, turning around and addressing his partner.

"Owney, I made you my partner long ago knowing that the share out for me and my partners would always be on the money, that's why I don't have to be here every second of the day!"

Luciano still smiling as he noticed the two new faces of Madden and Antonio, he then took off his overcoat and handed it to the smaller man as he then pulled up a chair close to Owney and began to talk in a low whisper.

He was speaking to Madden as if he were the only person in the room. When their secret talk was over, and it lasted all of three minutes, he looked at both Madden and Antonio and asked if they were the two.

Looking directly at Antonio Luciano extended his hand.

"Como te chiami(whats your name)"

"Antonio Piccolo"

"But please, Senor Luciano I was educated in Naples so I speak fluent English"

Luciano looked down at Antonio's hand.

"Ah! Now I understand. Camorra right?'

Antonio nodded yes.

"Who is your benefactor?"

Antonio squirmed uneasy in his chair.

"Is that a concern with you because I respect him so much that I would have to have a great reason just to mention his name?"

Antonio bowed his head in a most humiliating manner that Luciano had to respect that.

"Don't worry about that son, your secret is strong with me. Actually the only man that I knew that commanded that much respect is still in prison now, would that be the same man?"

Antonio looked down at the cross that adorned the space between his thumb and forefinger.

"His name is Benito Crespi, I will always honor him till the day I die, and did you by chance know him personally?"

Luciano stood up and began to walk around Owney's office as if he were addressing members of Congress. It appeared to Antonio that twenty years of Italian inbred feelings were about to erupt within Luciano's speech. As Luciano slowly paced Owney's office everyone in the office kept silent for here was the King of New York about to impart something special to everyone.

"Owney!" He looked directly at Owney Madden

"This man Crespi, was a man amongst men, I came here when I was a kid and my old man spoke of him in such reverent terms, YES,i knew of him and if Antonio were nurtured by him then I want him with me, is that ok with you being that he came here under your protection!"

The emotion in the room was so high that Owney, who was known to never show emotion in any situation, jumped to his feet and grabbed Antonio by the shoulders.

Owney smiled broadly while holding Antonio at arm's length.

"Son, I didn't know who you were but when my nephew brought you here I sensed that there was something special about you. Now it seems that you've come here to honor us like this and when Mr. Luciano puts his stamp of approval on you, Kid that's the golden invitation"

For the first time since his days back in Italy Antonio became emotional. As he glanced over at Tom and again at Owney instantly he realized that he finally was part of something, this was his new family.

For Antonio the happenings at Owney's club encompassed both gamuts of emotion from the strange way that Irishmen embraced him to the exhilarating thrill that a man like Luciano thought he was special.

Antonio instantly realized why Lucky Luciano was held in such high regard. Luciano had the ability to pull emotion out of a man, especially a man like Antonio who thought that from the day he was incarcerated back in Italy to the present he was incapable of true emotion, losing the love of his life coupled with the humiliating years in prison culminating with the elimination of an entire family, all stopped as soon as Luciano bestowed the look upon him. Antonio knew in that instant that he would go to the ends of the earth for the man.

Antonio was honored that Luciano acted as he did. And he could plainly see why Luciano was held in such esteem, he was truly the man.

As Luciano spoke his mannerisms were not rushed rather he spoke in generalities citing great men of the past in illustrating his various points.

"Years ago there was a man from Castelamare in Sicily. He came to this country and became a big man in both the street traffic like Gambling and drugs as well as some political influence. At the height of his power he had over four hundred men under him and each one of them were killers. Now to most people in our trade that would be considered successful, right?" Luciano looked at Owney who acted like a trained seal in acquiescing.

"What is wrong with that picture?"

Everyone, including Antonio couldn't figure what Luciano was alluding to.

"Diversification, that's what this guy never understood. Eventually his one way ideas about how to be successful for both you and your family got him killed. That was Joe Masseria. I did say family right?" everyone nodded but somehow Luciano was not convinced that the participants in Owney's office knew what he was talking about much less what all of this rhetoric meant.

"I believe in Family and honor, tonight I want all of us to bond, Antonio after this night you'll report only to me, is that clear?"

Antonio hadn't felt this loved since his initial days at Castel De Mare when he first met Benito Crespi.

Antonio stood up stretched out his hand by which Luciano grabbed him and in a bear hug embrace kissed him on both cheeks

"Antonio "tu si uno amico mio" you are now a friend of mine"

"Gentlemen, please sit I especially want to talk to Antonio and Tom, I have a very important job for both of you and you'll be assisted on this special mission with two very good associates of mine"

As Luciano spoke the room became quiet. In many ways it was reminiscent of some of the great orators who moved nations just by embodying thoughts that eventually turn into words and eventually turn into deeds. This ability Luciano had, and what Antonio did not know was that in that moment of clear vision he was spiritually indoctrinated into the Luciano family.

"Tomorrow evening my associates will be here to explain what has to be done and how I need it done. Does anyone know where the Wanamaker Building is located?"

Luciano had plans for Antonio that would eventually expand Luciano's influence into arenas that many of the gangsters of the twenties and thirties had never even thought of. Complete control over metropolitan cities in areas that no one had ever delved into before. Luciano's vision was to control and not just work at the multitude of avenues. Food, Unions, Garment's manufacturing and distribution but more than that he wanted to literally control the ebb and flow of commerce that surrounded those entity's.

Luciano never got a Ba or Bs from any university yet Antonio was amazed at the man's grasp of coupling emotion with logic.

As soon as Luciano talk was over Antonio was excited at the potential prospects in store for him as part of the organization.

"Mr Luciano I'd love to work for you but with one condition, wherever I go he goes" he pointed to Madden.

Luciano looked at Madden and suddenly the bulb went on.

Luciano then looked at Owney

"Ok, Ok your nephew right?" I do remember now you had mentioned that you had a nephew that was a policeman, is he the one and if you are that nephew are you still an active policeman?"

Everyone in the room knew why Lucky had asked. If Madden was still a Policeman then everything Luciano had said could be in jeopardy.

"I used to be now I'm unemployed."

Luciano raised his glass in a toast. "Gentlemen, after tonight you two will be working for me and your uncle, hopefully this marks the beginning of a very fruitful friendship."

CHAPTER 22

A PARTNERSHIP DOESN'T ALWAYS MEAN A SMOOTH RIDE

Two months had passed since the newspapers detailed the gruesome murder of gang lord Salvatore Marranzano. The murder and subsequent funeral was described in what the newspapers called the biggest mob funeral since the killing of Joe "The Boss" Masseria, a year before. Ironically the two killings were connected as Luciano had a hand in both. The daily newspaper accounts of the killing had stopped and the few lines attributed to the murder were now relegated to page six as the nation was absorbed with the economic depression that had a stranglehold on many Americans.

The mood in America in 1931 was somber at best. The White House was consumed with the inability of both Congress and the Senate to patch up their differences and come up with a solution to help alleviate the ill effects of the crashing stock market of 1929 and the increasing joblessness within the working class citizens of the nation.

Charles Luciano, on the other hand, was doing quite well as were his partners, surrogates and followers. His many business enterprises were flourishing. He was officially out of the liquor business as the Volstead Act was repealed. Businessmen from all walks of life had seen their fortunes dwindle as panic and depression set in.

Luciano had no such problems. He never invested in the market. He always kept his money in cash. He put his money out on the street and as businessmen after businessmen were losing fortunes he was right there to lend a helping hand.

Luciano devised a plan to reach out to the now not so prosperous businessmen who, prior to the crash, lived as though the gravy train would never end. He offered to lend them money at reasonable terms. As it turned out Luciano and his confederates were the only group that actually kept their money in cash and never allowed the greedy stock market big shots to handle it. In the end those same Broadway big shots came calling and for Luciano and his minions a new business was born, usury.

Since that dramatic meeting between Antonio Piccolo and Tom Madden with Luciano at the Cotton Club, many months before, the young and energetic duo were staked in business by Luciano. They were set up in business down in Greenwich Village working for Luciano.

The business was called "Jitney Escorts" In essence they would act as a limousine service for many of the finer hotels in the city still catering to the dwindled lot of still very wealthy people. Compared to the normal taxi cab ride that cost so much more and was less personal, Jitney created a working relationship with the hotel, Discretion was the byword and many times certain customers did not want to be seen by anyone. Many times that person and their escort needed privacy and they got it from Jitney.

In a matter of six months Jitney had cornered twenty of the top hotels in the city. It did not hurt that registered at the Waldorf Towers was a Mr. Charles Ross, alias for Charley Luciano. Luciano's rent in 1931 was $350 dollars a week, a tidy sum in Depression America. Piccolo's position was manager of Jitney and Madden saw to the actual functioning part of the business. At the end of each month Antonio set out to collect from each hotel, this part of his job was made so much easier since the true owner of Jitney was Mr Big shot himself Lucky Luciano.

Antonio, as was his custom each and every morning, was extremely quiet as he read the New York News and had his Biscotti and coffee. Madden couldn't help but observe that Antonio was still the non-conformist. He rarely smiled except on occasions when Madden would regale them both with stories about the incarcerated brethren he was forced to patrol when he was a cop.

On many a rainy and wintry nights those inmates, many of them so drunk, would make so much noise they would eventually wake Madden who used the evening shift to get hours of shut eye. The laughs were plenty and just remembering those incidents brought a smile on both of their faces.

From the outset these two men were different in so many ways. Antonio was quiet to a fault and Madden was just the opposite. On so many occasions Madden would offer his opinion on anything happening in the world and as he did looking to extract an either yea or nay from Antonio the end result was just the same.

"Tom, why do you always want my opinion, I'm a fugitive from Italy, what could my yes or no due to illuminate the conversation!"

This was a daily occurrence at the office sending Madden into fits.

"I can't believe that you show no interest in anything! God! the only time you showed me anything in the emotion department was when the boss spoke to you and me over two months ago"

On that special and historic occasion Luciano laid out an itinerary for both of them that for Madden it represented a radical change in the path that up until now had led him on the straight and narrow. For Antonio the new direction was a welcomed embrace of the future.

Luciano created the bond between himself and Antonio that would last for decades. As far as the personal side of their partnership Madden and Antonio couldn't be more opposite.

Tom Madden was raised by parents who believed in the Christian way of doing things. Going to church, respect your elders even if they were one hundred percent in the wrong. Antonio, since his Italian experience was forced to change everything he had ever known about decency and fair play. He became a murdered without conscience, in many ways it was inevitable that he would end up in New York working for one of the most famous Gangsters in History.

Antonio, without realizing it, automatically hated everything that resembled fairness. He had become a vessel to wreak havoc on command. From Benito Crespi in Italy to Lucky Luciano the string had not been broken.

That fateful evening whereby Luciano charged the two of them to murder, Both Madden and Antonio signed on but with different reasons behind their decisions.

Madden accepted because he felt the law had deserted him. Everything he had been about his entire life was centered on the fact that justice and the law would always provide for him as long as he continued to dedicate himself to the life that was chosen for him by his parents and close relatives.

Antonio, on the other hand, welcomed the order. He welcomed the fact that Luciano, like Crespi, was considered a man of respect. In so many ways the charge for Antonio to kill was a reenactment of what had happened to him back in Italy. Marranzano was portrayed as a potentate much like Don

Francisco, the man who had Antonio incarcerated. Killing him was something he needed to do so that somehow the deep pain and hurt he continually felt inside his being might somehow disappear. In Antonio's mind he knew the truth, the pain and hurt he inflicted would never disappear. Some psychiatrists might call that form of behavior masochism, Antonio used it as his calling card.

Madden tried to bring Antonio closer to him by trying to create the bond he thought they had between them.

Whenever Madden would invite him to a family function he would refuse Madden believed that after hearing all the horrors he went through back in Italy it wasn't that hard to figure out why Antonio was the way he was. But that didn't stop him from trying.

And lately the pattern that Antonio demonstrated lacked emotion and feeling. That was until the meeting with Luciano. Madden also noticed that although he and Antonio were partners that most of what their everyday life together was centered on business and business matters. They would never socialize outside of the Jitney Business. He also noted that Antonio, with all the modern money and acceptance within the small enclave of companies and their workers, he still stayed his distance.

To illustrate the great differences between the two. On one such occasion a man was shot and robbed in the street by two young thugs. Witnessing the shooting Madden, with his former policeman's mentality, chased after the two boys caught up to them and physically restrained them until the police arrived.

"God! Antonio why didn't you come out there and help me!?"

Antonio continued to read the Italian paper never lifting his head to answer Madden.

In one fell swoop Madden angrily slapped the paper out of his hand. Standing there emotionally charged he half screamed at his partner.

"What the fuck is wrong with you! Didn't you hear me?"

In seconds Antonio arose from his chair although this time Madden had gotten a rise from him as his face was now as red as Madden's

"Tommy, do me a favor. Yes, we're friends and partners but if you value anything in your life don't ever, I mean ever do anything like that again. I don't give a fuck about those kids, do you hear me! And neither should you! Stop it you're not a cop anymore that is unless you want to go back and be one again! Well! Do you!?"

And with that he sat down and picked up his paper again.

Madden was shaken up not by either what he said or what Antonio said but how Antonio said it. It wasn't a threat it was a warning. In the next two months with the Maranzano affair about to happen Madden saw at close range Antonio's volatility and killer instincts, and after all the bad men Madden had locked up, Madden knew that Antonio was more ferocious than any of them.

As the weeks passed culminating with the Maranzano killing Tom tried, on numerous occasions, to interject personal anecdotes that might bridge the gap between them.

"Antonio, do you remember the alkyl that was always being arrested every weekend so that he would have a warm place to sleep at night?" Antonio half smiled as he recalled the man.

"Yes I do remember, I often wonder what ever happened to him, how come your mentioning him? Have you seen him lately?"

Madden was beside himself and had to handle this diplomatically.

"Antonio, no I haven't seen him but can you sometimes interject a little humor into our lives, after all there has to be some life beyond the Jitney Business!"

"Tom, lately you've been quiet and moody what's the matter? Did something happen in the garage, what!?"

For the first time in their relationship Tom felt that perhaps Antonio was trying, in his own way, to bridge the gap between them.

"Look, as a partner no one could ever ask for anyone better. The money, which is at the heart of every partnership breakup, is never an issue with us. You make the pickups and hand the cash over to me. That trust is important to me but I still wish that we could bond a little more than just showing up each day and running this business"

Antonio put his newspaper down and it appeared to Tom that what he had said finally struck gold.

"What about tonight, how about both of us going to your uncle's place and catch a show, how about it?"

Madden sat down next to him and smiled. For the first time in weeks the mood was jovial.

"I seem to remember that there was one special lady in the chorus at the Cotton Club that caught your eye, right?"

His remark made Antonio smile. Tom had to laugh as Antonio rolled his eyes ala Eddie Cantor to which they both enjoyed a good laugh.

CHAPTER 23

ONE LOOK WAS ALL IT TOOK

"So, what town did you say you were from?"

The scene was reminiscent of every backstage drama depicted on the big screen. The dancers were scurrying from their backstage dressing rooms in order for them to be in perfect formation just before the curtain was about to rise. The typical girl y screeching sounds emanating from all fourteen ladies as they scurried announcing to one and all that they were so excited just to be there.

"Do you dance in this part of the show?" he was forced to raise his voice against the noise coming from the chorus of parading showgirls that ran past him and Ardelia like a side car ride at the circus. "What I meant was, will they miss you in the chorus?"

He asked the bronze beauty concentrating solely on her face as he followed each line that marked the contour of her eyes.

"Oh no not this number, I come out later in the finale when the entire chorus comes out sort of like what's happening now except at that time everybody's on stage all at once"

She looked nervously to her left and right as she spoke knowing full well that it was almost a forbidden rule that there be no fraternization between the entertainers who were all Negro and any white customer. The scene was eerie in the fact that Antonio, unlike many white men attempting to talk to any Negro entertainer, was emotionally calm and collected while Ardelia was nervous to a fault. In the first few seconds that they were face to face she couldn't help being distracted with the combination of chorus girls scampering from stage left to stage right and the constant blaring of the orchestra that was situated directly behind where she and Antonio had decided to talk suddenly made her tremble with fear.

"Please! Relax ok? You're all right back here with me"

Antonio was well aware of the rule but seeing that his partner's uncle owned the place who's going to squawk. But in the end the conversation was cut short by the backstage manager who, at first, gave Antonio a look that could kill then practically shouting into the young lady's face

"What you doing back here girl!" he suggested in a threatening tone as he inched close to her practically yelling in her face. His tone was menacing but it was more for Antonio's benefit, it was a warning for sure as he glanced over to Antonio as he was making his threats directly to her. Simply put it meant no white man allowed.

She began to get up and as she did the backstage manager helped her stand as he grabbed at her arm, smirking as he did so. He glanced over to Antonio, like a man would when he sees that his opponent has decided to back down, but Antonio looked back at him like a lion about to pounce upon a helpless doe.

In that instant, before the young lady had completely gotten up from her chair, Ardelia was slowly pushed back down by Antonio as he simultaneously stood up confronting the back stage manager.

The entire episode took all of twenty seconds but in the end there was the girl sitting down Antonio standing to her right and the stage manager standing to her left.

"I think the lady looks much better sitting down this way you and I can look each other in the eye and speak our piece, you agree?"

The man looked at Antonio quizzically not knowing how to answer. The question beckoned, was this White man a man of the law? Was he just a patron and did not know that most Negro men, although poor, valued their relationship with their women as sacred. It was New York and 1931 and White America dominated, but the average White man would think twice before crossing the color line especially when the colored man was bigger and stronger than he was.

Antonio slowly raised his hand and reached the man's suit lapels. Pulling him so close that their lips were inches apart.

"I really don't want any trouble from you, all we were doing was talking, do you want to pursue this right now?!"

Antonio let the man straighten up and gain a little composure. The manager swallowed hard trying to figure out what to say. Antonio, with eyes glaring asked him again.

"Do we understand each other?"

It was as if a cold shower devoured the man. He stepped back and quickly understood that this white man was not the typical foppish night club moron who frequented the backstage area hoping to get a cheap thrill. Or better a person who thought that perhaps their money and status would somehow make a young strong Negro buck fear for his life, no this man was different and he would not be trifled with. In that short span of seconds every noose around every poor innocent Negro ever assonated by the scores of southern white scum that lynched and killed innocent folks was suddenly felt by this rather adroit stage manager.

The intent was perceived and the manager understood and he was gone.

Antonio sat back down and as he did he made doubly sure that the stage manager was out of sight.

"Is he or was he ever a boyfriend?"

She smiled nervously and he sensed that she was uncomfortable after hearing what was said and what was implied. "No, we have never been involved but I think after tonight I won't be working here much longer"

"Why do you say that; you mean because of what I just said? No Never, first of all he will never look at you again in any manner but respectful, secondly I am a gentleman not a pimp! And lastly I'll make sure, that is if it's ok with you that you work more not less, is that ok?"

Ardelia was taken back. She had never met anyone like him before, the fact that he promised to do these things for her made her take him seriously and in a manner made her feel good.

It took a few seconds but her attention was now focused directly on him and she too began to follow the lines on his face feeling a bit more relaxed and confident that perhaps she finally found a man who would respect her for who she was not what they could get from her.

"What is your name?"

He looked at her and sensed that beyond her fabulous looks and charm there was an aura of spirituality that sent out emotional signals to him without ever having said a word.

"My name is Ardelia Reed and I come from Virginia"

He visualized her name in his psyche.

"Ardelia, what a beautiful name. I think that someday people will see it written on billboards and plastered all over the place. Places like Times Square, telling one and all that here, finally, was a performer who truly believed in her art."

Ardelia moved a little uneasy in her chair not being able to fathom what Antonio meant, was he sending signals to her that he was a bit unbalanced, as she had never spoken with any man, much less a white man, who spoke like that about her. She understood that perhaps a drawback in communicating with anyone might be that her language skills needed a lot of work. As she listened to Antonio speak it sounded to her that he was an educated man. The manner in which he spoke, so slow and methodical, made her believe that she might be listening to a teacher. But there were other aspects of this young and intense young man that piqued her curiosity.

"You asked me my name what is yours?"

"My name is Antonio Piccolo, and I was born and raised in Italy, do you know where Italy is?"

He could see that she was slowly settling in to the fact that no one backstage was pressuring her to get back in the lineup, that this young impressive man did in fact have some clout there at the Cotton Club. She observed another facet of this man's presence was that he never looked around as so many men and women do when they know that they are either being looked at or that because of the surroundings seem conspicuous at the least. The backstage area of the Cotton Club was not the best place for anyone, much less a woman of color, to be seen speaking with a white man.

"I've read some about it; it is in Europe right?" Seconds passed so slowly like raindrops running down a window Paine. And as each drop cascaded onto another Antonio's desire for this lovely creature increased.

He couldn't keep his eyes off her face. She captured a euphoric joy that was missing in him for so long. As each second passed he couldn't help inhaling her into his senses that reverted back to a time in Benevento where the sun the moon and the stars was all he ever wanted for.

Her hands were soft like velvet. Her long fingers that he slowly caressed into the palm of his hand did not waver upon his touch.

"Can we meet after the show? I assure you that my intentions are honorable"

Ardelia had never been put in this situation before where a white man was asking to be a friend with ramifications that could lead to more. At any other time in her life she would have probably said no and walked away but this fellow, who was both quiet and polite while demonstrating a fierce determination, did in fact have charm and good looks. The last part of him being good looking only manifested itself to her after she allowed herself to get over her serious case of nerves. This will always happen whenever a white man attempts to get friendly with a Negro woman.

His look and strong personality added to the fact that a white man could be so courteous piqued her curiosity even more.

It was 1931 people were starving, the Black man was only 70 years out of slavery and Ardelia really did not know what tomorrow would bring made her think twice about every decision she was ever to make about survival.

While the entire world was knee deep into a major financial depression this man wielded power within that arena.

"Of course we can, I get off at midnight"

Antonio got up from the table and as he did so he took her hand in his and raised it to his lips whereby he kissed it. "Till then" he replied softly.

And just as quickly walked away.

CHAPTER 24

RELATIONSHIPS

The same scene had played itself out over the next three weeks.

Each evening Antonio would wait outside the Cotton Club for Ardelia to finish work. They would then proceed to an apartment that Antonio had rented on the north side of Harlem facing Broadway.

In the same ensuing three weeks they had gotten to know each other quite well. Everyone at the Cotton Club knew about their romance much to the annoyance of the stage manager who, upon orders from Owney Madden, inserted Ardelia into the two main numbers featured at the club. This did not sit well with him as well as the girl Ardelia replaced. At first there was some minor tension but knowing that the owner wanted it and the fact that Ardelia had not pushed the issue made the transition, at least on the surface, amiable.

The girl that Ardelia replaced, whose name was Clarissa, actually made friends with Ardelia and on more than a few occasions Antonio, not wanting any resentment between the women, would slip her an extra $100-dollar bill just so there were no hard feelings. For all intents and purposes the world could not have been better for Antonio. Luciano had expanded his brothel industry using three men from his Unione Siciliano, (The Sicilian Mafia) to supervise the activity. The Jitney Express was so successful that Antonio had to hire four new people just to handle the extra business.

Luciano had expanded in so many new and different directions that lately Antonio was lucky to see him once a week.

Luciano had, as soon as prohibition was repealed, began to develop relationships with many of the people who purchased liquor from him and his associates. Men who had been giants in the stock market and now had fallen on hard times. Men who were in industry and used Luciano's services to cater everything from prostitutes for a large party in long Island to bringing in special bottles of the finest French wines at $1,000 per case. Many of these industry leaders much like the stock brokers were now broke and hurting for cash. So Luciano instituted the Usury racket. This enabled him to lend out, at a fair rate, money to these people knowing full well that their business acumen would take them back to the top all over again and Luciano would be there right alongside them in the ensuing years, after Luciano's deportation, many of those business men kept their word and made good on all the money they had borrowed from him. Antonio saw the potential in everything Luciano was doing and planned to do. Luciano conversely saw the potential in Antonio and began, by small tests, to see if Antonio not only could be trusted but in the end become a clone of Luciano himself.

"I never quite thanked you, I mean for doing this for me. No man had ever been this kind to me"

Antonio had just come out of the shower listening to Ardelia muse to herself as she lay across the wide bed in their apartment. The sun had come up and as was his custom he generally went to the corner of 129th street and Lexington bought the morning paper and sometimes a small gift for

Ardelia. After he would come back to the apartment, undress and lay in bed with her till noon.

"Maybe today I'll just be lazy today and lay here with you. And you don't owe me a thing. Believe me I was drifting and, depending how the wind blew that day, only God knows what I would do for sure I didn't"

Ardelia just smiled as God had indeed answered her prayers, here she was slowly falling in love with a man she knew little about yet didn't care. She had a job that she loved yet as long as he was in her life she couldn't care if she ever worked again. She wondered what their kids would look like if they were ever married. She had started to bring up that same subject once before but Antonio asked her to table it. She got the message and instantly understood that her kind was the lovemaking kind but never the marrying kind. Antonio objected to this kind of thinking.

"I need you to stop thinking like that" he looked at her without flinching a bit

"I don't want kids because of who I am not who you are. There is so much about me you don't know and will never know believe me it's not a world I want any of my kids to live in. if it's ok with you let's leave well enough alone ok? And furthermore perhaps you're thinking that the reason I said let's wait to talk about us and the future was because your Negro and I'm white. You're wrong! I don't see skin color. As a matter of fact, I was betrayed by my own kind and sent to prison to die. The love of my early life was taken away from me because of what my own kind did to me and what color were they? And you think that color is the issue? Ardelia I am a murderer! Do you understand! I killed a lot of people both in Italy and here. Do you still think that color is the issue? You have to decide if you want to live with that!"

Luciano had asked Antonio to meet him at the Greenwich Village office of a Juke Box Vending business he had controlling interest in. Also attending the meeting would be another gentleman named Aldo Debruto, a Mafia Kingpin who controlled the vegetable industry as well as a dozen other businesses in and around New York. The rumor had it that he also controlled much of the high end prostitution business but those were rumors.

The meeting was attended by just Antonio, Debruto and Luciano. After their cordial hugs, handshakes and kisses the meeting got to order.

"I am sure you know or have heard of who exactly Aldo is and what he represents" Luciano expounded.

"I asked Aldo to sit in with us because over the years he has worked with me and my friends where all have made a lot of money. Through the years the standing edict was that if he, an independent, needed my help for anything or had a serious problem then it would be within my power to help and in effect his problem would become my problem. Aldo's problem concerns a man who works closely with Owney and is friends with your partner Tom. I already spoke with Owney and he's ok with whatever decision we make here."

Luciano took his time in speaking and Antonio realized in him a rare study of a man who dealt from behind the dark shadows of evading the law yet and yet at the same time handled the English language as a man would caress his most prized possession, the ability to create a business environment in the United States.

"As I see the situation it is all fine with everyone as long as we handle it clean and with no problems. My problem here is your partner Tom. The man in question is one of Tom's best friends and when Tom was a policeman this friend of his could never be touched without repercussion but now. This man's name is Eric and it seems as though he's having an ongoing relationship with Aldo's secretary Maria. "

After the first two minutes of his meeting with Luciano and Debruto two things became evident to Antonio. First, he absolutely disliked Debruto and secondly he was simply fascinated at how gentle and concise Luciano handled the meeting. Debruto on the other hand was so crude and actually disgusting to a fault that Antonio, right in the middle of the meeting, asked to be excused as he had to relieve himself in the bathroom. Debruto epitomized everything Antonio had come to hate in Italian's who envisioned themselves as pillars of the community while in their spare time looking up young girl's skirts.

In reality what he simply needed was a breath of fresh air, Italy and everything in his past came to his conscious mind rushing to every sense in his body even as much as the smells of the carnage he left behind so many years ago. In Debruto he saw the reincarnation of Philp Testa.

He simply stepped outside the office and took a deep breath.

He took a little more than five minutes, taking his time before going back in. The anger he had for Debruto could not be measured in words. The simple idea of this pig of a man wanting another young woman brought back so many ugly memories that Antonio needed air to breathe.

"For Christ's sake how long does it take to take a piss?" Debruto bellowed as he looked straight at Antonio as he, returning from the men's room, slowly grabbed a chair and sat down. Debruto waited for the apology. But Antonio would not reciprocate, what he gave instead was the opposite.

"Apologize, for what!" He spoke directly to Debruto knowing full well his reputation yet tempering his tone, he spoke not loudly or bellowing but calmly and straightforward.

This was viewed by Debruto as totally disrespectful and he knew it. He obviously wasn't used to anyone speaking to him that way. In an instant he was up and standing over Antonio in the most threatening manner.

"Lucky! For God's sake who the fuck is this punk!" Debruto exclaimed

"Did you tell him who I was? Hey kid I'm head of the Unione Sicilano, that's who and I demand respect"

There was quiet in the room then Luciano spoke. "Ok Aldo I know he's sorry"

As Luciano looked back at Antonio and seeing that Antonio was nodding his head in compliance he then proceeded to quiet Debruto's anxieties. This show of respect from Luciano calmed Aldo down and he sat down. Luciano making sure that the tension had subsided began to speak.

Each word Luciano uttered was symbolic of a leader and in many ways Antonio would have followed him to the moon if asked. Antonio studied Debruto trying to unmask this pig of a man, feeling hatred for the man and in reality not knowing who he was. In actuality it really didn't matter who he was or what he represented Antonio knew in his heart that one day they would meet him and at that time he would kill him.

"Does that sound like something you can handle, I mean with your partner and all"

Antonio studied Luciano to see if there was anything that would lead him in any direction as to why he was chosen. Nothing was mentioned about Maranzano or Masseria and what part Antonio had in those dealings as well as nothing mentioned as far as Italy and all, no, Antonio felt there had to be more as to why Luciano with all his army of chosen killers and associates chose Antonio. Because of protocol Antonio couldn't ask out loud but all during Luciano's dissertation Antonio paid no mind to Debruto...

"Mr. Luciano if possible can you and I have a small meeting, just the two of us after this is over?"

As if a thunderstorm had suddenly crashed through the windows of the Vending Company Debruto chimed in.

"You see Lucky! What did I tell you! He's not the man to do this! God Dam it I've been a boss for more years then you're alive for Christs sake, I asked you to do something and you elect this amateur, for God's sake he doesn't even acknowledge that I'm in the room. What the hell are you looking at him for?" As Debruto motioned to Luciano

Then Debruto committed the most critical sin, he talked over Luciano and in an almost inaudible high pitched lament he screamed!

"Look Lucky you may be the boss around here but I'm calling the shots about this Eric kid, I will tell you when and how this thing goes down got that!" This was directed solely at Luciano.

Luciano sat emotionless acting as if he heard nothing concerning Debruto's violent tirade.

Luciano raised his hand, he had heard enough. This was the second outburst from Debruto in the past half hour.

"OK I get it! My decision still stands; we'll talk later this week!"

Debruto was dismissed and he exited mad as hell without saying good bye to either Luciano or Antonio.

Antonio looked quizzically at Lucky, waiting for his answer.

"You wanted to talk, so here we are"

From his tone Antonio couldn't read anything into Luciano's thinking. Here he could see that Debruto was a slug. A poor man's mafia representative a counterfeit killer, so why make all the fuss and help this guy. He was puzzled.

Antonio tried again to exact exactly what Luciano wanted from him.

"Mr. Luciano all I wanted to say was that I'd like to assess this situation before I act is that OK, I mean this man Debruto is off his rocker, if you know what I mean, am I out of line by asking?"

Luciano listened intently as if assessing his young lieutenant's merits. After a few seconds he abruptly ended the meeting and dismissed Antonio.

"You have one week, get back to me before that on your thoughts on this matter and how are we going to handle it, now go."

And that fast the meeting was over.

CHAPTER 25

The Truth

Tom Madden was so absorbed with running Jitney Escorts that lately it was as if he and Antonio were passing each other in the night. The business was flourishing and the total amount of people working the business had grown to eleven.

Antonio had settled down into a normal routine with Ardelia and for all intents and purposes the world he had left back in Italy was but a memory. As far as America was concerned Antonio was satisfied that he had finally found peace and although he was not in love with Ardelia she had become the vessel for emotion and warmth that he so desperately needed.

1931

Three years had passed, it was now 1931 and for everyone in the Luciano organization the world was a better and more financially secure place than it had ever been before.

Antonio and Ardelia had just left the small grocery store on the north side of Mulberry Street in Lower Manhattan. They both loved the fresh fruits and vegetables the store carried. Everyone in the neighborhood knew Antonio and in the last couple of years his prowess in the Luciano organization had gone from one of Luciano's men to second in command. Antonio wanted to buy a newspaper before they walked the eight blocks to their two story apartment on east 4th street. As was her custom she ran ahead to open the door as Antonio carried the two extremely heavy grocery bags up the steps.

Ardelia opened the front door and put the door stopper under the door to keep it open. She then proceeded to open the lights and go upstairs trying to get a jump on dinner.

"Hey babe" he shouted as he struggled to both juggle the bags and keep his composure

"Get the white wine Mr Cantalupo gave me yesterday we can have it with dinner"

Not getting to the open door in effect saved Antonio's life.

Three days later, Saint Clair's Hospital in lower Manhattan.

"Has he regained consciousness?" Chief of Detectives from the twentieth precinct Matt O'Connor waited for the head nurse to answer.

"Briefly last night then just as quickly fell back in this coma like state and today well. He's been the same all morning"The head nurse on the floor stated.

After seeing that there would probably be no answers today the two officers left.

Seconds later Antonio opened his eyes and quickly scanned the room. Seeing Tom Madden sitting across the room he tried to speak.

"Tom, can you tell me what happened, the last I remember Ardelia had gone upstairs, oh! God is she alright?"

Tom got up and walked to the bed holding Antonio's hand in his he shook his head No

ANTONIO FRANCESCA

In the next eight hours the room had visitors all wishing Antonio a speedy recovery and by nightfall he was appraised of exactly what happened. A bomb was set off in the basement of the apartment house he lived in. By sheer luck he avoided death. This was the second time in his life when a genuine relationship between himself and a woman was suddenly shattered and taken away from him.

Two months had passed, with Antonio fully recovered from his nightmare, he continued being the number two man in the organization. By now he had begun to fully implement the master plan he had devised two years previous when he discussed with his partners how the vast world of Aldo Debruto should be carved up.

It took six months but eventually Tom Madden through his police contacts discovered how and why did the bomb that killed Ardelia go off.

The perpetrator who set off the bomb was found quite by accident. Debruto's son, who was at the center of all this controversy was mysteriously killed in his own apartment house. He somehow fell down the dumb waiter shaft falling 6 floors to his death. The autopsy showed nothing extraordinary about his physical makeup except he had a small trace of narcotic in his system. The official report cited death by accident and the case was closed.

Antonio was now in charge of over 200 houses of prostitution, the ever expanding garbage business that touched every business in the city and in the latter stages of 1933 officially took over the management of five of the largest garment center unions in New York. Antonio's days as the head of Jitney Express were long past yet all profits from that enterprise and so many others all flowed directly to him, and after he received his share he dutifully brought the rest to his partners. This more than anything solidified his position as he had shown time and time again that the quest for money never came between him and his partners.

Luciano now at the pinnacle of power in the city beamed whenever Antonio's name was brought up. To Luciano's and all of his partners the businesses and profits derived from the vast diversified portfolio Antonio managed made Luciano's decision to have him run the day to day a stroke of genius.

6 MONTHS LATER

"How do you feel?" Luciano asked, as Both Antonio and he were relaxing at the Turkish Baths in Lower Manhattan. "I mean have all your bruises both inside and out healed?"

"Since Ardelia's gone I just haven't felt the same about anything. I do owe you everything and I hope you know that" Looking at his mentor Antonio started to well up and in that instant Luciano just by putting his hand on Antonio's lap and gently smiling meant that he understood Antonio's pain.

"I also want to thank you for Debruto'S kid........"

Luciano stopped him in mid speech

"No matter it's over, let's concentrate on business ok?"

Luciano could tell that although Antonio looked healed emotionally he still needed a little more TLC.

"Believe me, I know what it's like to lose someone you love but remember your still alive and she would not want you to sit and mourn her this way, no she knew you were faithful hell that's a lot more than most would do, you're a good man Antonio. Enough time has passed and you're still a vibrant young man, I think you need to be involved with your feelings and perhaps find another girl, I have an idea"

Luciano set up a meeting with Polly Adler one of Luciano's top business partners in the garment center. Polly's background had always been to get her customers what they wanted sparing no cost and in the end everyone was happy. Eventually Polly began to supplement her income by taking charge of a few of the houses that Lucky and Antonio controlled.

Since her teen years she began working for her father a haberdasher with a shop at thirty Eighth Street. Her father taught her the merchandising business as well as the raw material business she eventually combined the two and became, by1930, the largest wholesale supplier of raw goods in the city. Having Luciano as a silent partner didn't hurt.

Polly also had another talent. Polly was great at finding women for out of town men coming to New York to do business with Luciano and while they were here why not enjoy themselves and have a good time at the same time.

Antonio came to one of Polly's parties and for most of the night sat alone in one corner of the large room. At various times during the evening Polly tried to convince him to join and mingle with some of the guests. Reluctantly he agreed. There were a few women who looked at him but none of them caused him to give them a second look. Most of the women, he thought, wore too much makeup and because of the men, many of them millionaires, the women overly carried on like school girls. But there was a woman who caught Antonio's eye.

She was taller than many of the women there and when Polly made her return to see if Antonio had seen anything he liked the tall brunette was mentioned.

Her name was Catherine.

CHAPTER 26

Retribution

The week had begun for Antonio with Luciano commanding his presence at the Greenwich Village headquarters. Luciano had good news for Antonio.

"Well Antonio things are certainly looking up right? I hear that Polly and you have become good friends is that right?"

Antonio broke a smile. "That is true I really like her, but that is not what brought me here today, you said it was urgent"

Luciano began to silently pace as he had done so many times before. Antonio couldn't get over the wardrobe Lucky sported from morning to night a different change of everything from shoes to top hat. Lucky caught him admiring the wardrobe. "Like the suit?"

Antonio smiled.

"It's not only the suit boss it's you! Everything about you shows class and that's what I love about the vision"

"Well I am flattered but there are more serious matters at hand. I have decided that you are to share in everything I do, just like Frank, Benny and Meyer. In everything I do mean everything. I have discussed it with the partners. But I called you here for another reason. I want you to take over all and I mean all the houses of prostitution, everything from the girls to the houses themselves. Management to the end, what do you think"

Lucky looked at Antonio like a proud father does when rewarding a son with a new car upon graduation from college." I don't know what to say, you mean everything?"

Lucky picked up the ledgers from the large Mahogany desk and gave them to him. "Read what I've got there. I mean it's a gold mine and I need someone I can trust that can make those ledgers stay and go beyond those numbers. Antonio right now there are over 400 houses in the city, before long with you at the helm we'll have 500 or more and the dough will come back to us a hundred fold."

Lucky was beaming as he spoke. "Kid! You did this with your Debruto plan! Don't you see! I'm turning it all over to you for all of us, do us proud kid, do us proud!"

As both Charley Luciano and Antonio Piccolo discussed their future.

"Well my young friend are you aware that it is 1932! There are so many things happening in America and we, all of us, have to keep up with the times. This depression we're in, for most people in America it's the worst thing imaginable, but for us it can be heaven. Just look around and see what people want and need and just supply it to them. Have you settled on what direction we have to take? I mean the Debruto problem?"

Luciano, surrounded by his brain trusts, called the meeting so that his business partners could hear and see the face of their future. Antonio Piccolo was slowly being seen by Luciano and others as a force in their organization.

The assembled group, which numbered fifteen wanted to be at the meeting because history had shown them that Luciano had the golden touch to making money.

The group of men attending the meeting, many of whom Antonio knew personally, were all on their best behavior.

"There was Frank Costello, real name Francesco Castiglia, who was busy filing his nails. There was Ben Siegel, known as Bugsy but not to his face. Siegel was so different than both Luciano and Costello in that he was always mad at something or someone. But for some reason he never showed any contempt for humanity on Antonio rather he seemed to like him.

"Hey paisan, Well! Do you have the plan to assist Mr Debruto in his hour of need"?

Siegal said this with tongue in cheek giving Antonio the impression that he did not like Debruto in the least. And as he was speaking Costello still attending to his nails smiled.

Antonio had thought long and hard on Debruto's dilemma.

"Yes I do and here are my thoughts."

As Antonio began to speak and outline his plan everyone, even Costello, stopped doing what he was doing and stood quiet as Antonio spoke. All eyes and ears in the room were on this young lieutenant and what he was about to propose.

"First of all I want everyone to know that my ideas about Debruto are simply based on what I believe are your and Mr Luciano's needs. Now I need all of you to know that Mr. Luciano never told me to act and carry on a certain way, no, these are my thoughts"

Everyone sat up waiting to see what this up and coming mover and shaker was about to say.

Luciano hadn't said a word the entire evening. He was unusually quiet and introspective. When Ben Siegal questioned him about some gambling venture they had discussed weeks before he calmly asked Ben to wait. Still looking at Antonio in anticipation as to what he was about to impart on the group.

"Well my young friend have you decided what course is best for me and my friends?"

In the next two hours Antonio laid out his plan and to everyone in the room.

Prior to the meeting Luciano signaled that if he calculated the events that were about to unfold the general feeling amongst his partners would be euphoria at the prospects of what Antonio Piccolo was about to impart to all of them. Lucky labeled the plan as their future.

The Plan

The Fulton Fish Market, The Jewelery Exchange, Ten buildings owned between 34 and 35th street in New York, The Clark Inn, a national chain of restaurants that became popular as an inexpensive way to dine in the big city. The best kept secret in the city a string of brothels catering to the elite of Manhattan. These were just a few of the Debruto holdings.

Debruto, at fifty-five years of age, came to New York as a child from Palermo Sicily. Almost from the outset his cast as a member of the Italian Immigrant community tainted him with names like Dago and Wop, these names were synonymous with the perception that this new breed of immigrant was stupid and shiftless. The ruling class, being English with the Irish as their overseeing eye, dictated that this new breed could survive if they followed the rules.

By the time Aldo Debruto had become a young man he already gained a reputation as a rough and tumble fellow who would fight for what he believed in. The rules according to young men like Debruto were simple, if it wasn't nailed down it had to be stolen.

At nineteen years of age Aldo had his own gang and by the ripe old age of 29 he was already a convicted felon having served six years for robbery and attempted murder. At thirty-five he became the head of the Unione Siciliano, a Mafia organization started in Sicily and carried over here in America. To many of the old time Sicilians, who still believed in this organization, the laws and rules that accompanied this union was held by all as Gospel. By the age of forty Debruto had a family and had relocated to a palatial estate in the Bronx.

Through the years Debruto aligned himself with many Mafioso's from various parts of the country. But the two men who carried the most weight in Mafia circles were Giuseppe Masseria and Salvatore Maranzano. Both men were Italian with Masseria coming from Western Sicily and Marranzano coming from Eastern Sicily namely Castelmare. Both men supported Debruto and in time made him a multi-millionaire. The only strange fact about the alliance was that by 1927 Marranzano and Masseria were at odds with each other. Disputes over territory forced both men to divide with each man retaining over 500 men apiece. In 1929 the two men went to battle with each other in what the newspapers called the Marranzano Masseria war.

Before and during the war Debruto stayed friendly with both men making money with both and showing allegiance to both to which both Marranzano and Masseria both thought Debruto was exclusively with them. It was a fine line he walked but his cunning business abilities and ruthless tactics proved that in the end he stood alone with much of the fortune left behind by both men. Because his company was relatively clean both men, at different times, entrusted him with valuable tracks of real estate they had purchased in and around New York in which they put both deeds and title in

Debruto's name. They paid the necessary taxes to him and he used his real estate business to funnel from their companies to himself and legally paid each and every duty, tax and fine that was needed.

They entrusted him with Jewelry, stolen from wealthy Jewish merchants, knowing that if the police ever decided to raid any of their premises that they would find nothing. But the biggest item in Debruto's relationship for both men was that he eventually became exclusive caretaker for the two funds he held for both men. This fund, suggested by him to each of them, would turn out to amount to over a half million dollars. These funds were originally earmarked as slush funds specifically used for political payoffs AND WAR CHEST NEEDS, JUST IN CASE EITHER OF THE BOSSES DECIDED TO "GO TO THE MATTRESSES".

From Tammany Hall to the Mayor's office certain funds were dispersed by Debruto to the many politicians and Policemen in every precinct in the city in both Masseria and Marranzano's name.

At various times between 1928 and 1930 both Marranzano and Masseria demanded an accurate account of their vested money, to whom and to where did what payoffs go and what was left and where was the money at that moment. To all of those inquires Debruto had all the facts and figures to collaborate his work much to both Marranzano and Masseris's jubilation. To both men their political dreams were coming true and at the same time no evidence of any kind could ever link either one of them to any political payoffs of any kind.

By 1931 with the death of both Masseria and Marranzano Debruto stood alone, a millionaire many times over, a land baron controlling great parcels of rent paying tenants that added millions to his bottom line. The one arena that Debruto was not strong in was his opinion of himself. He envisioned himself as omnipotent solely based on his cunning and deft deception of the two big bosses in the city that he was impenetrable and that his secret would die with him.

Debruto trusted no one. His staff consisted of twenty men who were more bookkeepers than gangsters, his oldest son Vincenzo however, was more gangster than bookkeeper. Educated at the finest schools Vincenzo acted as if the world owed him a royalty. It was in this vein that Debruto came to Luciano for assistance.

Debruto explained to Luciano that he was enamored of his young secretary and that he wanted her young boyfriend to disappear. In reality it was Vincenzo, Debruto's son, who was madly in love with the girl but she spurned his advances so many times to a fault. Because of his rejection Vincenzo regressed into depression. None of this was common knowledge.

Debruto's thought process was that if the boyfriend could be eliminated perhaps in time the girl might see Vincenzo as her eventual husband.

Debruto had just left his usual late Friday night stops that entailed him collecting his tribute from all the madams by himself. This practice of he, himself, collecting the tribute did not stand in good with his son Vicenzo who consistently pleaded with him not to do the dirty work of collecting by himself. In the end Debruto, with greed as his motivation, ignored the threat posed by his son.

"Well signora, have you my small token of your appreciation for letting you operate and make so much money?" Katie MacGovern, a 41-year-old redhead and madam at one of Debruto's top grossing houses of prostitution, hated even the thought of dealing with this pig of a man. With disgust on every syllable that emanated from her mouth Katie made the obligatory gestures needed so that Debruto wouldn't stay any longer that he had to.

"What's seems to be the problem my child, your acting so skiddish"

Knowing that on occasion when he wasn't rushed Debruto would suggest that one of the girl's service him and tonight was no different. Besides being fat and unkempt Debruto kept many of the old European ways with him when he came to the United States. He bathing habits were atrocious and his body odor proved it.

Katie tried as persuasively as she could to dissuade Debruto from asking for one of the girls but to no avail.

"Well good night Katie my dear see you next week!"

As Debruto walked to his car counting his money suddenly he experienced a piercing pain in his lower back that physically made him drop to his knees in mortal agony, in slow staccato sounds he began to yell for help as he was unable to move. Louder and louder he yelled until he instinctively knew what was about to unfold and the fear of death had suddenly reached his senses, it was at hand. As he reached back to the focal point of his pain he felt what felt like a long metal object stuck directly between his shoulder blades. As his face crashed to the cobblestone pavement and his breathing had increased a hundred fold it had dramatically dawned on him that in minutes he would probably be dead. From what little breath he had left he muttered towards the only vision he could barely see. A combination of a solid brick wall and the cobblestone pavement beneath his face. In his last gasp of life, he asked.

"Why?"

CHAPTER 27

A beautiful face in the crowd

Polly had mentioned to Antonio that Catherine was a widow and the sister of one of her biggest customers. Antonio thought it strange that a man who frequented a house of prostitution would have his sister work there. Polly explained that Catherine was her customer's half-sister and after helping her for a while after her husband's untimely death he simply said he wasn't about to continue with the financial aid. In time he suggested that she get a job or starve.

After much discussion centered on the fact that they were all in the midst of a depression the brother convinced her to come to Polly for some part time assistance. He set up an appointment with Polly and introduced Catherine and the rest was history.

"Antonio are you really interested in her?" Polly uttered this statement with disdain."I mean there are so many other girls that would probably satisfy you......" Polly could see that she had hit a nerve and as soon as Antonio's expression changed Polly diverted.

As soon as Antonio's facial expression changed Polly knew that she had mistakenly crossed the line, in an effort to do instant damage control she blurted.

"Well on the other hand her clean look and all would appeal to any man. Look, I'll get her over here and you two can talk, OK?"

In seconds Polly hurriedly walked towards Catherine.

"Cathy! We need to talk. Do you see that man standing over there, well I want you to go over and introduce yourself to him" Catherine quizzically looked at Polly questioning her direction.

"Who is he, I mean is he a regular because I don't recognize him?"

Irritatingly Polly curtly answered her in rapid fire fashion.

"Did you hear what I just said? This fellow is the last word around here! Do I make myself clear?"

From her voice and attitude Catherine instinctively knew that this customer was different than all the rest. She casually walked over and in her most seductive manner asked him his name.

But before another word was uttered by either one of them something else happened that took her by surprise.

Antonio reached and gently placed his finger to her lips. "Please don't, don't try to be someone you're not, can we sit and talk"

He motioned to a group of couches aligned along the far wall to which Catherine, who was still in shock, just followed. At five foot six and one hundred and thirty pounds Catherine looked more athlete than prostitute. Her features were soft with blueish green eyes that seem to change color as their conversation continued.

"Do your eyes always react like they are doing right now?"

Catherine smiled coyly as it had been so long since a man wanted to be with her simply to get to know her. The fact that this was happening in a house of ill repute made it more bizarre. Catherine was not overly large busted but her height and proportioned weight was centered just right to Antonio's liking.

Catherine's strong facial lines would suggest Swedish or Danish in heritage. Her fair skin highlighted by her dirty blond hair pulled back to a bun gave her a rather plain Jane look yet with all of that there was a regal elegance to her smile that warmed Antonio's heart. Antonio, coming from Europe, where hygiene of any sort was sometimes the last item on a person's daily to do list was not lost on Catherine. There were so many things about this woman that Antonio was drawn to. He noticed that her hands were creamy white and appeared soft accentuated by her long fingers with nails neatly manicured. Her teeth were solid white and shiny accenting a face that warmed Antonio's entire being. The total package was not what many men, who frequented places like Polly's, would call enticing yet within that very framework the wholesomeness of this woman brought Antonio's to emotions to the surface.

"How long have you been working here?" He asked and that was the first of hundreds of questions they asked each other. Before they both realized it time had passed and Polly's assistant knowing who Antonio was informed that all the girls and the customers were gone and they were the only people left.

"You can go and thanks for waiting for us, please don't worry I will lock up"

After assuring the young lady that he was in fact the boss he gently slipped her a twenty for her troubles. As they walked the twenty blocks to Catherine's house they each told the other a little bit more about themselves and by the time they had reached her house Antonio was sure that this woman was everything he needed in his life right now.

"It's been three months! So when do we meet her"

Frank Costello in his typical gruff yet friendly voice and demeanor was simply echoing everyone in the combines sentiments.

"I mean if we're all partners Charley, Ben and I want to meet her, is that ok?"

Antonio, with tongue in cheek, uttered.

"Why so that you bums can rattle my cage as to when I might get married?"

This last line took everyone by surprise.

"You're serious with her?"

Luciano asked as a father might to his son.

"Yes Charley I think for the first time since Italy I might love her, it happened suddenly and oh I know what you're thinking she knows nothing about us our business or anything. She was a widow and had to fend for herself, I hope you all understand."

Luciano had hoped that this girl might fill the void left by Ardelia, and although Antonio had professed that he had never loved Ardelia he still respected her. In this light Luciano needed to know if this was the same type of situation or was it real love. In the end Luciano saw that Antonio was in deed in love with this girl.

The statement was made by Antonio and it was final but Luciano in the ensuing weeks did his homework and just happened to find out who she was and where she was from This direction by Luciano was not only from a man who viewed his relationship with Antonio as a father would have with a son but much more. Antonio had not only become a great leader for the organization but even more than that he was held in special regard by Luciano who looked at him in the most humanly connected relationship, in the past a man like Charley Luciano would never get this close to anyone, but in this case Antonio Piccolo was special and in the end Luciano gave his approval.

CHAPTER 28

ALL THAT GLITTERS

It was 1937 and for all intents and purposes Antonio piccolo had everything a man could ever ask for. His position with the Luciano group was beyond reproach, his financial status put him the million dollars' bracket and growing. His stature amongst the men in his society, mostly Italians and Jews was as strong as any Sicilian Boss could ever be.

His expertise and business acumen stretched far beyond the New York skyline. His business deals were now almost global in stature and nature. His involvement in activities that were clean far outweighed his nefarious interests. The original group was still intact with Siegel moving out west to open up territory in California and what was later to become Las Vegas.

The original group of Luciano, Costello and Lansky stayed in the eastern part of the country expanding their tentacles into any new business that looked as though it had potential.

In every venture the lure of easy money can sometimes get even the smartest operator in trouble. And so it would eventually be that Luciano and Piccolo, forever intertwined in both the legitimate as well as the not so legitimate would make the mistake that so many of their kind had fallen prey to and that was complacency.

Houses of ill repute have always been a target for every bible thumping politician wanting to turn the tides of what man wants to what God wants him to have. And in this context Luciano himself and Antonio Piccolo felt their position was coated with Teflon.

Antonio had over 100 men answering to him not to mention the real estate brokers situated all over Manhattan that too had to answer to him. Consistently mindful of the typical pitfalls that older Mafioso's had always warned about that could in a blink of an eye bring you and your entire organization down. Antonio moved out of his headquarters at the Jitney Express where Tom Madden held court and moved to a new office situated directly above a social club called "The Ravinite Club" on Mulberry Street.

The Ravinite Club was significant for so many reasons and all of them centered around Antonio and what he had to do on a daily basis just to survive for himself and the hundred or more men under him. This extremely stressful job of keeping everyone employed in troubled times would have been a test for legitimate businessmen much less a mob boss, as in fact Antonio was. Many a day Italians from all walks of life asked for his audience. And dutifully so he would oblige with a recommendation or a job either way these men swore loyalty and in the end that is all Antonio asked for.

On one such occasion an old friend, and employee at the Jitney Express, brought over a young man who had made himself quite a name in Italy having to flee before he was arrested. In America he needed a helping hand and his godfather who, having worked for and steadfastly a loyal soldier in the Luciano organization, came to Antonio for his help.

"Is this the fellow you spoke to me about?"

Giovanni Deluca, an old line "mustache Pete" character who was also one of Tom Madden's favorites came to vouch for this young Sicilian runaway. Deluca's was a man who had shown the organization throughout the years that he was associated with them that he was reliable and kept his mouth shut, a valuable tool to have in Antonio's world.

"Yes it is, his name is Carlo Gambino, and he hails from Castelmare in Sicily. He had a few troubles there but that was then and now he needs a little help"

Antonio studied the young man. He reminded him of himself so many years ago. Carlo was lean at 5 foot 10'" tall with an angular face and droopy looking eyes. When he heard his name, with hat in hand, he stood up. Carlo, not knowing the language that well, managed to smile when he heard Antonio call his name.

Antonio got up from his office chair and walked to Carlo who by now was still smiling hoping for a friendly acceptance.

"Como sta" (How are you)

Carlo, still nervous and squeezing his hat as he attempted to answer. Seeing Carlo's reluctance to meet his eyes he assured him there was nothing to be scared about.

"Carlo, non deprecoupare paisan"(Don't worry my fellow countryman you're in my hands now)

In minutes Antonio directed Giovanni to assign Carlo into one of Luciano's Companies selling vegetable goods as a front with Black Market OPA stamps on the side. In the next three months word got back to Antonio that Carlo was doing well learning the language and happy and grateful that he was able to meet such a generous and gracious boss as Antonio. Throughout 1936 and into 1937 Antonio held court and made decisions that would enrich his partners.

Yet within this turmoil of what many have called good and evil of the underworld stood the love of his life Catherine. She, and her two children from her previous marriage, were put in a beautiful townhouse in Northern New Jersey in Bergen County. The house picked out by Joe Dodo one of Luciano's closest friends.

There situated amongst young families, who knew nothing of the world that Antonio had come from, was the Piccolo family and although Antonio had never married Catherine she still introduced herself to all as Mrs. Piccolo.

The townspeople welcomed Catherine and her children and before long Catherine had associated herself with more than a few social groups including doing volunteer work at the local Catholic Church. Throughout the end of 1935 through all of 1936 Catherine and Antonio lived the life of middle to upper class Americans.

CHAPTER 29

SOMETIMES GREAT THINGS
SIMPLY COME TO AN END

Antonio had seen the writing on the wall and preparations were afoot to assure that the fruits of all the hard work he had done these past 12 years were not in vain.

The United States government had indicted Luciano and his group at the Jitney Express with the only charge that they could make a case out of and that was Prostitution. In the underworld there were many who could give testimony as to the power of the underworld but to have someone who actually witnessed a murder or witness graft of any kind was near impossible. The unwritten Italian law of "OMERTA" meaning death before dishonor was the law within the Luciano Empire.

There was, however, an Achilles heel to the Luciano story. During Luciano's hey days as king and Antonio Piccolo's as his chief lieutenant in the prostitution business the threat of bodily harm was used over and over and issued to prostitutes and their madams if they did not pay up. This one fact, in the end, brought everyone down.

Using this ammunition, the prosecution convinced an American public that being the kings of prostitution was worse than murder. The trial took 6 months and in the end the one outstanding witness, who just happened to be a madam that both Luciano and Piccolo confided in and partnered with, brought the entire Luciano Empire down.

Adler, who by the way introduced Antonio to the love of his recent life Catherine, was such a compelling witness that the publicity surrounding the trial made the prosecuting District Attorney Thomas Dewey a national political figure. In real life Dewey was at his best considered a stuffed shirt when it came to personality and charm but this trial made him a hero and eventually elected him Governor of New York.

The end result was guilty on all counts for both of them. Luciano received 50 to 90 years and Piccolo 30 to 40 years.

Antonio Piccolo realized that within the financial success of illegality eventually there is a price that will be paid.

While Luciano huddled with his staff of attorneys' trying to put together an appeal Piccolo spent his last few days as a free man on bail redirecting his focus and adjusting his sights on a long prison term.

Antonio came one last time to New Jersey to the house and family he set up there in Bergen County. He wanted Catherine to have no fears about her future in that the house she lived in was paid for, her children's education was paid for and a small nest egg put aside for her.

Antonio stressed one important fact to this woman that he had come to love over the past few years.

"Catherine please stop crying, I know how sad you feel and what I need to tell you hurts more than you know."

Catherine stood looking at the only man in her life that actually cared for her and wanted nothing in return but respect and love. This connection she had with Antonio would have made sense in any era of modern history, a storybook romance with the gangster and the prostitute.

"This has to be the last time we ever see each other, believe me it's for the best. I don't want the girls or you visiting me in prison. I want to know or at least hope that you will eventually find someone and this connection with me is over!" Catherine started crying before Antonio had finished his sentence.

"Take this envelope it will instruct you as to how you will receive the money as well as the deed to this property and some bonds I put aside for the girls, Catherine I will always love you, say a prayer for me" And in an instant he was gone.

The Friday before both he and Luciano were to turn themselves in at the federal building in lower New York there was a small get together at the Jitney Express. Earlier during the day Antonio expressed his admiration and respect for Tom Madden and how well they had gotten along since Antonio's earliest days. Antonio wanted to turn over his entire stake in Jitney to Tom but he would have none of it.

"Antonio, this place has given me life and a new beginning but none of this could ever be possible without you. Believe me I've made more money than I could have ever imagined and I've saved most of it and again I'm willing to spend every dime of it on getting you out if you think we can win!"

Antonio smiled at his friend and for the first time in months actually felt well about at least one person that mattered in his life.

"Thank you but no thanks, you keep it and spend it on your family"

Tom walked over to Antonio and embraced him, "Antonio before we go downstairs and you officially say good bye to everyone I want you to know something. I will keep your money and make it work for you so that when you come out you'll never want for anything!"

The following Monday both Antonio and Luciano were taken away to begin serving their long sentences. That was the last time either one of them set eyes on each other. Luciano was remanded to Dannemora Prison in upstate New York and Piccolo was sent to Atlanta Federal Correctional.

Luciano would eventually be pardoned 6 1/2 years later and subsequently deported. Piccolo stayed in prison until his release in 1973. He was 71 years of age.

While in prison he began to read. He became interested in just about everything, after all, he had nothing but time on his hands.

Antonio's interests ranged from agriculture to opera. Tom Madden had made at least one trip a month to Atlanta to keep Antonio in the loop as far as what his financial interests were doing. In the end Antonio's money had done both good and bad in the ever expanding economic landscape. Many investments that both Madden and Piccolo's money went into went broke but still others did very well. In 1963 Tom Madden had a heart attack and by November of that year he had passed away. A cousin of his took up the gauntlet and continued taking care of Piccolo's money knowing full well that although Piccolo wasn't active in mob circles his name and a phone call could change that in an instant. The truth be told Antonio had forgotten all of that as soon as his first night in Atlanta was complete.

Tom's nephew kept good records and minus the service charge that went directly to him the books were in order. In 1973, after his release, Antonio met Tom's nephew outside the prison gates where he was given all the documentation and after dinner that night he slept in his first bed outside of his prison cell in 35 years. He was given an attorney in Long Branch New Jersey that was familiar with Antonio's investments as well as his property. Antonio mailed all the documentation that he was given by Tom's nephew and soon afterward was off to his sister's house.

Antonio did have a small extended family albeit no relation to himself. When he was sent to prison Catherine, who had died roughly 10 years after Antonio had been sent away, had continually asked her two daughters to stay in touch with him.

And although not one of Catherine's daughters or their eventual husbands had ever come to Atlanta to visit Antonio still considered them family.

One of the daughters, named Seraphina did in fact contact him a week before his release. She wanted to know if he would like to stay with her and her son for a while as she was a widow with her husband having died so young. Antonio thought it odd that Serafina, who hadn't set eyes on him since she was a child would want him around her. She lived on Long Island and for better or worse Antonio accepted. It never dawned on him that perhaps Serafina's request might have nothing to do with family, he simply thought it generous.

Antonio did eventually stay with her and her only son but in less than a month he needed to leave as it had become clear to him that Serafina and her sister and all of the family involved were interested in his money only.

"Antonio! You just got here, must you leave so soon?"

Antonio sipped at his cup of tea before answering. At the same time Serafina's only son who still lived at home questioned Antonio. At first her son's attitude was joyous at the least. Her son's name was John.

"Uncle Tony, you were away a long time but before you were sent away did you manage to sock any cash away? I mean you were making millions the papers said"

Antonio's blood began to raise itself above the pissed off limit yet his years in prison taught him many things and restraint was one of them. It was at that precise moment he knew that he had to leave and that this family was only interested in what they could get from him while he was still alive.

"Well, in one respect your right John, I did make and spend a lot of money but between Luciano and myself the appeals took millions from us, I was left with nothing"

Upon hearing that John's demeanor changed.

He quickly got up from the table and stormed out of the house with his mother following closely behind. Antonio could hear the two of them arguing in the driveway.

"Fuck him, didn't I tell you I would get nothing! You bake for him do his clothes what can he do for you now he's an old man with arthritis and if you don't watch out he'll die and you'll have to pay for the funeral" His mother was dumbstruck, again she tried to placate her son.

"Johnny, Johnny, please stop your all I've got believe me things will get better. Look! He's got some property in New Jersey I saw the document while he was sleeping last night, yes he owns some stuff it's not like he's broke!"

In seconds they both came back as Serafina managed to calm John down and John spoke first. "Uncle Tony mama tells me that you have some property in Jersey? Is that right, I thought you said you were broke"

By this time Antonio, feeling some of those old gangland spirit coming back did not want to do anything that would put him back in jail, least of all to Serafina's son. In as docile a tone as he could muster he addressed the issue.

"Yes I do have a house that my old partner Tom had paid up for me, now whatever I owe him for that is between him and I and basically that's all there is to it" In seconds John stormed out of the house again.

In reality Antonio was far from broke. He had in cash roughly a half million dollars in three safety deposit boxes in New Jersey and a bunch of small investments in real estate managed by five separate re estate brokers all in New Jersey. In the end Tom Madden had turned out to be the best friend that Antonio had ever had. Through his shrewd investments Tom was able to negotiate real estate deals with brokers who would collect rents and pay the taxes due plus take out their commissions. Until Tom's untimely death the Piccolo holdings were intact. And even after Tom's death the contracts and deals that he had set up continued as planned.

On one such trip to Atlanta the two of them spoke candidly about Tom's endeavors in preparations for Antonio's eventual release, which was years away, as well as he and Tom's future together.

"Tom I meant to ask you what ever happened to that woman you told me about the one who had a small drinking problem but one that you actually cared about." Tom squirmed a little at the question but since they were speaking intimate Tom confessed.

"I am still trying to figure that out, I didn't tell you but she got pregnant and as of this week had not delivered yet."

Antonio smiled at the news. "Tommy, Tommy! That's great news God! Marry the girl and you had always talked about the Jersey Shore and how much you loved it there. Buy some property down in Jersey and eventually I'm going to get out and we'll all live near each other, how about that"

They had a good laugh and as usual Antonio showed his partner all the trust and faith a man could have in another, they said their good bys.

In Tom's master plan Antonio's name was out of the New York limelight and as planned he put Antonio in South Jersey near the ocean hoping that this new and relaxed environment would be good for both of them as he had originally planned to be near his friend whenever he was released from prison.

Sadly, Tom Madden didn't last the twenty years to enjoy it.

LONG BRANCH, NEW JERSEY

The house Tom purchased for Antonio was situated on Sycamore lane, a three-bedroom home boasting a magnificent view of the bay on one side and the ocean on the other. The house and the upkeep had been paid for and all that was left was for Antonio to eventually move in.

After leaving Serafina's house he took a train into New York. From New York he boarded a train for Florida and two days later landed in Miami. He tried to touch base with some friends who were released earlier than him. He stayed in Florida for all the winter months and planned as soon as the spring time came he began to make plans to eventually move back to New Jersey and eventually reach Long Branch. It never entered his mind to fly direct, in his thought process rushing to anyplace do not have any meaning whatsoever.

BOOK TWO

CHAPTER 30

FAMILY
1965

Sister Augustine, a Sister of Charity nun, was proctor of the Saint Anthony Orphanage in Harrison New Jersey. On this special day she signed the last set of papers allowing her pride and joy Richard Maguire to finally graduate from the orphanage high school and make his way into the world.

"Needless to say Richard you will be missed"

For most of her sisterhood life Sister Augustine made it a practice of never getting too attached to any one orphan as that could cause serious problems for that orphan as well as the other children who perhaps might get the wrong idea.

In this case Sister Augustine did favor Richard Maguire. As he grew and realized that his biological mother did in fact abandon him and for all intents would probably never come back he resigned himself to the fact that in the end he still had Sister Augustine. To most orphaned children knowing and feeling something like that could cause scars that no amount of love, caring and therapy could erase.

Never once did the fact that his biological mother abandoned him ever make him change into anything but a loving and grateful child.

It never entered his mind that by his own mother abandoning him to be cared for by strangers was an abnormal thing. Rather he was greeted by a loving and caring guardian who became both father and mother to him. And in the end that in itself served Richard well.

Sister Augustine had to, on numerous occasions during her 30-year tenure, attempt to explain to numerous distraught children, that although it seemed as though they were abandoned God had never forgotten them. That explanation only took Augustine so far with many of the children but not Richard. From their very beginning he trusted her and a bond was sealed between them with her promising that she would never abandon him and he promising that he would make her proud.

To many children of the orphanage that bond that solidified Richard to Sister Augustine was envied by more than a few distraught children. The promise that tomorrow would be a better day kept many a child up at night hopelessly praying that everything would change in their lives and that someday the right people would show up and adopt them.

Richard, unlike the rest of the kids, slept restfully during so many of those cold and wintry nights.

The promise that Richard would always be loved by Sister Augustine was kept in spades for him.

Richard was an exception whenever Sister Augustine had anything to do with the day to day goings on at the orphanage. She took special care of him from the time he came as an infant. She also made it a practice never to outwardly show her affection for him when others were around rather she waited for those special moments when they could be alone and she would bestow that love for this boy as he would have been had she been a mother.

Richard's mother, a recovering alcoholic and substance abuse addict, expressed to the orphanage that she needed to stabilize her life first before she could take care of a child.

This explanation repeated itself for the first year at least once a week when she visited. She explained to the sisters that Richard's biological father was a man of means and that he would pay to keep Richard there until she could get her act together. But soon after that she disappeared and Richard had never set eyes on her again.

The next 15 years Saint Anthony's proved a practical solution in the case of Richard Maguire, he studied hard earning a high school diploma and expressed his desire to go to college if possible. Sister Augustine encouraged Richard at every turn to push himself to be the best he could be. Sister Augustine dreaded the fact that Richard's day of reckoning would one day come. His departure was inevitable but Richards's enthusiasm for life and learning made it a joyous time for both he and Sister Augustine.

Sister Augustine knew that she would eventually lose him to the world but hoped that they would always stay close.

"So Richard, have you decided what your next course of action will be?"

Sister Augustine holding back the emotional signs she had for this boy since those very early days when she, as a younger Sister of Charity, took an extra interest in him. The interest could have been seen by many as meddling in a young boy's life but to Sister Augustine Richard represented all children who needed someone to love and believe in.

Richard also realized the fact that at an early age Sister Augustine demonstrated not only raw emotion but a genuine appreciation for him. He also recognized the fact that another human being took the time to go the extra yard all for his betterment. Sister Augustine made it her priority to make sure that many of Richard's needs growing up were met. She introduced him to many of the social skills she thought he would need as he eventually would enter the real world.

She taught him how to interact with the opposite sex introducing him and some of the other boys to the intermingling with females from various other Catholic schools. These mingle sessions were called Catholic Socials. These socials featured music and entertainment. Eventually at one of those socials Richard met a girl named Clara. They hit it off instantly the moment they met.

Clara came from a middle class home and her parents were working class. Almost from the very first dance they shared somehow Sister Augustine saw them as a couple. They were both studious and quiet sometimes to a fault yet within that quiet realm of togetherness there was an understanding that both of them quietly grabbed onto furthering their relationship.

From the very beginning Sister Augustine knew that she could never take his biological mother's place even though Richard's mother hadn't been around for years, still she had to be aware to never cross that line.

"Truthfully Sister I guess Seton Hall would be a great fit."

Seton Hall University was a Catholic University situated in the heart of North Jersey.

"That would be splendid and I had a talk with Father Manion, the Church's liaison to the orphanage, and he assured me that if you did choose Seton Hall that the transition there including room and board would be taken care of by the church, isn't that great!"

Richard could not believe what he had just heard. In a fit of joy, he actually forgot himself and jumped up and grabbed Sister Augustine in an embrace reminiscent of a professional wrestling match.

"Oh God Sister, Sister, I am so sorry "

The pure joy that a person gets whenever their dreams suddenly come true can sometimes manifest itself through sheer physical contact, so it was with Richard and Sister Augustine, but the one fact about that joyous embrace was that the thrill and excitement concerning Richard's Seton Hall revelation was as much a joyous celebration for Sister Augustine as it was for Richard. Sister Augustine, acting as if it was her biological son, reacted as any mother would when her only child elected to make her so proud.

Sheer emotion coupled with all the years of bonding between them erupted into a joyous celebration. For that one singular moment they were connected for all time. Teacher student suddenly became big sister to little brother. They both stood there smiling at each other. The cloak of sisterhood was gone and Sister Augustine was swiftly melted into a part of Richard's life now and forever.

"I think of you as I would if I ever had a son of my own, I bless you so go with God Richard"

As she began to tear up she quickly turned and walked away when she had gotten about 30 feet away she looked back and called out "Richard, Richard"

As she called, Richard looked up.

"God bless you Richard! and remember when your away at your new home there in Seton Hall, take a moment and just remember Saint Anthony's ok? Oh and don't forget to write"

Richard, who by now was as choked up as ever, looked at her with love and affection. "I will never forget you, please! Never forget me!"

CHAPTER 31

YOUNG MINDS AND YOUNG HEARTS

The Iron bound section of Newark, situated south of the business district and bordering the Newark Bay, was a haven for Immigrants coming from Europe seeking employment and a decent place to live.

The Saldutti family was one such family. They were first generation Italian Americans and the work ethic was part of their very existence. The Immigrants that formed the ironbound coalition of working families had a totally different motto about this new land they were suddenly occupying. Most Immigrants from the beginning of America's existence always looked at this country as a second home to their homeland. The majority of Ironbound Immigrants looked at that picture totally different. They felt it was an honor to be part of the United States. The roles of the young men, who came from the Ironbound that fought and died for their country, proved beyond a doubt that patriotism was rampant in that neighborhood.

The Saldutti family had two sons and a daughter. The Daughter's name was Clara. She attended Mother Seton Grammar and high school and throughout her scholastic life she excelled in music and sports. Basically Clara, at five foot six, was considered tall for and the traditional Italian American girl reared in that era. Clara, who wore glasses and was without makeup most days was not given the look that other Catholic reared girls were given from the few neighborhood boys that intermingled with Clara and a few of her friends. Dating, for so many Catholic girls, was an anticipation that was only spoken behind closed doors. Mother Seton and its faculty frowned on pre-college dating and warned so many of the girls about the pitfalls that could arise from inward desires that could only lead to disaster.

Mother Seton encouraged social events between the various Catholic schools in the area and the list included Seton Hall as well as Bayley Ellard, Saint Anthony's, Saint Catherine and a host of other Catholic schools in the Newark Area.

On this particular evening the social was a quad. Quad meant four schools all joining together for a social event. All the boys and girls invited were being supervised by the host school which just happened to be Saint James in the iron Bound.

It was Saturday night and Richard could not wait to test his new dance moves that Sister Augustine had worked so hard on with him. She taught him the box step which was a variation on the traditional waltz. They worked a little on the twist to which both he and Sister Augustine laughed so hard that tears were flowing for both of them

Richard wore his only suit a dark blue single breasted jacket and pants together with a white shirt and matching blue and red silk tie. He glanced at himself in the mirror at least a dozen times making sure his hair was perfect.

By the time the music had begun at 7pm he had eaten at least 20 life savers in the hope that his breath wouldn't give him away.

He had hoped that this night might give him hope in the social department. Aside from small childish crushes he developed within the last few years. His prior associations were simply with Catholic girls two steps from the nunnery. Tonight he held out hope that he would finally graduate and meet a girl that might stir his heart as well as other parts of his body.

Tonight, he hoped, that his manners and semi suaveness might just pave the way for him as he tried to convince a girl that he was sophisticated as well as debonair. It never dawned on him that perhaps most of the girls assembled in the Saint James auditorium felt exactly the same way.

The auditorium, which doubled as the Saint James cougar's basketball team official game site, was now renamed New Orleans Mardi Gras Jazz City.

The basketball hoops pulled high above the floor and decorated with fancy ribbons and balloons the loud New Orleans Music emanating from a three speaker set up strategically placed around the perimeter of the floor gave everyone the feeling that the theme of a New Orleans Mardi-Gra night was artfully accomplished. Refreshments were being served by the Saint James Sisters of Charity.

There was once facet of the evening that struck Richard as odd. Having been around Catholic Schools and Catholic teachers especially Nuns that the students participating at the dance were acting a bit strange to his way of thinking. Richard knew from past experience that for many Students, there was this invisible social barrier separating student and teacher. Tonight that invisible wall was nowhere to be seen, rather the atmosphere was jovial and friendly. Richard wondered did this oddity only occur to him. He observed so many conversations again between students of the school and the faculty where outright personal likes of each other were discussed. Throughout the course of the evening both students and the Sisters joked and simply acted as if they were all best of friends. Richard wondered would the torment begin again when they all came back to school on Monday.

Richard also took note that, just as sister Augustine had predicted, the girls would be lined up on one side and the boys on the other. Richard recognized some of the students and everyone boys and girls were all there for the same reason, to mingle chat and hope that love and excitement would reach each and every one.

Some of the boys were signaling to each other about that girl or this girl and throughout all of it Richard took notes and just stood like everyone else on the sidelines not wanting to be the first to ask any girl to dance.

As he went to get some punch that was offered at the south side of the gym he caught sight of a girl sitting alone almost to the end of the line of folded chairs. Aside from touching her dress a few hundred times to make sure that it was evenly distributed and draped across the folded chair she sat perfectly still looking straight ahead.

Richard liked the way she looked and before he knew it his legs were taking the offensive and he found himself walking directly to her. As he approached her their eyes met his and she smiled.

There was something special, he thought, about her. Her hair was "dirty blond" and pulled away from her face. She wore little make up and as he got closer he hoped that no one would ask her to dance.

To say that he was nervous was the understatement of the century. He stopped in front of her, his immediate inspection vaulted her image into his senses she was beautiful he thought.

Half stammering he managed to say

"Hi my name is Richard and I'm 18 years old, I come from Saint Anthony's in Harrison and I' don't have any brothers and sister and...."

He knew that he was stammering yet throughout the short speech he noticed that the young lady was still smiling.

"Well, hi my name is Clara, is Richard your only name?"

This was said in jest and for that moment the tension was broken and blushing Richard laughed and got his last name out.

"Maguire, its Maguire... oh I said that right it is Maguire!"

Clara started laughing and instantly caught herself. "OH I am sorry I'm not laughing at you, oh no I just thought it funny that oh my God, the truth be told, I'm just as nervous as you"

Throughout the course of the evening both Clara and Richard talked nonstop. It was odd in the fact that dancing, except when they danced the first and last number, was the last thing they were interested in. They sat together the entire evening as if they had been friends forever. If someone were to eavesdrop on this conversation one would think that each one of them had at least ten thousand words all stored up for such an occasion and like a freight train racing to the finish line.

They sat for hours and by evening's end they actually made a pact. They exchanged phone numbers, although Richard explained that he was exactly between schools and that the only number he had was in Sister Augustine's phone situated in the hall way at the rectory. He wanted to be honest with her and she wanted the same. They agreed that it would be he who called her and a time was specified.

The very next day, for Richard, was anticipation of the phone call that evening.

Six thirty came and Richard had his dime in the phone call box at the local diner.

"Hello Clara? Are you there" His heart was racing and feelings he had never experienced were running through his senses like rushing water cascading down a mountain side.

He waited for her to respond and the only thing he actually heard was the loud drum of his own heart, banging feverishly inside his chest.

"Richard! Oh God you called!"

Here he was thinking she'd not pick the phone and there she was thinking the same about him.

"Are you kidding? Why would I not call?"

There was an awkward pause.

"I don't know... perhaps you didn't like me today as much as you liked me yesterday, oh lord I really don't know what I'm saying... I am happy you called, OK that's all!"

"Clara I really think your great and all, is there... are there... any..."

Clara blurted outstanding "No there is no one else how about you".

He responded the same. In minutes his dime ran out she quickly called him back and by the time the diner owner asked him to leave as he had to close it was midnight. Before he said well by and arranged for their third encounter he professed.

"This cannot go on like this"

Clara, appearing hurt, stammered "Why? Don't you want to talk to me?"

Richard had to chuckle to himself" Are you crazy, no what I mean is I have to get a phone of my own!"

CHAPTER 32

Inseparable

Four years had passed and except for a fact finding trip Clara took, as part of her required course study for college to Florida, both Clara and Richard saw each other every day.

The following year after they both graduated Richard proposed marriage, she accepted and within two months they were married.

They were married on August 13th, 1973. It was always Richard's master plan to have a home of his own. Both he and Clara had spoken many times about home ownership so they made a pact just before entering college. Richard decided that eventually he had hoped to marry Clara and so with that in mind he set out to work and save every penny he could so that his dream of owning his own home would become a reality.

Being raised in an orphanage, even with the love he received from Sister Augustine, couldn't compare, in his mind and heart, with having his own family and living in his own house. The greatest feeling, he felt besides being married to Clara was actually their first night in his own house. Late at night after Clara had gone to sleep Richard propped himself on his elbows and simply surveyed the bedroom. Since he was a child he was forced to bunk with others. Many a night he would wake up and look to his left and his right and there was always someone sleeping just feet away from his bed.

This night there was only Clara and himself, life could not get any better.

In five short months Richard and Clara had made a pretty fine home for themselves. Long Branch New Jersey was where Richard's home office was situated as he had taken a job as an advanced insurance adjuster for company that represented insurance companies like Metropolitan and Prudential. This company made it clear that they wanted Richard and made him an attractive offer. The best part of the deal was based on the fact that this company needed him to stay and develop business in the shore area.

In six months Richard had moved up to Sales Manager and for all intents life was good. At the end of 1973 Clara announced that she was pregnant and although the eventual loss of a paycheck would be felt the addition of a child made the journey that much more rewarding.

As they sat and watched television Richard couldn't help feeling that he was the luckiest man in the world, a wife that he loved so much who was now pregnant a great job that took him to an office in downtown Long Branch only ten minutes from his home and a salary of twenty-five thousand a year plus bonuses, he thanked God every night for his good fortune.

"Did you ever think you'd be pregnant and living in Long Branch?'

Clara, reading the medical manual the doctor had given her, hadn't paid attention to what Richard had said. "I'm sorry honey what was it you were saying?"

I said I just hit the Italian Lottery!" Clara looked at him in disbelief" You never play the lottery so how could you have won?"

Richard started to laugh "It's you! You're the Italian Lottery"

Clara got up and walked over to where Richard was sitting and sat on his lap whereby she gently whispered in his ear" Well Mr. Maguire I'd like to think that I hit the Irish Jackpot with you!"

CHAPTER 33

April 1974

Clara was pregnant and the world couldn't hold Richard's excitement at the prospect of becoming a new father.

"Do you feel OK? I mean any kicks at all!"

Lately Clara had to fend off a remark a minute from her husband inquiring about the pregnancy and all. "No Rich "exasperated Clara became defensive. "Richard! Please darling, don't fret I'm all right believe me I am OK and yes I can do chores around the house I'm only 6 months pregnant and I'm not fragile" Lately it seemed that any excuse that he could use was used so that he could leave the office and check on Clara.

No sooner had they become occupants in their Long Branch home, a home that fate landed in their economic lap. It came to pass that the house that Richard originally looked at around the corner from Sycamore Lane was listed at $15,000 less but the realtor had told both Clara and Richard if they were interested in the Sycamore house the owners would give him a mortgage for $20,000 less than the price. The reasoning was that the owners wanted a family to move in not just single people and since Richard and Clara fit the bill the deal was made.

Richard had expressed his desire to his wife that he had a 5-year game plan concerning the house and raising their family in Long Branch.

His idea was simply. He wanted to have children, and the Jersey Shore was appealing, but in the end he still wanted to settle north of Long Branch. He expressed that he was not a shore person. He realized that the beach and its amenities was great when thinking about a vacation but to permanently live there was not a thought he relished. He was moving up in the insurance world and most of the major business in New Jersey was north not south. And although the company he worked for called Metropolitan he still wanted to eventually go to business in New York.

Richard loved the fact that his employers appreciated his work ethic. His dream of eventually was stalled as the employers gave him three raises in a row, Clara advised him to stay with the company as it was obvious that they liked his effort and success.

Richard's dream was to eventually move from the shore. As an added incentive Richard liked hiking and camping rather than sun bathing. He always felt that the Jersey Shore was so overpopulated and the property values were excessively inflated simply to enjoy the beach a few months a year to him was not worth it but to Clara, who loved the shore, it was. And for that alone he would stay the course. Resigned to the fact that pleasing his wife came above all else he threw himself into the maintenance of the property.

In no time Richard became a lawn genius. The grass and shrubs, the moment they arrived at the house, needed serious attention as the previous owner neglected them badly. Richard worked with a local company to develop and cultivate the lawn and shrubs even making the local papers as an owner who took pride in his property. The neighborhood was filled with families like Richard's with small children and in the end that was truly what mattered the most. And it certainly made Clara happy.

The neighbor to his left was a retired couple who seldom entertained and in truth hardly ever came out of their house. Richard surmised that either one of them or both were suffering some way or another. Their property was maintained by a Gardner and for all intents Richard was content in the occasional hello and good bye offered by the couple whenever they'd see each other. The house on his left was a puzzle to both he and Clara.

When Richard bought the house the Realtor described as best he could the makeup of the neighborhood. Locations of the schools and local houses of worship. The center of town Long Branch proper was heavily dominated by the tourist trade but that didn't start until Labor Day. Other than that the neighborhood was quiet and serene perfect for raising kids. When Richard asked about the house on his left there the Realtor was stumped.

"Truthfully Richard, I've been selling homes in this area for a while and that house has got me stumped. On more than one occasion I asked the Realtor board who owned it and why has it been vacant for so long. The other oddity is that the grounds are always kept in great condition winter and summer, so you know that someone has been paying to do that but who?"

Richard wondered out loud "I hope whoever comes to live here, whenever they come. I hope their young with kids" The Realtor agreed.

CHAPTER 34

New Arrivals

It was 1975 the Maguire's were getting accustomed to the newest addition to their family lovely Josephine who was now 6 months old and just getting into a routine. Richard's duties at Metropolitan now included heading up a new department the company called Estate Planning, a term that was slowly being talked about as to what people should do about concerning their retirement.

Robert welcomed the promotion and the extra 60 dollars a week paid for a lot of diapers. The commute was easy and it still left plenty of time each day for him to get away at lunch to see his growing family, in other words, Robert loved being married and having a family of his own. It had never escaped his memory for an instant how lucky he was in meeting Clara and marrying her. It also never passed his mind about the love and care given him by Sister Augustine and Saint Anthony's in general. No matter how busy he was he always took the time in calling the orphanage and Sister Augustine. In 1974 on three separate Sundays he invited Sister Augustine to a barbecue and twice she came. Richard was excited the first time he drove up to Kearny New Jersey to pick her up. That special Sunday was also important because it signaled closure on an episode in his past and began a brand new relationship with one of the most important people in his life.

As they were both in the car driving back to Long Branch he couldn't hold his excitement at the prospect of her seeing his new home and how proud he was of it.

Excitedly he exclaimed

"I can't wait for you to see the place"

She was silent for a few seconds and Richard sensed from her quiet demeanor that perhaps there might be something bothering her. "Are you ok? you seem a little distracted, you did want to come right Sister?"

She continued her silence as the y drove towards the shore. He began thinking that perhaps she was hurt in the fact that he might be more interested in showing off his new home rather than getting to know how she had fared since they last spoke. That specific evening, some 6 months' prior, was alarming in the fact that it was the first time Sister Augustine had ever confessed that her age was getting to her. She mentioned that Pneumonia had gotten the best of her and she had been bed ridden for almost two weeks.

As they drove he remembered the incident, perhaps she wanted him to ask her about her illness, and perhaps something else was bothering her. Either way he needed to pry the truth out of her. In effect, he thought, it had actually been a while since they spoke. Sensing this he tried to change direction. "I should have asked you and I'm sorry did the Pneumonia leave any lasting scars?" This brought the most alarming look from her to him and if looks could kill he's be a dead man.

Again he tried.

"The last time we spoke you mentioned that your right leg was also bothering you how is it now"

She moved uncomfortably in her seat then as he continued to look straight ahead she finally opened her mouth to speak.

"Well I didn't think you remembered, after all it was quite a long time ago" It was then that he knew something else was bothering her.

"Ok, what is it come on now I know you too well, tell me what's wrong!" he could see a tear slowly rolling down her face

"Oh I guess I'm just an old fool, thinking that our relationship was a lot more than teacher and student" Richard reacted quickly seeing where she was headed with this line of defense

"Oh God Sister Yes we are more than that we've always been more than that" he saw that she was crying and somewhere between exit 109 and the Long Branch exit he pulled over. In an instant he knew there was more she wasn't telling him. Her expression told him even more. She appeared frightened and pale as she sat there. "What is it Sister please! Tell me"

"I realized a long time ago that the vows I took prior to me becoming a Sister of Charity never prepared me for what I experienced the moment you were presented to me at the orphanage. Prior to you most of the charges I was responsible for were all great kids and I respected them as if they were my nieces and nephews. But you were somehow different. Oh I really can't remember how it started but it did. In your case I felt a closeness and a need to take care of you like a... Mother would. I looked at you as the son I never had. I thanked God every night that you came into my life and when your biological mother abandoned you I actually rejoiced at the thought, God please forgive me"

It all became clear now. Sister Augustine felt genuine love and abandonment all at the same time. Richard spoke gently "Sister, come here" he slowly slid over and embraced her and as she did she began to cry. He felt her emotion coming through her coat and in that instant he began to cry too, realizing that she in fact took his biological mother's place long ago and now it was certainly time for them to recreate that bond again.

"As far as I am concerned as of this moment I am looking at you as I would my mother. I hope you can accept that"

Sister Augustine was elated and thanked God for all of her prayers were answered. She leaned over and gently kissed Richard on his cheek. "Richard I can now go on living my life knowing that you and I will always be family"

CHAPTER 35

Florida

The meeting was set for Thursday evening at the Cabana Club portion of the Country Club.

Trafficante arrived early with an entourage and after exchanging greetings with everyone connected with the club, including the cabana boy, he subsequently picked out a large Bamboo lounge chair ordered an Ice Tea and just waited for the main man to arrive.

This meeting had been coming for months and after multiple delays, all based on Meyer Lansky's reluctance, finally a meeting was set. Florida, for most of the last 47 years, was considered open territory for any organized crime boss to plant his flag. The ruling had been put down and enforced back in 1929 by Luciano. Every other mob boss around the country agreed that it would be gospel, that is, until now.

The original conclave of organized Crime rulers took place in Atlantic City circa 1929. It was called by Luciano after the Maranzano and Masseria murders were committed and the old Sicilian edit of "Cappo Di Tutti Capi" boss of all bosses was eliminated. What took place instead was a ruling in favor of a combination of bosses from around the country who would set policy and govern their own provinces and when needed a commission would meet to discuss matters that were more global in nature.

Luciano created this idea and now some 47 years later it was slowly being challenged and an attempt to mold new directions. This new direction was being tested, in Florida by Santo Trafficante. In this instance Meyer Lansky who had been part of the original architecture that Luciano created objected. But again in 1976, with many of the old line bosses either dead or retired, Lansky had no one to help bolster his disagreement. And in 1976 Lansky was still the accountant for many aging Mafiosi around the country who feared that if Trafficante was given his way he would infringe on that constant flow of Capital.

Trafficante knew that he had money and guns and power and in reality did not need any sanction from anyone to move in any direction he desired but history dictated that cooler heads always outnumber the rash and outspoken, so he waited. Time passed and nothing was being done in any direction so Trafficante persisted and Lansky finally relented and consented to the meeting.

Up until this very date Lansky had, as his protective ace in the whole, semi-retired Capo of the Genovese family Jimmy Blue Eyes Alo. In his day Alo was a gunman and Mafia Captain in the organization. When Luciano got deported in 1946 he assigned Alo to stay close to Lansky for Lansky's protection but that was not the only reason. Luciano being 3000 miles away from the action in New York also left him 3000 miles away from his money. Lansky was in charge of taking care of the organization's money including investments and cash and Luciano wanted to make sure it stayed that way.

Recently, because of some medical ailments, Alo was forced to cancel a few early meetings. He finally agreed to meet with both Lansky and Trafficante at the Cabana Club.

Lansky arrived first and immediately went to a standing Trafficante and they embraced.

"It's been a long time Santo how have you been?"

"I'm pretty good if my stomach doesn't act up I've got to eat bland, you know no more late nights like we used to eh Meyer?" Immediate Lansky forgot the formalities and pulled out his briefcase and basically ignored Trafficante who was still standing there perhaps waiting for some other small tidbit that might otherwise connect them to their organization.

Lansky did not answer the remark basically stating by his silence that as his life style was nothing like Trafficante. As a matter of fact they had never had as much as a drink together. Trafficante was considered by Lansky as a new kid on the block. Even though Trafficante was a multi-millionaire many times over he was still an outsider to the original group and Lansky's I really don't give a shit attitude did not sit well with him. As he gently squirmed in his seat he instinctively did not like the little Jew. Lansky's attitude was one that Trafficante had to get permission to work the Florida areas and Trafficante's position was that nobody would ever tell him what to do and where he could or could not go.

Sitting in his seat and sipping his Ice Tea he chose to listen before making any rash statements based on emotion. Yet his background dictated that he would never take a back seat to this diminutive figure of an aging mob boss. "What papers have you got there Meyer, mind sharing what you're reading?"

Trafficante, blurted out in an almost condescending manner, "I mean I'm here waiting for you for twenty minutes and when you finally arrive your moving papers around when we have serious business to talk about!" This last statement was said in anger and Lansky finally paid attention to it.

"Santo I am sorry but when I originally put these papers together so that the figures would make sense they needed to be in order and I was just adjusting them, for the delay again I am sorry"

Trafficante's anger was muffled by Lansky's response and seeing that Lansky was indeed a businessman and apologetic at the same time Trafficante became relaxed and was now interested in what Lansky had to say.

"Santo, I want you to see these blueprints "As he handed the papers to him

"Here, I believe, is the future of Florida for all of us. Here is a prime example. The new Gulfstream Racetrack. Now you may say what does this have to do with me? Well just like Luciano's idea of cooperation with each other almost 50 years ago worked back then it can also work now! We can do the same thing today. Oh I know your ideas about expanding into many different businesses using both muscle and money will gain you some financial advantages but just hear me out. In the end you and many more like you will still be on the outside looking in. Answer this if you can, in the past 10 years what member of your organization or yourself, for that matter, has had any entry into any government projects that consider gaming as a base." Trafficante was speechless

"No one as far as I know, but what does any of this have to do with me?"

"Now for the first time in years I can arrange for complete cooperation from the government here in Florida. You and my partners and I can share Investments in Dog Tracks, H-li Arenas and Horse Racing, do you get my idea?"

Trafficante, pondered everything that Lansky was saying.

"So what you're trying to tell me is to back off in me moving towards the west coast and go in with you is that right?"

"Not only that. By you not moving in on our friends and allowing them their freedom you then will share in spoils that would outweigh any gains in the areas you're looking at now. And the best part of investing with me and my partners is that it's all legit! What this means is that without me the lawmakers would never consider taking you as a partner."

There was a long pause and Trafficante pondered what had been discussed and as was his nature he would wait. "Ok this is my decision I will talk this over with my family and get back to you in a week is that ok?"

Lansky got up and held his hand out. "I am sure that after you weigh all the factors you will see that this is the best course of action for all of us, let us say next week here ok?"

They were all agreed.

CHAPTER 36

WILL THE REAL BOSS PLEASE STAND UP? BAL HARBOR, AT THE CONTINUUM

In his luxurious suite overlooking the water Santo Trafficante needed to somehow get on that list of legitimate businessmen owing pieces of the new racetrack.

7 weeks had passed and Santo Trafficante was no closer to an answer from Meyer Lansky concerning the new racetrack bond offer. Gerolamo Santucci, the trusted Trafficante lieutenant who was the impetus behind Trafficante's original refusal of the Lansky offer, needed some space between himself Trafficante and the entire ordeal.

"As far as I am concerned that little Jew has a lot of balls in not calling you boss"

Trafficante, as if he was slowly coming out of a fog and suddenly noticing that Santucci was speaking to him, reacted vehemently.

"Balls!" He spouted directing venom right at Santucci where a frightened Santucci was speechless. "Are you kidding me? You're the reason I initially rejected the offer do you remember?"

"Yes I do but boss we both know that Lansky favors all those front……"

Trafficante picked up a large folder on his desk and threw it at him. "Lansky was and is the sharpest businessman down in this fucking state, and I should have agreed to the deal right then and there. Now I've got to posture and put pressure on this guy to see if I can get it back"

Trafficante began to pace the office and Santucci just stood there hoping that there wouldn't be any more attacks directed at him.

"I've made up my mind"

Trafficante picked up the phone and dialed.

"Hello is this Meyer? Yes, it's me I've been waiting for your call back for weeks what happened"

"Santo it is good hearing from you but the reason I did not call was simply that I haven't been back in Miami in over a month. I've been all over the United States drumming up support for some of the other projects we are all working on, what was so important that you wanted to talk about"

"Can we meet? What I mean is that it's important I want you there, we need to talk!"

This Trafficante said as serious as any mafia big shot can sound when he wants to covey urgency.

"Ok, tomorrow afternoon at the Card Club, ok?"

Santucci hoping that the Mafia side of Trafficante had emerged winning the battle between gangster and businessman and on that note decided that it was his time to rally around the gangster side.

"Santo, remember he'll have Vincent Alo at his side so I think you'll need me there, right?"

Trafficante hearing Alo's name brought back his early days and the some of the bad memories that accompanied them. He had become a young Mafia up and comer in New York. Back then, amongst some of the older members, he was ridiculed and laughed at when his height and slight body type was called into question reminding everyone that Trafficante might be the first effeminate member of the Luciano Family.

But many of these same seasoned mafia up and comers soon found out that his slight build and small stature was totally outweighed by his ferocity. And more than one occasion casual joking at his expense was met with the prospect of their eminent death at the end of a gun in their face.

Those memories rang true whenever Alo's name was mentioned for he was one of those who although didn't actually ridicule Trafficante but in effect condoned some of it to go on in the taste of just having fun, Trafficante never saw it that way, so this face to face wouldn't be a pleasant one according to Trafficante's thinking.

The meeting was set for 2pm. Trafficante arrived first with his trusted aid Santucci at his side. Within minutes an uncharacteristic Meyer Lansky arrived with his trusted shadow Vincent Alo. After cordial greetings were shared all around them all came down to why they were all here.

"Meyer, I asked you to come because I changed my mind about the deal at Gulfstream. I want in it's as simple as that. I realize that I did make a mistake but what I need from you is to acknowledge who I am and what I'm now asking you for."

Santo was calm and all the years of a Mafia chieftain was out in force. Meyer scratched his chin as he had always done while thinking. As they waited for his response Vincent looked at Trafficante and what Santo dreaded occurred.

Alo took a long sip of his Ice Tea looked over at what was becoming a snarling Santucci, as the two men did not like each other from previous altercations and brush ins. Alo got up and walked over to the large pained glass view of the beach and while he looked out at the many beach goers enjoying the Florida 0waters he remarked directly at Santucci yet never looked him directly in the eye rather still staring at the ocean.

"Gerolomo did you ever think you'd be sipping tea in such a place like this when you were a kid on the lower East Side?"

Santucci squirmed uneasily in his chair trying to find some agitation to Alo's statement but could find none. "Actually coming to Florida was never a thought, by luck I came here on my honeymoon and fell in love with the place, what about you?"

"Truthfully I love it here been. I've been down here with Meyer over 25 years and no I never thought I'd be anyplace even remotely connected to a place like this when we were growing up"

Trafficante could not hold his temper in anymore." Meyer, what the fuck is it with you I asked a question and I want an answer!"

At this point Alo, Santucci and Trafficante were all standing and looking down at Lansky, who was just sipping his tea and looking at the glass after he had three long gulps.

"My answer is that I don't know right now, I have to hear from someone else and when I get that answer we'll all know if there's room for you"

"Who is this person, is he a politician you have to grease?"

Lansky handed his glass to Alo and stood beside Trafficante.

"Santo I offered you this piece not because I had to but because I wanted to, I want you to know that. And yes I realize your relevance down here and make no mistake about it I had to weigh that and a lot more before I brought this offer and dropped it in your lap and what did you do you spurned my offer, right? Now in the 11th hour you want in, tell me who I kick out!"

Lansky, for the first time in a long time, raised his voice. To which Trafficante obliged by standing nose to nose and the threat came out.

"I don't give a fuck who was promised or what was promised I get that share because nobody is going to have the last word on this! And nobody is ever going to tell me anything about anything that goes down here! This is my turf you know it and everybody up north knows it! So whoever has that piece get it from him and jot my name down on it, I'm not asking you Meyer I'm telling!"

It was finally out in the open and anything that had ever been mentioned concerning good taste and manners was out the window. This was a potential turf war and the better man was going to win.

Meyer stepped back and slowly seemed to collect himself. He walked to the far side of the room as if to gather strength from the available air left in the room.

"Ok Santo, have it your way. The man will be here in a few minutes you can try to persuade him yourself"

Lansky sat down and just crossed his legs and never once looked at Trafficante who was still venting near the large pane glass panorama. In seconds everyone would know who the certain person of interest was.

In through the door cam the figure of a man that was partially hidden by the brilliant sunlight cascading through the window. In seconds three of the four men in the room immediately recognized the newest addition to the Lansky puzzle Lansky suddenly got up and a broad smile crossed his face. He then announced

"Gentleman allow me to introduce a friend from way back in the good old days this here is Antonio Piccolo"

CHAPTER 37

Humility

Antonio, suntanned and looking casual, was dressed in light vanilla slacks with a most startling bright blue shirt looked more like a movie producer than a 70-year-old retiree. He stopped short as he surveyed the assembled group. With their mouths wide open one by one their expression changed from expectation to pure joy with smiles all around. Even with the dark sunglasses Antonio wore he was a sight for sore eyes.

The only person who did not share the group's enthusiasm was Santucci, otherwise from Alo to Trafficante to Lansky it was just like old times. Alo shared his remarks first as Antonio slowly made his way to where everyone had been sitting.

"Wow, Meyer mentioned it once that he had seen you in Florida and now seeing you my mind can't stop racing back to the good old day's dam it Vinnie, how the fuck are you!"

Vincent got emotional in seconds. Whether it was his age or ailments or the thought that being in the last quarter of his life would be his last raced to Antonio and bear hugged him.

"God Tony!" he exclaimed "It is so good seeing you, I didn't realize how much till now"

As Antonio pulled away he looked at Meyer and embraced him. "Well Little man, you haven't changed a bit right? Always business, wasn't it Charley who used to tell you that you needed to loosen up remember?" Lansky looked at him and smiled "Yes I remember but the last time I saw Charley was in 61 just before he died, so you can see what the good life can do to you"

Then Antonio turned to Trafficante

"Well Santo how are you, let's see the last time we actually spoke was when your uncle came to me to sponsor you, you were a scrawny kid but you had balls and I loved that. How the hell are you?"

He walked to Trafficante and they embraced.

"Oh my God I wish Meyer had told me it was you, what an asshole I turned into, Santucci this is the man himself, and my goomba who started me, look! Go back to the office I'll call you later."

"Look Santo if you want him to stay it would be fine we have no secrets"

"No he's better off at the office, Antonio I just want to talk to you and with no interruptions and Antonio I am so sorry, after all I owe you please take the shares and great luck, you'll have no problem from me"

Antonio motioned Santo to sit down." I can see that you're a generous man but the shares belong to you"Trafficante tried to insist but Antonio stopped him.

"Let me finish, I know what emotion can do to a man believe me I've had 40 years to learn that. I want you to share this great opportunity with Meyer and his partners and believe me everybody will be grateful that you're involved and you will be satisfied, do it with my blessing.

The reason I need this deal to kick off this way is simple; my day is over. I've done a lot in the time allotted me and now it's your turn. I need this deal to evolve this way for one simple reason, we all need to be legit! It's as simple as that and Meyer's dream will do that. Plus, for the remaining years I have left I want to go back up north, Tom Set a lot of things up for me while I was away and I just want to enjoy them even though Tom is no longer with us. In the end we will always be friends."

There were so many questions from the group for Antonio. In the next half hour Antonio tried to answer many of those questions, he also wanted to illustrate what a good friend Tom had been to him all the while he was incarcerated. This last statement was framed for the group simply to show how and why he was settling up north.

"At least once a month Tom would come to Atlanta. At first he connected with the closest motel to the prison. He began by getting acquainted with the owner. Renting at first then he bought the place leaving the management to the people he bought it from, this way he'd always have a place to sleep whenever he came plus being a good businessman he created a great deal whereby everybody made out. 2 years before I got out and 6 months before Tom died he sold it for a big profit. He invested in real estate in New York and Jersey plus so much more and each month most of the visit was spent on what we owned and what we were going to do once I got out. He also bought in Florida, that's where I live now, Tom was my best friend and I do miss him a lot so you see gentleman enjoy life while you can and Santo God bless you and Meyer and Vincent make a million ok? I'm going up north"

And once again this man of vision used his humility to overcome adversity and leave a situation better than he found it.

The very next morning Antonio said his good byes to the few friends he had made for the past two years then headed to the Realtor who maintained his properties. Once there he instructed the Realtor to sell all his holdings in Florida and transfer them to his Attorney, Caldwell and Stringer's office in New York. The property in Atlanta was also transferred there. With an eagerness to Leave the hot and humid climate of Florida he anticipated starting out again in New Jersey just as he and Tom Madden had discussed so many years ago.

CHAPTER 38

New Place, New Start, New friends

The Maguire family had grown since they had first arrived at Sycamore Lane in Long Branch New Jersey. Richard Maguire's routine had not changed in 5 years, except his family had grown to two daughters and of course Sister Augustine. Richard wasn't at work he was tending to the family his garden and magnificent lawn. The mailman stopped each and every day to deliver the mail. On the days that Richard was not at home he would usually discuss anything that came into his mind with Sister Augustine, who by now was a fixture at the Maguire's, "Seems like we're going to have a great day eh Augustine?" The mailman directed this line to Sister Augustine.

With a look that could kill, she wickedly answered" My name is not Augustine its Sister Augustine and don't you have other mail to deliver"

This drove the message home and he was quickly on his way.

This was the usual verbiage that crossed between Mail men, milk delivery men, newspaper delivery boys whomever appeared at the Maguire's door Sister Augustine was there to greet them. Clara and the children loved having her there. Clara, since childhood, had always been devout in her religion and having Sister there made each day a joy for her and in that Richard thanked his lucky stars that Clara didn't balk at the Sister being a permanent part of the family. Richard was now a supervisor and at $35,500 per year he was one of the highest paid insurance execs in the North Jersey. But a conversation Richard had with the merry mailman made him take full notice of what was happening in his neighborhood.

o "I hear that you're going to get a new neighbor, have you heard the same?" The mailman was more searching for answers then revealing any information.

Richard could see what he wanted but just felt like playing along. "Well, maybe it will be another older couple like we had over there" Richard pointed to the house on his left. Seeing that he wasn't going to get any more information the mailman, resigned to his afternoon fate sighed, "Back to work, see you Richard!"

New Deal Realty usually opened each day at 9am, but this day John Carroll, owner of the office would be late. He was going to the Long Branch train station to pick up a home owner who, for the past 2 years, had only corresponded his needs to the real estate office by mail. The original maintenance of the property had been set up by Tom Madden years before with an expenditure schedule being taken care of by a New York Law firm.

John had been in the real estate business for over 20 years and never in his experience had he done business with a customer who did most of his business by mail. From the legal papers filed with his office everything connected with this property was mostly done in secrecy. From previous records John had been aware that the purchase of the property was conducted roughly 5 years before by Thomas Madden a business associate of the new owner. Since Madden's death the property and its deed automatically referred to this new client. At 10.30 am the train pulled into the station and the passengers all filed out. John strained to see if anyone resembled his client. But soon the train had emptied out and was on its way with no client in sight.

"Excuse me! Are you John Carroll" A voice came from behind him and as he spun around immediately knew this was not his client. The young man was dressed in a dark blue suit with matching tie. His shoes were polished to a luster but he was all of 25 and definitely not his client.

"Yes I am and you are?" The young man pulled out his business card, it read Steve Layman, pC Caldwell and Stringer Lawyer Firm

"My name is Steve Layman and it's a pleasure to meet you"

The next 10 minutes proved to be illuminating for John to say the least. One thing for sure whoever this client was John felt that he must be wealthy and important enough to have a big New York attorney come ahead and make financial arrangements in advance. In reality John did not know the new client's name the only name associated with the purchase of the house was Tom Madden.

"I am here representing my client who is in route to New Jersey from Florida. There are a few things we need to do prior to his arriving. My client has expressed a desire to have air conditioning installed in the house rather if there have to be separate units then perhaps you can arrange for a reputable firm that can handle these things. Reason being that my client suffers from Emphysema and breathing in humid weather could make it difficult for him, can we accomplish this? All bills for this and any other services he desires will be covered by my firm. What I'd like to give you is a cashier's check for $10,000 I'd like you to deposit this check and work off of it and if the expenditures exceed that amount a simple call to my office and I will rectify it, is that ok with you?"

To say that John Carroll was impressed was an understatement. They parted and most of the wants of the new client concerning the house were given to John with three months to make the necessary changes, John agreed he would take care of it.

Richard couldn't help but notice that although there was constant monthly activity such as gardening and landscaping not until recently had the amount of work suddenly increased to the point that there was serious activity again coming from the next door neighbor. And still no sign of the elusive tenant. Day after day he would come home from work and he would notice that there was another chapter unfolding in the ongoing saga of the mysterious house next door. Lately Clara had been noticing that Richard was becoming fixated with all the activity from next door.

"Seriously Rich, why are you so fixated on that house?" Richard looked at Clara as she was standing over the kitchen sink and wondered why it hadn't bothered her.

"Fixated? No I'm not fixated I just am curious, and I can't' see why you're not!" Clara continued to do the dishes not looking up as if the entire situation didn't interest her.

"Well! Perhaps the fact that we're living here for more than a few years and for all that time there has been no sign of anyone ever coming here to claim that as their property, yet there is constant activity there, and what makes it even stranger is that the property looks great and all. And you don't think it's odd? God! for years some mysterious person or persons pay a lot of money to keep it up and yet no one shows up to claim ownership, it's simply strange"

From the outer hall Sister Augustine, carrying the wash chimed in," Your wife is right Richard we can't do anything about it Clara only hopes that a family might move in bringing children and that would be great for the girls! And

Richard! You should be happy my God the property values surrounding that house have got to go up based on what they are doing to it right?"

"All right I can see that you're both ganging up on me, let's just say I'm nosey ok!"

But in Richard's mind the additions made to the house these past few months baffled him. All the outside improvements for sure added to the total décor of the property that was true and the total property values of that house and surrounding homes were increased that is all true, but the mystery still haunted him. For a neighborhood such as Sycamore Lane only the largest homes in the general area had the improvements this house was being fitted with. The thought of automatic sprinklers was strictly for the well to do yet his new neighbor had the unit installed. Central Air Conditioning was another item

Usually seen in the really large and opulent homes built in and around neighboring wealthy Rumson, but not Long Branch. He quizzed himself over and over again as to why someone would spend so much money for an average 2-bedroom bungalow. Ever since the constant flow of realtors, workmen and alike began flooding the neighborhood the rumors were flying as to who was going to live there, and again most of the talk was harmless and soon everyone at one point or another resigned themselves to the fact that eventually someone would come to live there. As time passed the only truly interested party was Richard Maguire.

Two months had passed and the summer was in full swing. The Blossom trees were flowing with their bright yellow plumage giving small shade to the inundated sun drenched grass surrounding Richard's property. It was Saturday and his normal chores included cutting the grass and trimming the hedges. The past few years a few of the neighbors decided that alternating barbeques would be a great idea and Richard loved it. This was a great time to relax enjoy one's family and meet and greet the neighbors who, and a few did, become good friends.

This Saturday Richard was busy preparing whatever he needed for the Sunday barbeque which was being hosted by him for the next day. As he ran the lawnmower he couldn't help looking over to his left and there standing not 30 feet from him was a man. At last, he thought, finally this must be the elusive new neighbor.

At first the new arrival hadn't noticed that Richard was looking at him as he was so fixated on the carrying on of the sea gulls fighting for some small morsel of food left by the sea bank probably by some of the early morning fisherman.

The man was just standing there smoking a cigarette looking across the front of the property to the vista overlooking the bay. The early morning haze that usually accompanies the Jersey Shore waterfronts gives the onlooker a most cerebral feel as the gentle movement of the bay current calmed the silky shore.

With one hand across his back the man just stood there mesmerized by the water and it's movement, it was as if he had never seen anything as peaceful as nature in the am. As Richard observed the new arrival he noticed his odd attire. He stood about 5 feet 5" tall. He was, to Richard's taste, looking unlike anything resembling a wealthy man, as he and everyone else in the neighborhood had originally thought.

He was dressed with red and yellow colored Bermuda shorts. He wore flip flops with aiguille socks. And to top this picture of sartorial splendor the man had on a white "wife beater" sleeveless tee shirt. As he stood there smoking a cigarette he slowly panned the terrain and happened to see

Richard trimming some of the flowers on his property. He looked and smiled and slowly raised his hand to waive hello.

This foray into a possible conversation gave Richard the impetus to say hello.

The man looked genuinely pleased that his arrival as a new neighbor was greeted with such a pleasant response. In his most deep and raspy voice he responded

"Hello, my name is Antonio and I am your neighbor and I am really pleased to finally get up here from Florida. As much as I've seen, and that's not anything at all, looks great to me. A lot of my furniture has not arrived as of yet, it's supposed to arrive today."

They parted and said good bye to each other and as Richard made his way back to his home he didn't know why but he was emotionally moved by meeting the man. Although Richard's initial impressions concerning Antonio's home and the apparent money spent on its décor might have originally influenced him into thinking this man was probably some wheeler dealer. But after meeting the man he was moved by something that wasn't said. Although the man was suntanned and outwardly looked fit and healthy there was something else that gave Richard the impression that there was true sadness running through his body.

Richard's first reaction came from the man's eyes. He appeared despondent and pensive and add to that his odd wardrobe and in Richard's mind flamboyant was not pictured here. To him the man reeked of loneliness. In Richard's though process he reminded him of a simple soul and not some flamboyant individual as everyone in the neighborhood expected.

The emotional factor immediately entered into Richard's psyche right from the very first moment he laid eyes on this stranger. Richard sensed the sadness when he looked into his eyes. Although the conversation was brief the man's rather odd and colorful demeanor reminded him of his past and how on more than one occasion whenever prospective parents would come to the orphanage to pick out potential candidates to adopt. That exciting, at first, yet strange and lonely feeling usually found itself into his own sensibilities especially after the prospective parents had gone, and of course he wasn't selected. After a few years he simply resigned himself to the fact that no one outside the orphanage would ever adopt him.

It was way too soon to ask the man personal questions but there was one thing that impacted Richard's original opinion of him. Although Antonio appeared suntanned, in decent health, and owner of a home that was subsidized for years without ever having lived there he still felt a deep emotional connection as if this man had been on an island all of his life and only now he needed a friend.

Although their initial encounter lasted but a few minutes this compelling feeling made him feel that this man somehow needed help of some sort. All of this in the face of a situation that told everyone in the neighborhood that here was a very wealthy man who had minions doing his bidding. He walked away feeling that somehow someway he would need to extend himself to the man.

CHAPTER 39

REVELATIONS

The summer was three quarters over and every household at the Jersey Shore had a different idea of how the rest of the summer should be spent. Some of the neighborhood wanted to end the season with a block party and some of the older gentry objected, too much noise. Then another suggestion from Richard that the entire block rent out a local park for barbeque. This like all the other suggestions were met with rejection.

The Maguire's were totally ambivalent about all of the ideas as the prior years had shown that in the end everyone stayed at home and enjoyed the family. Life had to go on so the Sunday barbeque was the thought that joined everyone together.

But barbeque aside the one thought that totally consumed his every thought was connecting with his newest neighbor, Antonio.

Richard was focused with making the connection.

It turned out that Richard's obsession with closing the emotional gap between him and his neighbor was actually consuming his everyday actions. Whether he was working or just puttering around the property his constant vigilance was centered on his neighbor's door. It began at the crack of dawn and ended every night as he pulled the covers over his shoulders and fell into unconsciousness.

Each day as soon as he got home from work Clara would usually comment on his peeking through the window at the house next door.

"Richard! Will you please stop! It has gotten to the point of annoyance"

"I'm not hurting anyone am I?"

Clara, exasperated "Your hurting me, will you stop!"

It had become an emotional connection with his new neighbor. With Sister Augustine in tow the family prepared for the end of their first summer where the girls now 2 and 4 were able to partake in so many hot weather activities that previously because of their age they couldn't. Richard was still a driven man when it came to his job just trying to be the best that he could be. And he still radiated passion whenever his landscaping duties came into question. Clara was fixated on fixing her house and raising their girls and Sister Augustine, by now fully accepted by both Clara and Richard as a true member of the household, was still trying to keep religion he would ask this mysterious man as a mainstay in this family.

As Richard assessed his life and family and everything holy on Sycamore Lane he still hadn't been able to have a heart to heart with his elusive neighbor. Until the last week in August when the opportunity presented itself.

At first their conversations were short and to the point.

They had first begun talking usually as Richard was about to leave for work early in the morning.

Antonio, obvious to Richard, kept the conversations short yet still creating an atmosphere showing Richard he wanted to be a lot more than just neighbors.

"Richard, it looks to me like you've got a beautiful family"

Richard, still half asleep, tried to understand the direction that this line of conversation could bring.

"Yes I thank you for that, I did notice that when you arrived here you seemed to be alone, any family to speak of?"

There was a pause as Antonio was pensive as he began to respond. "No wife, no kids I do have somewhat of an extended family back in New York State. The two women I am referring to are the daughters of a woman who I was very fond of years ago. We separated and lost touch but her daughters are doing ok. Other than them there are just a few old friends that's all. Why do you ask?"

This was Richards chance to bridge the gap in this entry level relationship. "Oh I just felt that if we are to become friends, heck we are already neighbors then I would want to know more about you, if that's ok?"

"I've got a good feeling about you Richard, I don't know just call it intuition but you seem like a good fellow and from what little I've seen about your family it looks to me like you've done a good job there, family is really important"

Their morning meetings became more frequent and on one such morning Antonio greeted Richard with hot cup of coffee.

"Wow, I usually go to 7-11 why are you doing this? Oh don't get me wrong I appreciate it but why…?"

Antonio just looked pensive at him, and for the first time in their brief relationship Antonio's gesture touched Richard.

"Thank you, I have an idea if possible and if it's ok with my wife, I'd love to have you over to meet my family, how does that sound?"

A smiling Antonio responded quickly" I think that's a great idea.

Ever since Richard found out who his newest neighbor was he was magically drawn to this stranger. It wasn't the opulence he saw and it certainly wasn't anything flamboyant about the man. Richard questioned himself numerous times about is true feelings concerning Antonio, who he was and why was he so drawn to the man.

Richard initially only wanted Antonio to join his family after seeing that he was obviously alone.

As each day passed and their casual relationship began to slowly turn into something close to a true relationship Richard felt that conversation alone would not do.

"Antonio, you and I speak each day. When I leave for work in the morning it seems like you're the last word from our neighborhood and when I come home from work it seems like you're waiting for me and we small talk again, right?"

Antonio smiled slightly and nodded yes

"And every night when I sit down to have dinner with my family I feel bad, hollow is the only description I can give you"

"Hollow, why?"

"Because I haven't asked you into my house, because I haven't formally introduced you to my family, who by the way, ask about you every day, that's why I feel hollow, Antonio there is something here as to why you moved next door to me, why I chose to live in this house and for a million more reasons of which I have no answers for. Oh I do have a reoccurring thought that perhaps you could have been my biological father"

Antonio looked confused and tried to speak but Richard stopped him

"All I know is that I'm inviting you to dinner for now ok?"

"I'd be honored"

CHAPTER 40

A BEGINNING

Four weeks had passed and the continuing saga and love fest between Antonio, Richard, Clara, Sister Augustine and the children was on and life for the Maguire's couldn't be better. To the uninformed this rather odd pairing between this 78-year-old mysterious neighbor who would, much to the disappointment of the entire family, politely excuse himself immediately as soon as dessert was over and make his way home.

"This is the fourth time in two weeks that you're leaving right after dessert, how come?"

Richard's 4-year-old also expressed her dismay "Yes both my sister and me like it when you here, and we're sad when you go home, we miss you" Both Clara and Richard were surprised at their 4 year olds statement.

Seeing how distressed the child was Antonio offered an answer.

"Since I got to know you all I have genuinely been honored to be a guest in your home and the last thing I ever wanted to do was to intrude and overstay my welcome"

Upon hearing this all five of them verbally jumped down his throat at the same time. Sister Augustine started first, she complained that she felt bad that he left the house so early in that she wanted to converse with him to get to know him better. She spoke of her status in life and being retired and instead of living the rest of her life in an old age convent she was given a second chance.

She was so proud to be part of and loved by the Maguire family. She emphasized that Antonio having no family to speak of, less 2 not related sisters who he hadn't seen but twice in 25 years, it might be a comforting adjustment knowing that there was a family who did want to see him more, and maybe within this small coterie of people perhaps he could find some of the same happiness.

Once Sister Augustine was done speaking Antonio looked at her and smiled warmly. "Sister, you have touched me tonight"

Clara continued. She chimed in wanting to know about his family and with her kids not having any relatives except Clara's family, who came once every 6 months, she too was sad when he elected to leave the other evening

"The word "company" meant a lot of different things to so many people. To some people company means strangers who are coming to visit, to others company means people who when they come to your home they become family. In a lot of ways, you, Antonio, are being looked upon by our family as we would a close family member."

Antonio got emotional hearing all of this was, Clara just wanted Antonio to know he was looked upon as more than just a neighbor.

"So you see Antonio" Said Clara "You staying a little longer really does mean a lot to all of us."

Taken back by this rush of adulation, Antonio looked at this middle class family and wondered out loud.

"There is a lot about me that perhaps in good time all of you might think different in your opinion, that's all I'm saying"

Richard wanted to know more." What can we possibly find out about you, are you a criminal?"

Antonio laughed "And what if I had been a criminal, what if I had paid my dues to society I would still be the same man you see right now, right?"

There was a pause, Sister Augustine asked "At this stage of your life seeing you for who we believe you are what you've done in the past truly doesn't concern us, what does concerns us is what you're going to do in your future, and how it will impact us. We truly love having you here and we feel that you are a friend so imposition is out of the question!"

At night's end there was a lot of love in the room, there were hugs all around and suddenly the relationship between the Maguire's and Antonio had reached a new level of respect based strictly on what the Maguire's had perceived as a man in need of a family.

At night's end, and after everyone had gone to sleep, Richard and Clara discussed the evening and their dinner and in so many words tried to express to each other and reflect on everything that had occurred that evening.

"What do you think Clara, I tell you the truth, to me, Antonio is a sweet man and no matter what he did in his past if anything there are too many reasons for me to root for this guy, what do you think?"

Clara sat on the end of the bed and smiled. "Rich, I feel the same way. Do you think that we come off as needy to him? I mean the way we almost begged him to stay later for dinner and all"

"No! Never! Can't you see that Antonio is a lonely man, I think he needs to be here as much as we love having him here?"

Clara looked at Richard and noticed that every time Richard spoke about Antonio his eyes lit up light up like a

Christmas tree, "Richard tell me the truth, what is it about this man that gives you that look!"

"What Look!"

"The look that tells me that whatever you've been searching for has arrived, it's as if Antonio represents all the fathers who never picked you from the orphanage"

Richard looked away and suddenly Clara felt that she had hit a nerve." Oh baby I am sorry; I didn't mean…."

Richard spun around and Clara noticed a few tears well up in his eyes. "Clara, sweet Clara, there is no one who knows me better than you and I guess I'd have to say that your observation is so close that it scares me"

CHAPTER 41

A FAMILY COMES IN ALL SHAPES AND SIZES

It was 1979. The children were getting bigger and Sister Augustine was as proud as punch at their excellent academic development not to mention their Catholic Studies to which Sister Augustine oversaw every aspect of it. Clara had joined a few clubs in the Long Branch city that gave her a sense of giving as some of those clubs were geared around the Catholic Church in Long Branch. Two of the clubs were volunteers for the needy, one worked at an abandoned home converted to a shelter for homeless people and the other club did the same except this club was there to help kids of all ages. Clara divided her time between each and Sister alternated with her whenever the kids were in school.

Richard continued on his job being promoted again to field Vice President of general operations in South Jersey. Because of his promotion he was spending a lot of time at the local office training future entrepreneurs who wanted the insurance business as their life vehicle.

Antonio had left New Jersey for a few months travelling down to Florida. He explained to Richard that he was needed down there by some of his friends. The explanation was subtle and Richard wanted to know more but decided not to ask.

Antonio sensing the curiosity needed to quell the questions "Richard you look like you lost your best friend, so sad? I'll be back in a month, ok?"

"Oh I'm not sad, but for so long you've been part of my family and if you leave us we get nervous thinking that you're not coming back, I know it doesn't make sense it's how close we all are that's all.

Two months had passed and as he had promised he had come back. Antonio arrived coming out of a cab looking suntanned and smiling.

As he approached Richard their embrace was a little different than any other time where embraces and salutations had been in order. This time Richard sensed that Antonio was acting a little different then when he left Long Branch 2 months earlier. It was immediately apparent to Richard that Antonio had an emotional issue as he simply couldn't make eye contact and quickly turned away right after they had said hello.

Instinctively Richard knew that it just wasn't the right time to point it out. He decided that he would not just brush it away so he pressed the issue as Antonio acted as if he wanted to run away from any confrontation dealing with whatever was bothering him. But Richard cared too much to let this slide.

"Antonio, your acting a little distant what is it? Is there some problem?" Richard sensed he hit a nerve and that there was something wrong but Antonio was not ready to talk about it just yet. As Richard was speaking Antonio turned around and started walking away towards his house.

Richard, taken back momentarily, left standing there and seeing Antonio simply just walk away needed an answer as to why so he raced after him. Finally catching up to him he grabbed his arm.

"Antonio! Please, if there is something wrong please let me in God I feel like we're family"

Richard could see that Antonio had the look that there was something going on inside of him and private or not Richard was going to get to the bottom of it.

There was a pause "Richard some things a man likes to keep to himself, I am not in trouble or anything so please don't worry ok?"

"Ok I promise that I won't worry but I sense something is wrong, was your trip to Florida about what's going on with you?"

"Richard, believe me there is nothing wrong. Hey I've got an idea to celebrate me coming back"

In an instant Richard was caught off guard forgetting what he had just seconds ago sensed and fell into the invitation

"I want to take the family out for dinner tonight is that ok?"

Richard loved the idea they both agreed that it would be fun. "5 pm we'll leave being that the kids need to eat early, is that ok Antonio?"

Dinner was set.

After discussing everyone's needs it was agreed that Bella Luna Restaurant was chosen in the heart of Long Branch for the 6 of them to have dinner.

CHAPTER 42

The Streets Never Change

The Bella Luna was packed and even though Richard had called ahead there was still a long wait. After 15 minutes Antonio finally went to the maître d and asked how long a wait simply because there were 2 children and an older woman, who just happened to be a nun, and he just wanted to feed them on time. The maître d said he didn't expect it to be that long before they would be seated.

The dinner was on and the family were enjoying both the meal and Antonio's return. The banter between everyone centered around Antonio especially Sister Augustine's desire to finally work with Antonio to develop much of his backyard and perhaps devoting some of that portion of the property to growing vegetables. The main course was practically over when Richard's oldest needed to go to the bathroom and no sooner had Clara gotten up to take her hand she enthusiastically proceeded to run towards the back of the restaurant to where she thought the rest rooms were as Clara caught off guard attempted to catch up to her. No one at the table paid much attention to them as everyone else concentrated on the pastries the maître d had brought out.

Within a few minutes Clara and her daughter had come back and Richard, looking up at his distraught wife, knew something had happened. Sensing it must have happened as his wife and daughter were at the bathroom. Everyone's attention was now focused on what had alarmed him. As he looked at Clara he could see that she was visibly shaken." Clara, you look like you've seen a ghost"

Clara, after making sure that her daughter was seated back in her chair, looked up as she adjusted her own chair and looking back at one of the tables in the rear of the restaurant turned her head back towards Richard. "Rich, please let's pay the check and go, ok?"

Antonio addressed Clara like an old uncle would address his favorite niece." I can see that you're upset did that rather large gentleman sitting with that group back there say something to you?" Antonio was referring to the group of 4 men who were sitting and quite frankly enjoying themselves obviously not paying any mind to the Maguire's and what possibly could have occurred between themselves, Clara and the child.

"I'd much rather go Richard Please!" Richard was about to go back and find out what this brute of a man had said when Antonio stopped him." Richard take everyone out to the car I'll attend to the check. In minutes everyone had left the restaurant and they were all waiting in the car.

While they waited both Sister Augustine and Richard listened intently as Clara recounted what had gotten her so visibly shaken.

It took all of 10 minutes but Antonio finally came out of the restaurant and as he got back in the car everyone wanted to know what had happened. As Richard drove everyone home Antonio explained.

"Clara, I am truly sorry for what happened back there. That man that said those crude and disgusting things to you is truly sorry. As a matter of fact, he offered to pay for our meal and the owner who was also sorry ripped up the check, so you see it was all a misunderstanding and that man swore that if he ever saw either one of you two on the street he would publicly apologize to both of you, so you see all's well that ends well."

Clara looked at her older neighbor and thanked him. "I told Richard what that man had said to me and how uncalled for it was but truly I could not understand why? Why me and with the child next to me, God it was freighting. Antonio if I can ask you what did you say to the man to make him apologize? And want to pay our bill. Did he all of a sudden have a change of heart?"

They were practically home as Antonio offered his explanation." I simply reassured him that we were all part of the same family and truly nonviolent. I also noted that I would persuade you not to go to the police and sue him for harassment, I also noted that he wouldn't want any man to talk to his wife like that. After a few minutes he thought it over and looked at me, God he must have been six foot four and two hundred and fifty pound if he was an inch, and stuck out his hand. "Mister, I really appreciate you taking the time to come back here and explain all of that to me, I promise if I ever see her again I will apologize"

Clara smiled at Sister Augustine "Well! I guess God answers all of our dilemmas and perhaps tonight before we go to sleep we should pray for that man"

Antonio nodded an agreement as they pulled into their driveway.

(20 minutes ago, at the Bella Luna restaurant)

Antonio walked slowly towards the back table. The four men sitting there all obviously Italian and from the Long Branch area. Antonio had seen one of them in the downtown area before. It appeared to him that this food fest they were enjoying must have been a weekly event either way they were familiar with the restaurant and the ownership catered to them as they must be big spenders.

As Antonio walked towards the back table he passed a couple eating that had ordered a rather large Porterhouse steak. As deftly as a magician he slid his hand across the table and grabbed the rather large steak knife without missing a stride, it automatically reminded him of an altercation he had some 25 years ago in Atlanta Federal prison. In that altercation he swiped a spoon and used it as a weapon against another inmate. As he was upon the giant of a man, whose back was to him he quietly came up behind the man and with his right arm grabbed him around the neck and with his left hand plunged the steak knife directly into the man's left thigh. As soon as the knife was deeply imbedded, and the big man screaming in agonizing pain fell the floor, he proceeded to grab the half-drunk wine bottle on the table and in a split second smash it on the table and simultaneously plunge the half broken bottle into the man's stomach who was seated directly across from the wounded diner.

The table surface as well as the entire area below it was covered with blood. The restaurant, now empty of patrons, except the two men writhing on the floor was a scene right out of Reservoir Dogs.

The other two men who had been having dinner with the two victims were stunned and scared at the same time. One of the two men shouted out, as if he had just come out of a coma, in a panic stricken voice half pleaded to the owner who was just standing there in shock "Somebody call 911, please they are going to bleed to death!"

The other man who sat next to him just stared in disbelief.

As they witnessed the carnage they hadn't noticed that Antonio was still standing there above the two fallen men. In an instant he looked up at the two men sitting there.

"Are you two assholes related to these two pieces of crap on the floor?" The two men nervously nodded no!

"Then get the fuck out of here now!" The two men ran out of the restaurant. The three tables who had diners who were at different stages of finishing their meal stopped eating and like a movie they were seeing the reality put them all in coma like condition.

Antonio had ordered them all to leave now!

The owner was just standing there with a plate of hot bread he was about to place on one of the diners table.

"Are you the owner! "There was a second pause whereas the proprietor hearing the question couldn't answer right away, a few moments later as if a delayed reaction he quietly said "yes"

"Ok, obviously you know these two bums!" The screams from the two bloodied victims had subsided to loud groans and pleadings of mercy.

"Oh…yes yes I do! Oh my God please allow me to call 911 please!"

Antonio leaned down next to the big man who he had attacked first

"Hey big man, I want you to remember my name it's Antonio Piccolo! Go to whoever you want and tell them what I did to you both. And if anyone comes near me or my family I will find both of you and I promise that both of you will have the most agonizing death, this will teach both of you two how to act whenever your around innocent people, got IT! Hey restaurant boss call the fucking 911" And just as quickly Antonio walked out of the restaurant and into Richard's car.

CHAPTER 43

REVELATIONS

The two newspapers that most south Jersey families relied on were the Asbury Park Press and the Newark Star Ledger. The Maguire household was no different. Upon reading the headline in the Ledger Clara exclaimed to Sister Augustine oh my God Auggie! Last week we must have just missed the fireworks at the Bella Luna. Sister Augustine affectionately called Auggie by Richard and his wife, asked what!

"What are you telling me? There was what?" As she leaned over Clara's shoulder as they both read the headline.

"MOB STYLE MAYHEM"

The article went on to read about the incident, although no names were mentioned it was noted that the two men accosted were part of the South Jersey laborers union 565. It went on to say that there was an attack of the two men. The writer of the article intimated that the attack had a lot to do with the Long Branch Pier project where several companies had complained to the Attorney General about bid rigging on the construction project. The article went on to compare the mayhem seen here to the violence seen on the construction of the Jacob Javits center in New York.

Just then Richard came in and Clara recounted the same story to him. Bewildered Richard sat down hard on the kitchen chair.

"It must have happened right after we left."

During dinner that evening Richard directed the same query to Antonio, who had become a frequent dinner guest at the Maguire's "Antonio did you read the Ledger today? The same night we all had dinner at the Bella Luna there was a huge brawl, can you believe it?"

Antonio, not wanting to elaborate on what he thought could have happened, deflected and turned the subject to Richard's recent promotion. "Look every day throughout most cities there are always going to be problems whenever people mix food and alcohol, but Richard you never finished telling me about the promotion, was it something you campaigned for?"

Richard showing exasperation tried to bring the conversation back to the topic of the evening. "Clara, don't you think it was a weird coincidence that ….." In an instant Richard harkened back to the group of men who had originally made some nasty remarks to Clara.

"Clara, I bet that the men who said those stupid things to you were also the men who are involved with this gangland thing"

"I'm tired I'm going home, see you guys tomorrow" And right in the middle of Richard's speech Antonio begged to leave.

"That was strange wasn't it? I mean the way that Antonio was acting"

Sister Augustine opined "Perhaps he was tired.

The weekend gave many of the homeowners on Sycamore as well as most of the Jersey Shore the only real opportunity to do any maintenance on their property. The

Jersey Shore, because of its proximity to the ocean, and all of its neighbors needed to be extra mindful as salt sea spray was never a great ingredient for growing anything green.

Richard was no different than any of his neighbors. From the very first day that he and Clara settled in to their first home he made up his mind that as long as he lived there he would try to change and upgrade, for the better, as much of the house as possible. It was Saturday and his huge row of hedges that permeated the property needed serious pruning. He hadn't seen much of Antonio since the evening he ate dinner with the family, some four days ago, Richard wondered if he wasn't ill.

The automobile is the one staple in America today that can notify friends and neighbors in most neighborhoods that someone is either home or their not. That is except Antonio Piccolo's home. Being that he did not drive and was the only inhabitant in the house one would have to actually knock on his door to see if he were home. With everyone's busy schedule no one bothered to see if he was home or not.

Richard rang the bell but no answer. For some unknown reason to him it bothered him not knowing where Antonio was. The past three months were very special for Richard. Antonio's presence in all of his family outings, dinners and barbeques rounded out, at least in Antonio's mind, the full effect of having family after all both Antonio and Richard were somehow cut from the same cloth.

In Richard's mind, he not having any family to start off with, he welcomed an older man reminiscent of a father figure and as far as Antonio was concerned not having an immediate family to speak of having Richard as a next door neighbor and seeing the obvious respect that Richard continually gave him made him both happy and thankful.

It took another day but finally Antonio had come back. That evening Richard rang the bell and Antonio welcomed him in.

"I looked for you these past 4 days are you all right?"

Antonio had a bunch of what looked like legal papers and had them spread out on his dining room table.

"Richard look here! The past few days I've been in Trenton to the State of New Jersey Immigration Department. It's been so long since I left the old country and the last time I saw my family was in 1925. I was actually trying to get any information on my sister, they said they would get in touch with me."

Richard noticed something strange on the paperwork, the name on the application was Thomas Madden

"Antonio the name on this app is Thomas Madden, who's he?"

Antonio picked up the application and just looked at it without saying anything." Are you all right? You're looking at that piece of paper but you seem a million miles away, who is this person?"

"Ok Richard, sit down and I'll try to describe what this document means. Simply put I did a few things in Italy that I wasn't proud of some 50 years or so ago. You could say that I left Italy in a hurry. Someday I'll explain in detail but now just take this explanation and know that what you don't know won't hurt you"

Richard was even more puzzled than before,

"Antonio" Richard exclaimed "Don't you trust me!"

Antonio walked to the large window above the sink in the kitchen

"Trust? You're the only one that I trust, but this happened a long time ago and I don't want you and your family painted with the same brush, so please let's just drop this for now and help me fill this paper out it's the only way I have to search and see if my only sister is still alive"

"I only have one question, why haven't you done this before?"

Antonio, stared impassionedly through the window overlooking some children playfully acting out life's dramas. As they laughed and ran around in circles Antonio thought back to his very first days in Benevento when he first set eyes on Anna. He hadn't thought about her in such a long time. Just watching the children laughing and carrying on brought back so many thoughts about what it was to be young. All those vivid memories, but in an instant he realized that Richard was talking to him.

"Antonio! Antonio are you listening to me?" Antonio, as if he were just coming out of his reverie, looked back at his young friend.

"Richard, I am listening really I am but I need your help, can I rely on you? Will you help me? Believe me my friend at this stage of my life you're the only friend I have and the only friend I can trust, and above all I need you to know that I truly love your family. God, even your religious conscience, Sister Augustine is a blessing. I do promise in time you will know everything there is to know about me"

CHAPTER 44

THE TRIP

Three weeks had passed, and again, Antonio was nowhere to be found.

Finally, on Friday night, Richard got a visit from his elusive neighbor.

"What a surprise" This was said sarcastically as their last conversation was so positive about the future and what secrets Antonio would or would not reveal.

"I went to Philadelphia to visit some friends and I am sorry for not telling you about it but the two-day visit turned into three weeks, sorry" Richard wasn't buying the apology but after living next door to this man for all this time told him one thing, take his excuse and forget it. Richard got to know Antonio and in that he instinctively knew that pressing him was not a good idea. Seeing that Antonio wanted Richard to believe him without question he acted as if the apology was real, so because of that Richard softened his tone.

"Oh no big deal the kids and Clara just missed seeing you and all and of course Augustine' been bothering me about you, it seems that she asked you about the deep cough you have and the last time we all ate together she had mentioned to you about getting it checked? We were a little concerned that's all"

Antonio deflecting, "I'm as strong as a horse"

Changing the subject quickly "I wanted to run something by you, I inquired with the taxi service in Long Branch how much it would cost to run me back and forth to New York's Little Italy. They quoted me $200 dollars 100 going and 100 coming back. I'm thinking that perhaps you'd like to make that trip and I would give the $200 to you, what do you say?"

Richard looked at Antonio quizzically," Why didn't you just ask me?"

Antonio smiled "Richard that's one of the reasons I am so happy that we became friends, because you are a very truthful fellow. You like the fact that we are friends and you're offended that I didn't ask you and that makes me smile again because you care and that is rare in this society."

"I haven't been in Little Italy in New York for over 40 years, have you ever been there?"

Richard thought and nodded no. "Actually we were supposed to go on a class trip to an Italian festival being held on Mulberry Street back when I was a junior in high school but the trip was cancelled. Do you know where Mulberry Street is? I am sure it's in Little Italy, either way I'd love to go with you. What shall we do when we get there?"

"Basically I want to go shopping, I want to buy some Italian Pastries and real authentic Italian bread, plus there are some other things I need to do and we can accomplish it all in one day"

Saturday had come and the two of them made their way to New York. They took the Holland Tunnel and after asking a few New Yorkers for direction they had arrived on Mulberry Street in Little Italy.

Mulberry Street, probably the most famous street in lower Manhattan, was once 6 square city blocks long. It had originally been the haven for Italian Immigrants coming off the boat affording both comfort and reliability. The comfort factor came from the fact that mostly Italians lived there and the reliability factor came from the few Italians who were politically connected.

The politically connected Italians were savvy enough as to see the potential in these new immigrants. These few who managed to convince the ever growing Italian community that they, the political bosses, could insure them a better future managed to bring jobs and economic prosperity to the Italian community.

And of course it all paid off again and again once election time came around.

In time Mulberry Street and the rest of the vibrant Italian community was slowly being encroached upon by the ever expanding Chinese community. By 1960 Little Italy had been reduced to 3 square city blocks, still a vibrant community but much smaller in size.

After they parked the car they walked almost the entire length of Mulberry Street. The most amazing thing that caught Richard's eye was the almost continuous line of small restaurants some right next to each other. In front of each restaurant was a barker who recited in Italian the house's favorite meals. Another factor in Richard's education about Little Italy was that the dinner and specials menu, usually posted inside the front window of any restaurant in America, was conspicuously written on a rather large chalk board positioned directly in front of each restaurant.

Each step they took on this magic tour of what Mulberry Street was and still is today fascinated Richard as nothing he had ever seen. Richard saw that tradition and The Italian way of life in New York was alive and well.

"Well Richard what do you think about the tour so far?"

"Oh my God Antonio it is magical, simply magical."

In the next 20 minutes they stopped at three Italian Grocery stores. They stocked up on non-perishables for both Antonio's kitchen as well as the Maguire household.

The next stop was one that Antonio had actually dreamed about. "I have been thinking about coming here for the longest time. Many years ago I used to have business meetings here and drink Cappuccino and eat a pastry called "schvoladella" a pastry that has layers of thinly crusted sweet bread outside of a small amount of sweetened cheese, it's unbelievable."

The name of the establishment was called Ferrara's, and the moment Antonio walked in the shop he just froze in silence as he closed his eyes, it was as if he suddenly had been transported 40 years back and he was a younger man of 35.

"Richard, I can remember the first time I walked these streets, it was magical. The smell of roasted Espresso and the sweet fragrance of cooked bread and pastries so early in the morning gave me the feeling that the community down here was friendly and I had nothing to fear."

As they walked passing window after window of gastro invitation Antonio stopped walking and in that moment he became pensive, as Richard had continued to walk and talk finally noticing that Antonio had stopped. Richard walked back to him" Are you ok, what's wrong?"

They were standing in front of a red building situated between two restaurants.

Antonio put his hand on Richard's shoulder and Richard was taken aback by the total emotional look that had suddenly taken over Antonio's entire being.

" .. What I wouldn't give to go back to that time once again. This house was where I lived for a time with a beautiful girl who danced at the famous Cotton Club, which was a club in Harlem, have you ever heard of it?" Richard hadn't heard of it

"Can't say that I do! What was the Cotton Club?"

Antonio smiled, standing next to a most familiar landmark, as he looked up to a red brick three floor walkup.

"Antonio! You're ignoring what I asked you, did you hear what I said?"

Antonio suddenly changed the subject, "I can't get over that this house is still here!"

"But I asked you about the Cotton Club"

"Wow, that's a great question and it would take hours to explain how important that club was to me in those days. It was special and one of the best things that ever happened to me in New York was to meet a man who would eventually become my oldest and dearest friend Tom Madden. Because of Tom Madden everything that was good that ever happened to me was made possible because of him He was my partner in business and in life and most of all when I was away from him ...." In that instant Antonio, in his reverie, had forgotten that he and Richard were still on Mulberry Street and as far as where and when Antonio was away and everything else connected with his past would, for now, go unanswered.

"Antonio," Richard exclaimed "You just faded from me for a moment what did you mean when you said you were away from him where did you go? What was that all about and what did Tom do for you?"

Antonio waved the question off "Oh forget it someday I'll explain, lets walk!"

Richard couldn't stop staring at his older friend, as they continued to walk and talk as they approached the corner of Mulberry and Spring Street. While they waited for the traffic to subside Richard couldn't help noticing all of the tourists with their cameras marveling at yet another landmark that made New York so great.

As they stood there, like so many tourists, Richard took a moment and tried to imagine what it was like for Antonio some 40 years ago to a time when he, then a younger and ambitious man, was attempting to plot out his future. And again that word stuck in his conscious mind, what did Antonio mean away? That was puzzling him.

In that rarest of moments when two friends, who are simply walking together and ingesting the overwhelming ambiance of this exotic yet humble neighborhood, suddenly blot out their age difference and intellectual experience and just concentrate on whatever mutually emotional admiration both were enjoying as they spoke and listened to each other. Those subtle looks, which Richard consistently noticed in every mannerism that Antonio made further solidified his feeling that their friendship was growing by the minute. The age difference between them was quickly washed away and all that was left was this pure relationship. The mutual feeling intensified as they continued to walk, talk and reminisce.

CHAPTER 45

THE CLUB

    Angelo's restaurant turned out to be a convenient choice for a late afternoon lunch. It was situated directly between Bayard and Mulberry and a few blocks west from the parking garage they had used where they parked. The ambiance in Angelo's was old world to say the least. Plain tables with white plain tablecloths a seating capacity of 80 people and an assortment of photographs depicting the more than 75 years in business. The male waiters were all European, mostly Italian, and that coupled with the ambiance and neighborhood made for an exciting dining experience. As they were seated the head waiter approached ready to take their order.
    "Antonio I will defer to you as far as what we should order here" Antonio, never lifting his head from the menu
    "Richard this place is no different than any other Italian Restaurant, believe me order whatever you like once you understand that Mulberry Street is no different than any other commercial arena this restaurant is strictly for the tourist, once you realize that then ordering a meal is a simple thing,"
    Their late lunch lasted over two hours and conversation between them ranged from Long Branch to Richard's job to Sister Augustine and how she arrived at the Maguire household.

"Richard, this dinner was great, but seeing that we're here in New York's Little Italy I'd like to see if we can connect with an old friend of mine is that Ok with you?"

Richard, unfazed, asked who that person was. Everything about the day including driving from Long Branch to the city coupled with a fantastic meal made for such a great day and the fact wasn't lost on him that in the end, he was still Antonio's guest and going anywhere new would be an added treat.

"Great, I'm in, who is this person"

"Let's walk as we talk"

They paid the check and proceeded down Mulberry and they turned onto Bayard and as they casually walked and feeling as though they had just eaten half of a horse Antonio mentioned. "There used to be a social club situated, I believe, down Bayard called The Ravenite club"

As they walked Antonio spoke of his early days in the neighborhood when he maintained a semi residence and ran a small office out of the club. "There might be some older members who might just remember me from back then"

Many of the buildings were old but in mostly great shape. Stucco and cement were the fabric of the day. As they walked it became apparent as the restaurants slowly gave way to more and more residential properties. Slowly the building Antonio was looking for appeared at the end of Bayard Street.

The Ravinite Club, a private social club in the predominate Italian neighborhood, stood as a reminder of what the past was all about and it also gave anyone who was even remotely interested a glimpse of what the future was to hold. Basically the club and its inhabitants from the mid-20s to the present day continue to carry on the silent tradition of the "Mafia". Unless the building got torn down or befell some unfortunate accident that by itself destroyed the structure the wants and needs of every member since the inception would always be the same, to carry on the tradition. The building itself represented what the American Mafia should have stood for, strong, forceful and dedicated to the original theory that the law of "Omerta" (never revel the true identity of any member) could never be broken.

That of course was the theory, when in fact the opposite was true. All one had to do was read the transcripts of the various Mob informants throughout the years to realize that the Mafia in America was anything close to resembling what the founding Mafia fathers ever had in mind. The original fathers of the Mafia used words like strong willed, quiet strength and various other adjectives describing the character of the core of Mafia men known men who addressed each other as "Men of Honor"

Antonio turned to Richard as they were both taken by the old world carving on the front door. The Italian code of arms adorned the large Mahogany engraved front door.

"The inhabitants of the club, dating back to 1929, have always been of Italian heritage." Antonio was suddenly pensive as Richard surmised that Antonio must have been drawn to an earlier time when he frequented the club. Richard had another thought

"Have there ever been any functions of the club that I would be interested in? I mean like softball or baseball or maybe athletic league activities? Just like the Saint Anthony Orphanage used to do?"

Antonio smiling at Richard's comment, half catching himself as he drifted thinking how absurd it was thinking that Mafia fellows would ever play baseball? "No, my young friend this club never got involved in any of those activities" Antonio attempted to give Richard a better explanation as to what the Ravenite was all about but no sooner had he begun to explain they found themselves in front of the building.

Antonio knocked at the door. In seconds it opened and the biggest man Richard had ever laid eyes on appeared.

He was dressed in black and sweating profusely. He stood there bigger than life. Richard surmised that the man had to be at least six foot five or six and must have weighed at least 300 lbs. He wore thick black glasses and coupled with his slick black hair made him seem even bigger than he was.

"What do you want?"

His attitude alone would throw fear into anyone who ever thought about disagreeing with this type of fellow.

Antonio spoke first. "Is Carlo in today, I mean is he here"

It only took a second but his reply was as brusque as their initial encounter, angrily he bellowed

"No he's not here!"

And just as quickly the door slammed shut>

"Let's go, maybe we'll come back another day"

Antonio started to walk away in the direction of where their car was parked. But Richard just stood there and after a few steps Antonio noticed that he was walking alone." Looking back, he couldn't help but smile.

"Richard, these people are the way they are for a reason, forget it we'll come back another time, ok!"

"What does that mean? God! Antonio that guy was just rude, am I not correct?"

By now Richard, still trying to figure out why that brute of a man spoke to them like that, had caught up to him. They weren't 20 feet from the Ravenite door when they heard a voice. As they both turned around, expecting that same brute of a man, they were surprised.

There standing in the Ravenite doorway was a well-dressed man, possibly in his mid-40s, calling out to both of them to come back.

"I am sorry can you both come back?"

Standing inside, the club they were introduced to Gino, obviously the caretaker of the place." My name is Gino Covelli and I run this place." Just then the hulk of man who was so rude to both Antonio and Richard came out of the back room with his head hung low, like a school child just coming off a time out.

"Seriously Gino I didn't know…"

"You! Get the fuck out of here and as a matter of fact I don't want to see your ugly face for the rest of the AFTERNOON, GOT THAT!"

The man quietly passed Antonio and Richard bowed his head and proceeded to leave the building.

"Again I am sorry. Can I get you anything, coffee, cappuccino, wine?"

Just then coming out of the shadows of the darkest part of the room was a man. He appeared thin and frail. He stood 5 feet 9 or 10 inches tall he wore a dark suit and a black mock turtle beneath it, his face was long with a scraggy face and white hair. All this on a skeletal frame that looked more cadaver than alive. The man's white hair, laid high above his head, gave Richard the impression that this man's hair as a young man must have been vibrant and impressive.

Richard had another thought as he stood frozen in the center of the room. He thought this man resembled that famous actor named John Carradine, who played Dracula in the movies. To anyone seeing this man at that moment the initial sight of him would be scary. But in the next few seconds it became apparent that his initial assessment was wrong. As the older gentleman came closer, with the sun light that emanated from the bay windows high above the room illuminating his every move, Richard saw a kinder more benevolent looking man smiling and holding out his hand.

"Hello, my name is Carlo what's yours?"

Almost tongue tied in his response Richard uttered "Me oh, my name is Richard and this is…"

Before Richard could finish his sentence the older man stopped him in mid speech.

"Please young man" And before Richard could utter another syllable Carlo uttered" I would recognize your friend anywhere, how are you Antonio, my old friend?"

The two men began to slowly walk towards each other as Carlo spoke and as he did Richard noticed that he was crying.

He held out his arms and in an instant he and Antonio embraced.

As they stood there just holding each other Antonio uttered under his breath "It's been a long time my friend, too long"

The older man asked Richard to please sit down and allow both he and Antonio to have a private conversation and as Richard sat and had another coffee and piece of cheesecake both Carlo and Antonio renewed their 40-year friendship.

Carlo led him to an obscure table at the very back of the club. There they both seated and as they did Carlo called to his second in command, Gino, to sit with them.

Carlo spoke first. "Gino, I want to introduce Antonio Piccolo you've heard me speak of him many times" Gino nodded with secure recollection.

They spoke for nearly one hour. Each needed to reminisce.

Carlo spoke at length about the past years and the legacy that Antonio had left behind. Carlo Gambino, who was now being mentioned as the number one Mafia kingpin in America. "The newspapers have me listed as the boss, they're still writing that same crap can you believe it"

Antonio looked around the room as if he were inspecting and reminiscing at the same time. "Carlo, the place hasn't changed"

"Gino, I've spoken to all of you about this man. And that discussion, to you Gino especially, how important this fellow was to all of us way back then"

Gino asked again, "Yes Padron (BOSS) but you never really elaborated, maybe since Antonio is here now perhaps you could now?"

"When it comes to Antonio and his role in all of this there is something I never spoke to any of you about. Many years ago Antonio not only did he make it possible for me to move up the ladder, but was instrumental in saving my life do you have any idea what I'm talking about?"

Antonio smiled and nodded yes. "Was it when I made the ruling about Albert's regime?"

Carlo got up and putting his hands on his hips he slowly began to pace inside the small area around the table they were seated at. To both Antonio and Gino Carlo it was as if he were reliving the episode all over again.

"Yes I remember it as if it were yesterday." Being as animated as Gino had ever seen him Carlo began acting out the story. Richard, still nursing his Cappuccino and Danish, sat nervously in the front of the club Looking bewildered as he tried in earnest to overhear what the three of them were saying.

"It was just after I had arrived and put into Gagliano's regime. He was a pig and like all pigs wanted everything for himself. Gino! You have to understand from my point of view I had no say as to what direction they were going to send me. Gagliano was a boss and when the boss commands you respond. There was a loft job about to go down and I was part of the initial crew to rob the place over on Eleventh Avenue. My uncle, who had originally sponsored me, didn't want me to go but Gagliano insisted. My uncle came here to see Lucky and plead his case but instead of Lucky my uncle appealed to Antonio"

Antonio smiled remembering the incident. "I do remember him Vincenzo right?" Carlo smiled like a proud father hearing that his child was selected for a great prize, as everyone else suddenly acknowledged the same thing.

"Antonio I am impressed after all these years you remembered".

Gino smiled at the obvious respect and mutual admiration each man had for each other.

"After all I'm not 90 years old right?"

Everyone agreed." I do remember Vincenzo and his wanting you to leave Gagliano's regime, I saw no problem with that and after consulting with Albert, Gagliano's top enforcer, and expressing my desires he agreed and that was that."

Carlo fidgeted in his chair, "Gino there is a lot more to this. By Antonio granting that favor it saved my life and for that I will always be in your debt"

Antonio went on to explain that on the night in question there was a robbery all right but that was just a ploy to get Gagliano alone. That night there was an execution, Gagliano and whoever was loyal were to be killed. Luciano had given the order and being that Antonio knew what the outcome was to be he actually spared Carlo's life, as all or any of Gagliano's crew that were there would also go down with him.

"So now that you are here I have given your visit a lot of thought and I feel that at this point of your life there should be some sort of payment or rather compensation for all the years you were away"

Antonio got up and as Carlo did the same he embraced his old friend and Gino could see genuine emotion emanating from men.

"Carlo, I appreciate you telling the story and more than that telling it in front of this young man. I actually love and appreciate the thought but I need nothing and I came here simply to say hello to you, believe that I want nothing"

"Antonio, I have given this tremendous thought and being that the buck now stops at me I'll have it my way ok? Allow me this please!"

What was proposed was that Richard or someone who Antonio could trust would come up to New York to The Jacob Javitz center in Manhattan. The center was under construction and there were many New York Mob families that were enjoying the spoils being created there. Carlo had issued an order that Antonio should get an envelope every two weeks and all the New York families would have to participate.

Once there the messenger would pick up the envelope and that's all that would be needed. Antonio insisted that he didn't need it but Carlo insisted that he and the other New York families would be insulted if Antonio rejected the offer.

CHAPTER 46

THE AGREEMENT

Sister Augustine arraigned the barbeque bricks so the flame on the grill would be uniform. It had been over a year since that eventful day in Little Italy in New York and because of it so many things had taken place in the ever evolving relationship between Antonio and Richard. The Maguire's were all getting bigger, Sister Augustine was still a full time nanny to Richards's girls and Clara had taken a full time position with the Long Branch division of Children services. While all of this was going on Richard had quit his job with the insurance company after Antonio had offered him 5 times his salary to simply be at Antonio's beck and call each day. This was greeted with surprise, optimism and in actuality pure joy. As Antonio's offer was greeted with a yes there was so much more behind the gesture. Ever since both Antonio and Richard had become friends it was apparent to Clara that Richard loved the relationship. To Clara Antonio represented the father Richard never had.

The relationship between the two of them had quietly begun to change the way Richard looked at everything in his life. His wife and children were top of the list and of course Sister Augustine was close behind. His working life was, also, taking a much different path he had ever imagined. The other fact that had surprised Richard was that Antonio had the kind of wealth that could afford giving Richard the offer. For the past year part of Richard's job was to travel up to New York at least once a week and pick up an envelope at the construction site where the future Jacob Javits Center was to be built. Richard never looked inside the envelope as he quickly gave it to Antonio and never a word was spoken about it since.

Richard leaned back in his recliner enjoying the hot summer breezes. He looked at Sister Augustine working feverishly in the backyard preparing for their usual Sunday barbeque. It had been so many years since she arrived and truth be told Richard loved it both for the fact that she had been a part of his life since birth but more important that his wife of almost 10 years loved her too.

Richard had a lot of time to think about his life and the many twists and turns it had taken him these past few years all because of an aging neighbor that he grown to love and respect.

A year ago as both he and Antonio were driving back from New York he popped the question that had been festering in his mind the entire afternoon.

"Antonio, I need to ask you something?"

"Ask whatever you like"

"Was that man Carlo, the man we both met so many months ago at your old club, the same man that the newspapers are writing about as being the king of the maf........"

Before Richard had finished his sentence Antonio cut him off.

"I really don't like that word, it cost me a lot in my life! I would prefer you just mentioned his name and remember he was and still is a good friend of mine"

As he sat back on this hot summer day he recalled that question and answer.

Richard just smiled, a smile that acknowledged that his neighbor, best friend and these last 12 months his boss, would be coming over to break bread with him and family. The fact had never entered Richard's mind that perhaps Antonio could also be part of that infamous organization, in the end Antonio represented something Richard had always known he thirsted for.

Antonio, much like Sister Augustine, had slowly become an integral part of Richard's family and in the end this made Richard very happy.

CHAPTER 47

A MEETING OF THE MINDS

"For more than a few years I wondered who owned that property of yours. And what was more mystifying being the fact that besides who owned it who would, year after year, maintain the upkeep without ever having anyone living there, boy that sure did bother me!"

Sister Augustine, in between bites of her hot dog, finally had Antonio all to herself. It had turned out to be such a beautiful day with Richard and Clara taking the girls for a short walk around the neighborhood thus giving Augustine the quiet time she desired to simply talk with the elusive next door neighbor.

"Sister, can I please call you something other than Sister Augustine?

The question caught her a little off guard but she quickly recovered as she finally swallowed her last gulp of Coke.

"Richard affectionately started calling me Auggie as soon as I got settled here and I guess it would be all right if you called me that too, is that ok?"

Antonio smiled, knowing full well Richard's endearing term was something special between them, made him feel special too and that fact alone warmed Antonio's heart.

"Well Auggie, I guess I'd have to thank my ex-partner who actually picked this house and made all the arraignments.

He went as far as to pay the bills and make sure that there was up keep all the while I was away from New Jersey, and I guess that's all there is."

Augustine was a little confused.

"Why do you think your ex-partner picked this house on Sycamore, is there some significance in why he chose this house and this neighborhood? was he originally from here?"

"As far as I know no! he was actually from New York and as far as I know he always lived there"

Sister Augustine had so many questions to ask after all after having lived next door to this mysterious man she wasn't going to let this opportunity pass before asking as many questions as possible. Making sure he was comfortable with both her questions their rather quiet surroundings she plodded on.

"What was your partner's name?"

"His name was Tom Madden and truthfully there are times when I really do miss him."

As Antonio sipped at his Coke he noticed Sister Augustine's complexion turn pallid and in seconds her facial expression changed from the happy and robust Sister of Charity he had grown to know respect and care for to a woman with an expression that was devoid of anything.

Antonio noticed the instant change thinking that perhaps something medical was happening to her perhaps her heart or possibly a stroke!

In seconds Auggie's cheek color turned into a dark and clammy sweat. Antonio jumped up and went to grab her arm

"Auggie, Auggie are you all right? You look like you've seen a ghost!"

In a second she quickly left Antonio and ran into the house. Just then both Richard and Clara and the kids appeared.

"Richard, I think Sister Augustine is ill, God we were just talking then suddenly she appeared as if a ghost had taken over her entire being, she ran into the house"

Richard quickly ran after her.

CHAPTER 48

REVELATIONS

For the better part of the next day Sister Augustine was morose at best. Richard and Clara knew that Auggie's behavior was odd simply for better or worse her attitude had always been positive and upbeat, this was strange.

When confronted about her sudden change in behavior she was pensive before even uttering a syllable, looking down as she wiped away the excess water from the dishes in the kitchen sink.

"No there's nothing wrong, oh yesterday! Well I just got a headache and I needed to get inside, the heat and all" And just as quickly she was gone into the living room

This last line, as abrupt as it was, was not let go by both Clara and Richard and perceived as perhaps Auggie was evading and something a lot bigger.

Here it was Sunday again and the same cast of characters were all seated again at the same barbeque table.

Richard again questioned Auggie as to her abrupt behavior.

"What's wrong Aug, Antonio said that right in the middle of your conversation you excused yourself last week and quickly ran into the house. He didn't say anything inappropriate right?" As Richard spoke everyone looked at Auggie for the answer.

Clara sat quietly as Richard spoke. When Clara tried, softly, in asking Auggie why she had done it Augie responded in the same fashion. Auggie denied acting any differently. She simply stated that she suddenly had a headache and begged to leave the barbeque. Richard had expressed his desire to find out from either Sister Augustine or Antonio if there was anything more to the story, finally convinced he dropped it.

The one overwhelming feature surrounding the story was that for the last 10 years Richard could never remember anytime where Sister Augustine had ever deviated from her character, this last episode had him mystified.

The next week did pass quickly and both Clara and Richard needed answers.

CHAPTER 49

THE MYSTERY

It took two months but Antonio finally found out what the mystery behind that strange barbeque some months ago was all about.

It was Sunday and as usual the entire Maguire family went to Saint Teresa's Church in Long Branch. As mass was letting out and most of the parishioners were saying good bye to the priest outside the church Richard quickly took Sister Augustine's arm and led her back into the now vacant church. He picked an empty pew and sat Sister Augustine sat right beside him.

"Richard! What has gotten into you! why did you pull me away from the family?" Richard leaned against the pew and angled himself so as no one else could hear what he was saying yet directed the conversation directly to her.

"We are here in the presence of our lord, I want to know what happened at the barbeques between Antonio and you?"

Clara knowing what Richard had said he was going to do simply took the girls home.

In the next two hours Sister Augustine outlined what had become the secret only she knew about and had thought that she would take that secret to her grave. The secret that had all but vanished from her memory.

The Second World War was raging, it was winter and Saint Anthony's orphanage was doing God's work, saving children.

A young woman appeared at the orphanage door. She appeared disoriented until one of the nuns discovered that, wrapped in three thin blankets was an infant, almost blue from the cold. As snowflakes fell gently on her head she explained that she had to bring the child there as her parents would not allow her to have it. She swore that as soon as she recovered financially she would be back to reclaim the child. The nuns brought her and the child inside where they ministered to the girl. After she had regained some sense to the knowledge that the orphanage would take the child and care for it and it was then that she told the truth as to who she was and the man who impregnated her. She went into detail as to the illegal profession she had been in and that the father was a gangster and that if the father knew of the boy he might want it destroyed.

Sister Augustine, after hearing the girl's story, felt a sort of kinship with her especially since she learned they were both from the same town in New Jersey, at least that's what the girl had told her. And because of that Sister Augustine took more of a hands on approach to taking care of the child. And most of all she assured the mother that no matter what the child would always be hers and that the orphanage was only interested in its well-being.

The girl went on to fully explain about the father and how vicious he and his gang were. He was some gangster from New York and that he originally demanded that she abort the child once he found out she was pregnant.

Knowing his ferocity, she decided to run away with the child. Having limited funds, she decided to bring it the orphanage. Before she left she vowed to return as soon as he got on her feet. She did, in fact, return one year later and again disappeared this time she never returned.

"I raised that child until he became a man and proud of everything he ever accomplished, that boy was as much mine as that young woman"

Richard was amazed as he listened to the story thinking and hoping that perhaps he could have been that little boy. Anticipation as to who the child was and the rest of the story crowded every sentence and he hinged on every word that came out of Auggie's mouth.

"God Auggie, don't leave me in suspense! Am i the boy? And If so then who is my father? Do you know his name? And more important what happened when you and Antonio were talking that Sunday afternoon, why did you get all upset and all?"

Auggie paused knowing that this day would someday possibly arrive but in her heart of hearts she had hoped that this secret would die with her.

"Richard, would knowing who your father was make that great of a difference right now?"

As soon as she uttered those words Augustine felt stupid and utterly ashamed. Before Richard could respond she cut him off.

"Oh God!" She exclaimed and immediately hugged Richard as tears flowed from her eyes. Half crying and sobbing in between words she tried to explain.

"I am stupid, childish and angry, yes angry!"

Richard, bewildered, asked why "Because you should have been mine, oh I know that biologically it would not have been possible but truthfully speaking I guess in my subconscious, deep down inside of me, I guess I wanted a child so badly yet my vows wouldn't allow it."

She could see the bewilderment across Richard's face. "But you took that vow, if you wanted children why did you stay?"

She was crying harder than before "I could not leave the children; it was as simple as that. Oh I thought about it so many times but each time the thought crossed my mind your face appeared and I just could not leave you. One year followed another and as each year passed the thought of marrying and having a family faded. And I am ashamed at what I just said to you, I'm a fool for asking you would it make a difference if you knew your biological father, I am sorry for saying that"

Richard sat back trying to absorb everything Auggie had just dropped on him. "If that's all there was then why act so strange when you and Antonio were speaking at the barbeque" Richard could see Auggie mentally categorizing her thoughts like a librarian does when she's filing.

"Simply because, for an instant mind you, I thought that perhaps Antonio could have been that gangster so many years ago. Perhaps he could have been your father and the thought of a man with his background being your father simply shook me up"

Richard sat back in semi shock. "Do you think?"

"No he is not your father; I know now that he isn't. Your father had B positive blood, the orphanage found this out and from Antonio's last doctors report from Florida it showed that his blood is a negative. I am sorry for all this but bringing back all that happened so many years ago shook me up a little"

CHAPTER 50

WELCOME TO THE REAL WORLD

Everyone at the dinner table sat quietly as they ate. The entire dining room table's eyes were all on Richard. Everyone seated just ate in silence and the conversation was polite at best. Antonio, knowing full well the entire story as Auggie had secretly retold it to him, thought it better to change the mood and talk about anything else, because in the end result nothing can be done about the past the only thing that can be managed is the future, it's the future that we may possibly be able to shape.

Two years have passed and with the Jacob Javits center in New York City still only half built there were more than a few taxpayers in the state of New York that were infuriated at the outlandish callousness exhibited by both the politicians and the labor force allowing the total disregard for the state and its people. One group of participants who were not surprised or angry were the 5 New York Mafia families, who together with union officials, all shared in the project. The millions that were gained in construction profits as well as the systematic slowing down of the general construction made it abundantly clear that the city was run by the powerful not the people.

And according to Carlo Gambino's wish Antonio had an envelope coming to him each and every week and as an employee of Antonio's company, Piccolo Realty, Richard's job was to make that trip into the city each week to pick it up. Richard's responsibilities, including the weekly pickup, was to inspect and collect rents on the various real estate properties that Antonio controlled. One such property just happened to be the family's favorite Italian restaurant in Long Branch, The Bella Luna. As Richard went about his duties it seemed odd to him that immediately after the entire family had its first dinner at the restaurant that Antonio alerted him that the owner wanted Antonio to be an investor in the place, upon hearing that Antonio said yes. And now some two years later somehow the owner decided to sell the restaurant to Antonio who rented it out to another Italian family and here he was collecting rents from the place. Richard never asked why Antonio liked the place or even how the relationship began as his was never to ask but simply obey and move forward.

To Richard his job meant a lot more than the money. Richard felt that Antonio truly valued his expertise and decision making. Whether it involved picking up money or making decisions as to what properties were to be spruced up and what properties weren't. Richard also loved the man for his insight. Antonio knew that Richard would need more money as time went on what with an aging, call her aunt Auggie, getting on in years and two growing daughters the road to some sort of financial freedom would be the order of the day.

Antonio, after knowing that Richards' last salary bump brought him to $30,000 per year, made him an offer he could not refuse.

"Rich, the three things you will always have to remember is Never Rat On Your Associates, always keep your family uppermost in your thoughts and try to conduct yourself as honestly as possible going through life"

Richard smiled knowing that everything that Antonio had promised to him had actually come true. Antonio told him that within time he would be able to accumulate enough money to pay off the mortgage on his home. He also stated that if he saved well that his two daughter's education would be taken care of also. The once a week trek to New York was pleasurable as he would always stop at Antonio's favorite pork and grocery store located on Mulberry Street and top it off with a visit to Ferrara's bakery for great semolina bread as well as some Connolis and scfolgia della, great Italian Pastries.

The front lawn of Antonio's house was filled with a dozen men all carrying badges and guns. Richard, who had converted part of his garage to an office complete with a phone system and all, walked outside to see what all the commotion was all about.

"Excuse me! Who are you people?"

One of the men closest to him pulled out a billfold wallet showing his picture on one side and the large red lettered words F.B.I. on the other,

"My name is Jack McGowan FBI and your name?"

"My name is Richard Maguire, why are you here?"

"We are looking for Antonio Piccolo your neighbor here do you know where he is?"

Richard instinctively turned around quickly and half shouted "NO!"

Seeing that he had struck a nerve with Richard and his rather quick answer he pursued the questioning as he followed Richard back up the driveway.

"How long have you known Mr. Piccolo?"

Richard suddenly stopped walking knowing that he had to answer these men but also in the forefront of his thoughts were the three things Antonio drummed into his head. Never rat on your friends, always be honest and truthful and be the best family man you could be. So as he turned to face the FBI agent he decided to speak to him.

"Gentlemen I am busy but I will tell you this, I've known Antonio quite a long time and although I've come to know him extremely well I can't believe that he is at fault for anything connected with breaking the law! Simply put I just love the guy, have a great day gentlemen" He quickly turned away and walked back to his office. In seconds the array of plainclothesmen and other police officials had disappeared.

As soon as Richard came into the house Clara could see that he was trembling.

"Oh my God Honey what was that all about?"

He quietly went into the living room not wanting his children or Auggie to hear what he was saying.

"Clara, "He began to tremble again "This is serious I can feel it. Antonio is in some sort of trouble and I need to find him to warn him to help him"

For the first time in their relationship Clara questioned his loyalty

"Rich, you don't owe him anything" And as the words came out of her mouth she instinctively knew that she had said too much and just as quickly tried to smooth things out a bit.

"Honey! I didn't mean it that way, what I was trying to say was that you have always been a great friend to him and that friends don't have to feel as if because of the friendship either one has to go to the ends of the earth to prove it, that's all I meant!"

Richard looked in disbelief at his wife.

"Clara, these past two years have been two of the happiest I've had since I first met you at the Saint James dance, Antonio made all of that possible" Before she could respond Richard got up from his chair and started pacing.

"What if they put him in jail? He's in poor health God I hope he's all right?"

CHAPTER 51

1929 all over again

The county Sherriff's office had left the subpoenas in Antonio's mailbox. In essence the courts demanded that he voluntarily appear before a warrant would be issued and if the charges proved to be real and enforceable the courts would then issue a bench warrant and he would be arrested. Again, if the charges proved to be enforceable, the authorities smelling Organized Crime would jump at the chance to catch a man with a background like Antonio Piccolo.

In all of this Antonio had, as he had done so many times in the past, disappeared.

Two weeks had passed and everyone in the neighborhood couldn't help but notice but Antonio's mailbox had so many pieces of mail in it that more than a few had fallen to the ground. At different occasions the mailman would try to organize the mail but to no avail. As all of this turmoil began to unfold the fact still remained that Antonio was still at large and Richard and his entire family feared the worst.

Sister Augustine, bothered by the fact that no one had heard from Antonio, also noticed that a lot of Antonio's mail had fallen on the ground, deciding that having Antonio's mail scattered on the ground was not a good thing arose to take action. Her fears centered on the fact that even if a strong wind should arise important documents might get lost. She decided to gather his mail and keep it for him. Auggie noticed that much of the fallen mail was indeed junk mail and felt foolish at the way she had suddenly panicked, but in the next instant she suddenly regretted being the Good Samaritan. As she began to separate the junk from the rest of the mail she noticed three postcards that were addressed to Antonio all from the same address and each with a different date. The three postcards were all dated each two weeks apart. As she turned one after the other she quickly got a sick feeling in the pit of her stomach.

The one postcard dated the earliest asked Antonio to report to the Oncology department at Jersey Shore Medical Hospital. The other two dated more recent asked that he immediately call the office for a consultation. As she perused and began to categorically put the rest of his mail in order of the dates she couldn't help but notice a letter from that same oncology group. Against all better judgment she did the unthinkable, she opened his mail.

It was late Saturday afternoon when the Yellow Cab from Newark Airport arrived in front of Antonio's house. Immediately behind the cab was a black Cadillac with one man behind the wheel. Antonio came out of the cab and the other man from the Cadillac followed him into his home. Within 15 minutes the same contingent of police officers and county detectives that were there weeks before appeared only this time they had warrants and search permits for Antonio's home. The man in the black Cadillac was Richard Stringer, Antonio's New York attorney. Richard his wife Clara and the entire family watched from their respective windows next door.

Within minutes Antonio appeared in handcuffs and as he was being led out from his house his attorney ran to Richard's front door rang the bell and as soon as Richard answered he handed him an envelope.

The Park Avenue office of Richard Stringer bordered the corners of Park and 46th street. The Stringer Associates occupied the 15 and 16th floor. Stringer had originally known Antonio through Meyer Lansky in Florida as Stringer's dad, also an, attorney handled Meyer's trials and tribulations covering almost 20 years.

The meeting was subtle and after handshakes all around Stringer asked Richard to walk a ways with him. They walked down three separate corridors before getting onto a utility elevator. The elevator went up to the 32nd floor and it was there that the two men got out.

Expecting perhaps another private office Richard was surprised that the floor was empty and in transition. As the two men walked in between the half-finished sheetrock partitions Stringer began to discuss his plan for Antonio's release.

"Richard, can I call you Rich?"

"Yes you can but Mr. Stringer why am I here on the 32nd floor speaking to you as if both of us are spies and the Government is watching?"

Stringer stopped walking and it seemed to him that Stringer needed a few seconds to compose himself before speaking. Once he had his mind made up he stopped ad looked directly into Richard's eyes.

"Ok here it is! I am sure you're fully aware that the US Government wants to put my client back in jail, correct?"

Richard nodded yes

"OK, with that in mind I want to expound on an idea, mind you this is purely speculation and I am not advising you or asking you in any way to say yes, again this is simply speculation. If Antonio gets found guilty, and I do believe he will, he will die there. He is sick and I am sure he has not shared the extent of his illness with you but believe me he's seriously ill and if he's not treated medically immediately he will surely die"

Richard looked around for something to sit on and in the corner there was a crate, he sat down to fully digest what Stringer had just told him.

"You started the conversation by saying you were expounding on an idea, what is it?"

"Because Antonio is Italian, being an ex-inmate and connected albeit 30 years ago with the man who created what we know today as Organized Crime Lucky Luciano, believe me, the Government will label him OC (Organized Crime). If convicted, he will stay in jail forever.

What I propose is for you to assume the responsibility here and in plain words take the fall for him. Oh I know I am asking a lot but three things here work in your favor. First you're Irish Not Italian, second you've never been arrested and lastly you have never been connected to anything resembling Organized Crime. I realize that this is a shock and for your information I gently broached the subject with Antonio late last night. Believe me he was so mad at me he actually threw me out of his cell. I proposed this while we were waiting for the ball bondsman to post bail. If he knew that we were having this conversation.... well I'd rather not speculate"

ONE MONTH LATER

There was a knock at the door and Clara opened it to find Antonio standing there. She looked at this man who seemed as if he had aged 20 years in one month. Instinctively she reached out to him and they hugged like a Daughter and father would have after a long separation.

"Please come in Antonio, everyone's here"

CHAPTER 52

THE DEAL WAS MADE

It actually only took 5 seconds but as soon as Stringer had finished the sentence Richard said he would do it. In the back of his mind he always felt that Antonio meant a lot more to him than just a next door neighbor or great boss or even a good friend. No! Antonio meant a lot more to him then even he understood. Call it the loss of a father figure or the potential loss of a man if sent to prison would surely die there, could he ever have that on his soul. It so much more than. Monday morning came and Richard, together with his attorney Richard Stringer, turned himself over to the authorities.

The deal was made; he was sentenced to four years in federal prison.

At first his early days as an incarcerated felon were, to say the least tough, but through inside intervention arraigned by Antonio Richard was spared the usual hazing and torture any new prisoner undergoes without friends inside. Even with friends this Irish Catholic man, who had never been in trouble with the law, was now a convict, # 667.

8 months later

Everyone sat around the table excited as Sister Augustine was about to read Richard's weekly letter from prison. Sister Augustine, now up in years, had to focus with her new extra thick reading glasses and as she did she attempted to hide the fact that reading had become a rather difficult thing to do lately. But it was Richard's letter that everyone wanted to know about and Sister Augustine's eye problems, although critical, took second place.

"Folks, how is everybody. Jail is not for the faint of heart. Yesterday was the best day so far in this place. I met a man named Bayonne Joe his last name escaped me but he did know you Antonio and that was all he needed to know. I can't thank you enough for all that you did because for a while my time here was really tough but the end result of all of this turned out to be a positive thing. Clara I didn't want this letter to ramble before I tell you how much I miss you and the girls and rather than tell me what is happening each week as far as the girls go just save it all up and when I come home I want to hear about every minute of their lives since the day I left you guys. To Auggie, not a night goes by that I don't say a prayer to Saint Francis, remember him? When I was growing up you always used to say that Saint Francis would always look over me when I went to sleep, it still is the same today, I love you Auggie. And last but not least Antonio. You have been in my heart ever since you came into my life, if I ever had a father I'd like him to be just like you. The prison bosses changed my job status last week to laundry and it beats cleaning the floors. I know that everyone will be out to see me at the end of the month and I will look forward to that, God bless you all and until next week, God Bless!"

CHAPTER 53

THE END OF ANYONE'S LIFE IS SAD NO MATTER WHO THAT PERSON IS

21/2 years later.

Antonio was visibly absent from the quarterly visit. Clara elaborated to Richard that Antonio had been sick and for a long time only this time the combined allotment of Cancer fighting drugs had finally failed him and he was in sharp decline unable to travel. Richard hoped that Antonio would still be alive when he got out.

The Attorney General's office of New York had issued the second set of indictments concerning Jacob Javits and to Clara and the family's sigh of relief Richard's name was not part of it.

Release from prison was in sight with actually 6 months to go and as each day passed Richard prayed that his release would be in time to say his farewells to his most trusted and loving employer and not to mention his best friend. The fact that Antonio continued to pay Richard his salary while he was away said a lot about him and how he felt about Richard.

With two weeks to go until his release Richard got word that Antonio had been taken to New Brunswick New Jersey's Robert Wood Johnson Hospital.

Release from prison had no fanfare and like the day he had entered his retreat was the same, quiet.

At 5.30 am Clara greeted Richard with his two daughters and Auggie not far behind. The occasion was bittersweet because Antonio's condition was listed as serious and day to day status were summed up by daily telephone updates to the family.

The ride from Atlanta Federal was long, almost 15 hours, Richard drove all the way except for the last 150 miles. They drove directly to Robert Wood.

Once there everyone got out to stretch their legs Richard walked briskly to the entrance Clara knew better not to follow so close.

The eleventh floor was the ICU unit and Antonio's room was the last on the left.

The strong smell of antiseptic hit his senses as soon as the elevator opened. The wall directions led him directly to the last 4 rooms on the left at the end of the corridor, Clara had told him Antonio was in 1104.

IF Richard was expecting to see his mentor and close friend lying there smiling and extending his hand for a royal handshake he was sadly mistaken. Instead of getting a big hello he witnessed a shrunken version of his close friend weakly turning his head and faintly smiling.

Antonio's hair had turned all silver and the sunken cheekbones demonstrated the havoc that the Cancer had bestowed upon the man.

Antonio's right hand lay on top of the sheet. Richard's first impression was to grab it and hold it in his own. In that instant an overwhelming emotional rush overtook his sensibilities. Instantly he found himself welling up inside. His stomach began to ache an ache he had not felt since the days when he was an orphan. As a child hoping to be adopted Richard hopelessly watched as one couple after another passed on him. That hurt that stung so bad and buried so deep inside of his chest erupted in emotional outpouring and it just needed to be released. The tears started slowly coupled with a sob and he simply could not control the pure emotion that followed.

Looking at the man that he learned to love obviously dying right in front of him scared him. In that instant Antonio opened his eyes to see Richard visibly shaken and trembling in front of his bed. Antonio raised his arms and without saying a word Richard knelt down next to him and both men embraced like a father and his son.

Although Auggie had never been able to tell Richard who his real biological father was she, as well as Clara, had guessed because of the obvious circumstances surrounding Antonio's arrival into their lives that it must have been him.

Barely able to raise his head from the sweat soaked pillow Antonio cleared his throat as if to give Richard one last speech for good luck.

"Rich, Rich," He slowly spoke choosing each word carefully. "I don't have much time so please let me get these thoughts out to you ok?"

Richard teary-eyed tried to stay composed for he had never been with anyone who was at the end of their life, dying right in front of him.

"Take your time Antonio, we have all the time in the world I made all my collections yesterday no need to hurry now"

This last statement was meant at levity as Antonio had always instructed Richard to make collections on the first Monday of each month and since this was Tuesday it meant that their relationship in business would survive till next week but both of them secretly knew this was the last week.

"I don't know if I'm going to be around next week, inside the drawer near my bed is an envelope. Don't open it now wait until tomorrow morning ok? in about 20 minutes a man from my lawyer's office will be here and he will conduct whatever time I have with you"

Richard didn't understand but no sooner had he begun to ask

"Please just trust me ok?"

Just then Michael Caldwell, eldest son of Richardl Caldwell Antonio's lawyer, came into the room and a woman stenographer with her machine followed.

"This must be Richard, hi I'm Michael, Antonio's lawyer. What this is simply is a swearing in of you. Antonio has requested that you be his legal heir, wait I can see that there are questions so let me answer some of them first. Antonio would like to legally adopt you!"

Richard totally blindsided, questioned as to why?

"Antonio wants to legally adopt me why because I went to jail for him? Is that why because if it is he doesn't have to do that. I did that because I knew that if he did go he would have certainly died an early death."

The attorney pulled out some papers from his briefcase and as he did he looked up at Richard.

"What you did for him was something only a loved one would do for his own, no! Antonio always wanted a son, so in this case if you agree you will legally carry his name and in essence be his son! It is as simple as that. Now the formalities are such but in reality the actual name change will take a few months but you'll be notified, are you in agreement."

All eyes were on him.

At that precise moment he accepted his fate and in holding Antonio's hand the bond that had been created some 10 years before was solidified by that simple gesture.

"It would be an honor to carry his name"

CHAPTER 54

PROLOGUE

The loss of Antonio Piccolo was felt ever so strongly in the Maguire household. It took many months but Richard finally allowed himself to resume some type of normal activity within his household and Long Branch in general. The job market didn't fare much better for him. The fact that he had been to prison hampered him from getting any worthwhile job. Some of the money he had saved from his job with Antonio was all but gone and the small menial jobs he was getting hadn't gotten him that far. Clara supplemented the household income by assisting at the local children's hospital and that money did help.

It was spring time and as each day passed Richard wondered if his luck would change. He wondered if his past would ever be forgotten and perhaps someone would step up and decide that he was a worthy candidate for employment.

On more than a few occasions his thoughts brought him back to his life before prison but that type of thinking can only get a man in trouble. The truth be told he was never a gangster and although he was portrayed as such in his heart he knew different. Everything that happened to him before being sentenced some four long years ago was all done on Antonio's behalf.

The mailman brought him his mail and besides the usual advertisements there was a clean white envelope mailed directly to him from Caldwell and Stringer. The letter stated that his presence would be appreciated at the New York office in two weeks. The reading of Antonio Piccolo's will be the subject at hand.

"What do you make of the letter?" Clara asked Richard quizzically

"I really don't know. What I do know is that as soon as Antonio was hospitalized I saw a slew of his family show up, they were there every night! Yet in all the years that Antonio lived next door I never saw any of them ever come to visit! so strange. Every time I was at the hospital his relatives made me feel like I was interfering. As soon as either his sisters or their offspring saw me they looked at me as if I were some stranger hanging on for the money, God! That was never the case. On one occasion I whispered in his ear that because he had so many visitors that it would be wise if I left! Do you know what he whispered back? He said that I should throw them all out!"

Clara sensed that Antonio's family and their obvious financial issues had really bothered Richard but she knew that it had been a long time since Antonio's death and by this time Richard felt that Antonio's money grubbing family must have taken whatever wasn't nailed down from whatever holdings Antonio had that were not part of the will.

The day had finally arrived and as Richard parker his car in the underground garage adjacent to the law offices he just sat there in a fog. He harkened back to everything that had happened since the very first day he had laid eyes on Antonio Piccolo.

LAW OFFICES OF CALDWELL AND STRINGER

As Richard entered the elevator and pressed 17 he couldn't help but look over at the few people who had entered the elevator with him. What made the entrance and, what people call elevator quiet time, even more interesting was the fact that the three people who entered the elevator with Richard also pushed the same floor. As the group of three led the way Richard followed the group into the offices of Caldwell and Stringer.

The room was filled with about 20 people all seated and as the three entered many of the 20 in the room greeted the three cordially.

Richard found a chair in the rear of the room and as he did many of the people seated eerily looked at him as if he, not only, was not a member of the family but certainly did not belong there. Richard recognized one woman who he had seen at the hospital the first night he had visited Antonio and in seconds was certain she was that same woman after hearing someone call her by the name of Serafina. Antonio had mentioned that this woman was the eldest daughter of his girlfriend Catherine who he lived with prior to being incarcerated.

Just as he was beginning to daydream about the upcoming summer season down at the shore the young man at the front of the large meeting room asked for quiet. His name was Michael Stringer.

"I am glad that all of you decided to come. This hearing will be short and to the point and I must remind all of you that whatever happens today the rules of conduct apply. Mr. Piccolo had given our office strict instructions about this will and his written wants will be carried to the fullest."

There was a murmur riffling through the crowd. To Richard many of the seated visitors seemed excited at the thought and anticipation of what was to be read. Michael Stringer opened the large legal envelope and began to read.

"I Antonio Piccolo being of sound mind do hereby bequeath this my last will and testament in this manner,

To the people I mention I want you all to know that I have given careful thought and made preparation so that my estate can be executed properly and fairly."

Upon hearing those words, the euphoria demonstrated amongst the people seated was like a small tidal wave starting from one side of the room to the other. And as the quietly repressed gaiety began to build hand slaps amongst some of the male members accentuated the reading to which Michael Stringer stopped reading and just glared at the few younger male members attending.

"There will be probably be a lot of time afterwards for any joyous celebration, remember this is still Antonio Piccolo's last will and testament please show him some respect!"

Eventually you could not hear a pin drop and Stringer continued.

"To Serafina, who I raised as child, and now is a mother herself I bequeath my house on Mulberry Street in New York. The property has a rental to insure that she would always have a steady income. To Her sister Adele and her family, I leave an assortment of stocks and bonds that I personally saved for her and all of the certificates have a cash value equal to Serafina's inheritance. To the children of both Adele and Serafina and their offspring there is an endowment I set up that can compensate for at least 10 college scholarships. This endowment has to be used for higher education."

Stringer began to turn one page after another and in the dead of silence the crowd that moments earlier, had shown anxiety and excitement at the potential of a windfall was now wondering is that all there is?

"Ladies and gentlemen that concludes our business here. Please as you leave the office be sure to make sure that your correct addresses are listed with my clerk, all the official documentation will be mailed out certified mail this week, thank you all again for coming"

And that was it.

As some of the people assembled there began to file out grumbling along the way more than a few of them looked back at Richard with contempt. As Serafina and her son were almost out the door she angrily slammed her fist down on Michael Stringer's desk.

"Listen buster! This mock trial you put on here is bullshit! Antonio had a lot more than that small stinking house on Mulberry! He had cash and lots of it! Where is it dammit?" Just then she disgustingly looked back at Richard who was still sitting silently in the back of the room.

"Can somebody tell me what he's getting? Who the hell is he?"

Just then two men from the outer office came in "Is everything all right Mr. Stringer?"

"Yes, please escort these people out!"

20 MINUTES BEFORE THE READING

Richard found a seat at the rear of the conference room. As he sat and looked at some of the arrivals he allowed himself to daydream about the last 10 years and everything that happened on Sycamore Lane since Antonio Piccolo's arrival.

As he reminisced he began to well up inside.... He truly missed the man.

He remembered the many talks they enjoyed as they discussed everything from politics to entertainment. Richard often thought that Antonio missed his calling. He should have been a writer. The stories, oh how he loved to hear Antonio talk about the past. Richard's revere was interrupted as Michael Stringer began to read the will.

THE PRESENT

"Mr. Stringer it seems as though I am the last one here and yet I thought you brought me here for a reason? Correct? Yet in this will reading my name was never mentioned, why?"

Without ever looking up or addressing Richard's question Michael Stringer took two large manila envelopes from the inside desk drawer. He handed them both to Richard.

"Here are two envelopes. They are numbered 1 and 2, in envelope 1 there are papers that are very important plus 2 separate lock box keys both boxes are in Chase Manhattan Bank in midtown. The two boxes both have your name attached and your signature is needed to get into the boxes, oh I know you have questions about the boxes but truly I am unaware as to their contents. In envelope 2 there are papers concerning your adoption and a letter written to you from Antonio and again except for the adoption papers the letter and its contents will be known only to you, please go and good luck"

CHASE MANHATTAN MIDTOWN BRANCH

The keys to the specific boxes were easy to access. Once Richard presented identification the manager attending the safe deposit section of the bank allowed him to pull both boxes out and once done showed Richard to an adjacent private room to view his belongings.

The two boxes were not equal in weight, each box was approximately 15"long and at least 7 or 8 inches high. Richard selected the heavier box of the two to open first.

The contents startled him at first. He had never seen thousand dollar bills before but there right in front of him were, what looked like hundreds of them all wrapped and labeled. Each label wore a $10,000-dollar dark purple ribbon around it. It took more than a half hour to count but the final count was just under two million dollars. He was floored and amazed at the site. There was a note attached to the very last stack of bills on the bottom of the box. It read.

"Richard, by now I hope you realize that you very special to me and exactly how I feel about you, but there is a little more. Before you leave the bank I want you to see a Vice President at this bank named Joe Morton he's familiar with me and he will give you further instructions, enjoy this my son I wouldn't have it any other way."

The site of all this money had him swirling in circles and he needed a chair to sit down and collect his thoughts. He looked at the second box and wondered how much was in it. He opened the box instead of cash what he found was just as valuable. There within tightly banded packages were deeds and leases from parcels of land as far away as Atlanta to buildings and apartments as far north as Syracuse. The parcels of properties listed him as sole owner and that all the rents collected were kept in trust for him and his heirs in case of his death by Joe Morton, VP of the bank. It seemed that Antonio had an outside investment company handle the day to day affairs of the properties collect the rents minus their commissions and forward the rest to the bank.

By the time Richard arrived back in Long Branch it was late that night. Everyone was asleep as his tip toed into his office. Once there he quietly closed the door and took the remaining envelope and laid it on his desk.

For some strange reason he was a little apprehensive about opening that manila envelope. His instincts told him that perhaps it contained a few or more items that might confuse or change him in some way. Perhaps it was Antonio's way of saying he loved Richard and that perhaps he was Richard's real biological father. Richard was now surer than ever that the incidental facts that led to Antonio to move next door to him was all planned. The overwhelming fact that, in Antonio's final hour, he would ask Richard to be his legal heir spoke volumes about Richard's theory.

THE FINAL ENVELOPE

My son Richard, I have always thought that that if I ever were lucky to have a son in this life that I would treat that relationship as most special. Meeting you and being in your presence was the most special thing that could have ever happen to me.

It is in this context that I reveal the truth to you.

I did adopt you and if I could have had my pick of any boy I couldn't ever have picked a boy that I could love as my own as you.

With every breath left in my body I want you to know how much I have really come to love you. From the very first day that we formally met I knew you were special culminating with that most grandiose gesture of spending 4 of your most precious years in prison for me. When I think about that I cry so hard that it hurts. But this letter is also about something else. Although I did adopt you and in fact look at you truly as my son in truth I am not your biological father. Your real name is Richard Madden. You are the son of my oldest and dearest departed partner Tom Madden. Tom was a fantastic individual, friend and partner. If I had the time I could regale you with stories about his character and bravery. The only problem that Tom had was that your mother, who did in fact give you up to Saint Anthony's, kept your whereabouts a secret.

    She would never tell him where you were so for years he tried in vain to find you. This he confessed to me thousands of times. Finally, when he did discover where you had been living and that you had gotten married he put his plan into action to secure your future.

    On his last trip to Atlanta to see me he told me about his medical condition and that it was critical. He wanted us, you me and him to all live together. Once that could not happen simply because I still had a few years left on my sentence he set in motion a few maneuvers especially in real estate that would make you and your wife choose your home on Sycamore. Of course the house next door belonged to us, don't you remember how long it took for me to finally get there. And we also owned the insurance company that hired you right out of college. The plan was for me to get out and take Tom's place. He truly loved you and on a few occasions he would drive by the house just to look at you cutting the grass, like I said he truly loved you.

    I hope you're not mad

    God! You could say you were the son of two fathers. Rich, I have always loved you even before we officially met, as Tom would consistently speak about you. But there is one thing I need to share with you. This was the last thing he said to me.

Tom looked at me across the glass reinforced window separating prisoner and guest.

He was quiet for about a minute the he got up and put his hand against the window. Good by old buddy, he said then he just stood there frozen contemplating, he then smiled and leaned over, Antonio, perhaps Richard can be our mouthpiece when he gets upstairs, how can God refuse anything from a boy like him"

THE END

CPSIA information can be obtained
at www.ICGtesting.com
Printed in the USA
BVHW071410090321
602096BV00010B/579